# FANTASTIC FOUR

## Doomgate

Read these other exciting Marvel novels from Pocket Books!

# FANTASTIC FOUR®

## Doomgate

### a novel by
### Jeffrey Lang

### based on the
### Marvel Comic Book

**POCKET STAR BOOKS**
NEW YORK   LONDON   TORONTO   SYDNEY

Pocket Star Books
A Division of Simon & Schuster, Inc.
1230 Avenue of the Americas
New York, NY 10020

This book is a work of fiction. Names, characters, places, and incidents either are products of the author's imagination or are used fictitiously. Any resemblance to actual events or locales or persons, living or dead, is entirely coincidental.

First Pocket Star Books paperback edition December 2008

POCKET STAR BOOKS and colophon are registered trademarks of Simon & Schuster, Inc.

For information about special discounts for bulk purchases, please contact Simon & Schuster Special Sales at 1-800-456-6798 or business@simonandschuster.com.

Cover design by John Vario Jr.
Art by John Van Fleet

Manufactured in the United States of America

10   9   8   7   6   5   4   3   2   1

ISBN-13: 978-1-4165-4025-0
ISBN-10:       1-4165-4025-3

This one is for my guys: Joshua and Tristan for their insightful comments and feedback; Kai and Keiran (my most awesome fans); the always enthusiastic Josh S.; but mostly for Andrew, who *finally* said, "Yeah, I'll read this one."

STANISLAW KLEMP SAT CROSS-LEGGED ON THE drab, gray, polyblend carpet that covered the floors of the Stacks' lowest levels, inhaled as deeply as he could (which, due to his asthma, wasn't very), then released the breath in a long, ragged exhale. Klemp loved the Stacks, especially the windowless depths where the mingled odor of paper mold and library glue was strongest and no one, not even the bawdiest and most desperate freshmen in search of privacy, ever came. He listened to the timer that controlled the overhead fluorescent fixtures go *click, click, click,* and waited for the moment when the lighted row would flick off and the world would be plunged into a profound darkness broken only at the far end of the row of shelves by the half-visible "Exit" sign.

He glanced again at the wadded-up ball of university stationery that lay to his left, just beyond arm's reach. Klemp could see the outline of the official seal of Empire State University through the back of the page, and he briefly wondered if he might somehow derive satisfaction from burning the damned thing. He'd started to reach into his pants pocket for his butane lighter when he reconsidered. The fire suppression system would activate and flood the room with inert gas, which, while not enough to suffocate him, wouldn't do him any good, either. He remembered reading about how Reed Richards, Empire State University's most famous (as opposed to *infamous*) alumnus, had designed the system and paid to have it installed. Apparently, Richards had spent almost as much time down here amongst the rows and rows of books as Klemp himself had. Once, that thought had delighted the young man, but tonight the idea only filled Stanislaw Klemp with self-disgust. In what now seemed the distant past, he had imagined that someday people might speak his name and Richards' in the same breath, as in "Wow, did you hear what Klemp has come up with this time? We haven't seen a mind like his come through ESU since . . ." And et cetera.

But now what were they going to be saying? What word was going to most likely be said in the same sentence as "Klemp"? He tried to remember the exact words the dean of the Graduate School of Engineering had said, but the only ones that stuck in his memory were "lax" and "disappointing" and, most important, "funding discontinued." Klemp's grandmother, a tiny, shriveled, desiccated, beetle-shaped woman who wore only black and had a mustache thicker and darker than the feeble one Klemp had sported for a brief spell last semester, had used similar words when describing him. "You're a lazy boy," the old hag would spit at him during one of her volcanic tirades. "Just like your father—God rest his worthless soul. He was lazy too. Got by on good looks and charm, but wouldn't ever turn his hand to an honest day's work." The implication here, Klemp understood, was that he didn't even have the advantages of good looks or charm to help him get along in the world. He was, he knew, a sunken-chest, no-chin runt, with a hairline destined to end in a comb-over. Girls didn't just turn away from Klemp or pretend he wasn't there; they actually seemed to look right through him, as if he was invisible.

Invisible. Like Susan Richards, the Invisible Woman. Except, of course, Susan Richards wasn't always invisible and when she wasn't, she was one of the most beautiful women on the face of the planet if you believed what every celebrity rag and Web site had to say on the matter. And who was she married to? Why, Reed Richards, of course.

Klemp lowered his face into his hands and mimed

a scream. *ARGHHH!* he thought. *If I lose my grants, I'll have to go back* there *and live with* her! His grandmother was the only member of his family still alive, if "life" was an attribute a scientist could truthfully ascribe to the shrunken, leathery old gargoyle. Klemp had not communicated with her for years, not since the day the acceptance letter had arrived. He tried to find an iota of savor left in that single moment of triumph, but found the memory as dry and desiccated as the mold covering the pages of the ancient volumes that surrounded him.

After being accepted, unfortunately, Klemp had learned two profound things about himself—1) he didn't like to work and 2) he had a talent for slipping between cracks. For almost four years, he had exploited the system and learned to exploit his "invisibility," though in the back of his mind he had always known that someday the dearth of measurable progress would come back to haunt him. Sooner or later, he knew, the Powers That Be would notice that the grant and scholarship checks were going in one end of the machine but that nothing useful was coming out the other.

The odd thing was that some part of him had truly wanted to work, to try to live up to all his "unlimited potential," but then there was this other part of him—the more persuasive and powerful part—that took a simple delight in wandering the Stacks like a goat in a grassy meadow, grazing on whatever random bits of knowledge fell under his glassy gaze.

Klemp was quite sure he knew things—*important* things—about a wide array of anomalous and (seemingly) unrelated lore. He sensed that this knowledge was all *significant* and would someday lift him above the common drudges who struggled so arduously to finish papers, impress their professors, and get good grades. In the pit of his soul, Klemp knew he was destined for greater things. The problem was that academic institutions tended to want a very specific and tangible proof of greatness, the exact kind Klemp did not possess. He had to come up with something soon—very soon—or they would ask him to pack up his meager belongings and shove him out the door into the incomprehensible, unforgiving . . .

*Click.*

The timer on the lights ran down and the world disappeared. Klemp did not curse the darkness—that wasn't his style—but he suddenly became aware that the sixty-four-ounce diet cola he had recently finished was sloshing around in his nether regions. He patted his pockets, found the LED torch he carried on his key chain, and flicked the switch. This time, he *did* curse the darkness, as the damned thing flickered once and blinked off.

Rising slowly, pins and needles pricking him under his skin, Klemp muttered a few choice imprecations and took a cautious step toward where he believed the light switch would be. Something crinkled underfoot and he realized he had just stepped on the wadded-up letter. "Good," he sneered and took another tentative step. He had expected to find a wall and was confused when all he found was empty air. "Wonderful," he muttered and was surprised to hear a small crack in his voice. Klemp didn't think of himself as superstitious or phobic and generally took pride in what he considered to be an unflappable nature, but somehow the darkness seemed more palpable than what he was accustomed to. *This darkness,* he thought, *has texture.*

He shook his head, took another half step forward, and this time his searching hands found something familiar: a bookshelf. Klemp frowned, annoyed. Somehow, he had gotten himself completely turned around. Instead of finding the wall with the light switch, he was staggering deeper into the Stacks. Just above his head, he heard a sharp, ringing sound, a *thunk!* that sent a quivering shiver down his spine and made him take a single unplanned step backward. His foot caught on the edge of what must have been an oversized book and Klemp's knee buckled, sending him tumbling into the shelf. He pawed helplessly at the precariously balanced volumes, but they tumbled to the floor and crashed into his bony shins, sending jolts of pain up his spine. Surrendering to the inevitable, Klemp fell forward under the hailstorm of archaic information, all the time trying (and failing) to protect his face with his forearms. A couple more largish tomes thumped down onto his neck as the headline for tomorrow's student newspaper flashed through his mind: "Scholar's Career Cut Short in Tragic Library Mishap."

The idea held so much appeal for Klemp that he found himself wishing for that last book—something really big and comprehensive with extra-weighty color plates—to come crashing down and provide him with a simple solution to his problem. Unfortunately, fate was not so kind, and so Stanislaw Klemp lay there for several long minutes, the unappetizing options not just for the immediate future, but for the rest of his life, slogging through his mind. The idea that death was the solution retreated and another one took shape: None of this, he decided, was his fault. The world was to blame. There were predators and there was prey and all his life Klemp had allowed himself to be treated like prey. At that very moment, he felt the darkness pressing down on him as if it were a tiger bearing down on a gazelle to break its back. *Maybe,* he decided, *maybe the solution is to let the predator in, to become one with the darkness. Maybe . . .*

And then the lights flicked back on.

A security guard—one of the heavyset retired cops who sat in a booth near the entryway turnstile—was standing over him shining his giant black flashlight into Klemp's face. "What are you doing down here?"

Klemp's fractured brain parsed the question, but momentarily had trouble making sense of it. Fortunately, his mouth was able to work independently and found an answer. "I'm a student." *Technically,* he added mentally. *For the foreseeable future.*

"That's not an answer," the guard growled. "I asked what you're doing down here."

Again, Klemp's mouth came through in a pinch (*Way to go, mouth!* his brain cheered): "Studying," he offered.

"On a damned Friday night?" the guard asked, his face twisted into disbelief. "Ain't you got anything better to do?"

"Is it Friday?" Klemp asked. "Boy, you can really lose track of time when you're . . . you know, working on something important."

"But why the hell you gotta do it down here? Ain't you heard of computers?" The questions were still coming, but Klemp could feel the guard's curiosity losing steam.

"Well," Klemp said, "not *everything* is online." He pawed the ground to his right and grabbed the first volume he found: something hardbound, but surprisingly light and floppy. He held it up and saw by the sharp light from the guard's flash that it was some kind of notebook. "Take this, for example."

"That's what you came down here for?"

"Sure."

"Then why'd you knock over all this other stuff?"

"Lights went out. I tripped."

"Yeah, I know. I *heard* you trip from like two floors up." The security guard frowned again, but was out of questions. Moving the flash so he wasn't shining it into Klemp's eyes, he reached down and offered his hand. "I think it's time you called it a night. Maybe go out and get yourself a life or something."

"Sounds great," Klemp replied. "I'll get right on that."

"Right after you pick up all them books and put 'em back where they belong."

"Of course," Klemp said. "Naturally. What else would I do?" He started to pull the books together into a disorganized pile as the guard lumbered toward the light switch and clicked it on. The fluorescents seemed unnaturally bright to Klemp and he held his hands up over his face to block the light. The guard asked, "Do you know where all those go?"

"More or less," Klemp said.

"I thought 'more or less' was one of those things you didn't say in a library. Isn't that how things get lost?"

Klemp considered. There might be a quicker way to get this done. "Maybe I should drop these off at circulation and put them in the pile for books to be reshelved. Just so they get put back right."

"I should make you put them back yourself," the guard growled, "but my wife's supposed to call in a couple minutes and you can't get no damned cell signal down here, so, yeah, that sounds like a plan."

Klemp patted the edges of the books into line, then crab-walked to the corner where he had been sulking, stuffed his crumpled letter into a pocket, and slung his backpack onto his shoulder. Returning to the pile, he hefted them up to his chest in a single jerk and felt something in his lower back go *twang!* He looked over at the guard, who was standing by the doors to the stairwell, his mouth twisted into a knot of barely contained impatience. Klemp grinned and said, "heh, heh, heh." He didn't chuckle, but actually said the word "heh" three times, as if somehow the two of them were ironically detaching themselves from the same silly, stupid joke.

Klemp pushed through the doors. The guard sighed. They plodded up the stairs, one in front of the other, to the first floor, then wound their way through the empty tables and study carrels to the circulation desk. The guard sighed at least three more times, long, slow, weighty sighs that were designed to communicate his profound weariness, his disappointment and contempt, with the world and all its occupants and especially one in particular.

An eternity passed and then finally they reached the circulation desk. Klemp dropped the pile on one of the carts, his arms and back muscles aching from the strain. He turned to look at the guard and hoped he was projecting something like manly bonhomie: two guys who'd just pulled off a tough, dirty job and now needed to go their own ways, but not without a moment of mutual recognition of what had been accomplished. Even in the dim light, Klemp could see that the guard wasn't feeling bonhomie-ish. He was leaning on the main desk and was pointing the unlit flashlight at Klemp's chest. "What about that one?" he asked.

Klemp looked from side to side, confused. "What?"

"That one," the guard repeated. He flicked the light on and the beam picked out the book on top of the pile, the flimsy hardbound book that Klemp had picked out of the pile when the guard had found him. "Wasn't that what you went down there to find?"

Klemp stared at the book and then slowly reached out and picked it up. "Oh," he said. "Yeah. Thanks."

"Don't you need to check it out?"

"Wha . . . Uh, no. No, I already checked it out electronically. A, uh, precheckout."

The guard sniffed, flicked off the flashlight and headed for the front door. "C'mon. Let's get you out of here. My wife's probably already called me three times and I'm going to have to tell her this whole boring-ass story . . ." He continued to mutter to himself as they walked through the main lobby, their footsteps echoing loudly in the cavernous space. Long banners announcing a seminar called "Fantastic Visions of the Future" fluttered in the air-conditioned breeze. Apparently, the dean had lured back Reed Richards to give a speech or donate a patent or cut a ribbon or some damned thing. Klemp felt a knot of shadows twist in his stomach.

"G'night, kid," the guard said as he unlocked the door, then pushed it open. "Go out and find yourself something else to do besides study. Can't just study your life away."

"No, sir," Klemp said. "You sure can't. Thanks for the advice."

The moment the door slammed shut behind him, a stiff wind born in the northernmost climes of the Arctic Circle swept up 114th Street, slunk up Klemp's untucked T-shirt, and made the skin on his back crawl. Flyers and notices tore off of kiosks; newspapers rattled, scurried, and swirled around Klemp's legs. Shuddering, wrapping his thin arms around his slumped shoulders, he plodded back across campus toward the tiny apartment he shared with two other students. Jerry would be playing some kind of MMOG and Riley would either be sacked out or down the hall hanging out with his girlfriend. Both had completely given up on speaking to Klemp about anything except the current location of either a) food or drink missing from the community refrigerator or b) the lateness of the rent. He decided he would simply creep into his room, lock the door behind him, and never come out. Sooner or later, someone would find him, if only because of the smell.

Passing a trash receptacle, he looked down at the book in his hand and decided that there was no compelling reason to carry it any farther. The prop had served its purpose and even if someone found it in the garbage, they wouldn't know Klemp had thrown it there. He shoved the book against the spring-weighted flap, but the can was overstuffed and he had to press hard to get past the empty plastic water bottles and the Styrofoam food containers. Another stiff wind snagged the flimsy cover and flipped the book up into a tiny vortex.

Reflexively, Klemp grabbed the book in midair before it was swept away. He felt several pages tear away from the spine. A part of him, the scholar that occasionally struggled to emerge, groaned, and he flipped the book open to inspect the damage. With only the unsteady light cast by the wind-shaken street lamp to see by, Klemp had to hold the book close to his face. Only then did he realize that the print was not typeset, but the very regular, evenly spaced printing of an engineer. He also saw that there were two small, carefully rendered illustrations: a circuit diagram and a mechanical drawing like the kind Klemp had only ever seen in old patents.

The first paragraph on the verso was continued from the previous page and read, ". . . of the second trial will require a complete reworking of the switching mechanism. I told Victor that I would need to consult with one of my contacts in the electrical engineering building and he responded with his usual condescending manner that he did not have the time. Instead, he found a piece of scrap paper and sketched out the design I have reproduced below. I've checked the library and am now convinced that if we can lay down the resistance coating in a thin enough layer, he may have just tripled or quadrupled the speed of our fastest circuit boards. The man's mind is extraordinary. Von Doom may be the most arrogant prig I've ever meant, but I'm learning more working with him these past two months than I did in the previous seven years of my so-called higher education."

Klemp reread the last sentence three times before the meaning penetrated, and he had to read the first two words seven more times before he would permit himself to believe what he was seeing:

*Von Doom.*

He scanned back up the page and confirmed that he had read the first name right, and there it was: *Victor.* A high-pitched giggle burbled up out of his throat. *Right,* he thought. *Like another Von Doom attended Empire State.* He flipped to the first page and confirmed his suspicion: He wasn't holding a textbook or a memoir or even anything that had been published by the university press—this was a lab notebook. Before the proliferation of laptop and handheld computers, every science student on the planet had filled up countless thousands of them with their aimless scrawls.

He read the name on the inside cover, written in the same precise hand as in the main text: Frank Forester. Klemp tried to remember if he had ever heard the name before, but nothing came to him. Every man and woman who ever attended or dreamed of attending Empire State University knew the names of its two most famous alumni . . . well, one famous and one . . . infamous. But, Frank Forester?

Who the hell was Frank Forester?

Even with the seemingly boundless resources available at Empire State and through the wondrous Internet, it took Klemp a surprisingly long time to find the answer to his question. When he finally uncovered the truth, he knew that some person or agency had done their level best to erase every vestige of Frank Forester's existence, and most particularly his relationship to ESU, from all public records. Study of the notebook explained why: While Victor Von Doom had been the creator of the experimental machine that had damaged his face and (many said) his sanity, Von Doom had not been the one to throw the switch. That dubious honor belonged to Frank Forester.

As every ESU student knew, Von Doom blamed Reed Richards for the accident, though it was unclear whether he believed Richards had committed a sin of commission or omission. Several years later, Richards and his best friend, Ben Grimm (another ESU grad); his girlfriend, Susan Storm; and her brother Johnny had "borrowed" an experimental rocket, gone into space, and been doused with an unknown form of radiation that transformed them into superhumans: Mr. Fantastic, the Thing, the Invisible Woman, and the Human Torch, respectively. A short time later, Von Doom—who had more or less disappeared from the face of the planet—reappeared as the armored Doctor Doom and quickly established himself as the Fantastic Four's archnemesis.

That's the story everyone knew, and a good story it was, too. The single new detail that Stanislaw Klemp had uncovered was that Von Doom had an assistant. In retrospect, this made perfect sense: How could an underclassman—even one with a reputation for resourcefulness and brilliance like Von Doom—have had access to the expensive equipment he needed to build his device? Von Doom might have been able to procure some of the electronics, but how could he have signed out the lab space and booked the time he would have needed to log on to the university's mainframe and perform the extensive calculations? Simple answer: He couldn't have, but an advanced-degree student like Frank Forester could have and, according to his notes, did.

As far as Klemp could tell from the notebook, Forester had been a diligent but unremarkable student. From the bits and pieces of personal comments scattered through the notebook, Klemp decided that Forester's greatest talent was recognizing talent in others. No other details about him were available. His alpha and omega were simple: He helped Von Doom build his machine and then, boom, he was dead. End of story. What had happened to his possessions, his research, his notebooks, his stuff? Klemp found nada, zip, zilch, zero. Doom's hyperreality seemed to have robbed his assistant of some level of tangibility. Klemp sympathized with the departed and almost wished he could do something to honor Forester's memory. Almost. Maybe after he became rich and famous, Klemp decided, he would pay to have a plaque to Forester placed somewhere down in the Stacks, something tasteful and discreet. Above all, it would have to be discreet.

In the indeterminate interim, Klemp had work to do, and he knew he could not make, *would not make,* the same mistake that Von Doom had. He would not be smug or proud or vain. He knew how to take good advice where and when it was offered, and there it was on the second-to-last page of the notebook, a margin note written in blue pencil: *Victor,* it read. *Recheck this set of calculations. I think you've substituted the wrong equation.* And then the signature: two initials— R.R. And then, under that: *This is weird stuff. Be careful.*

In his heart of hearts, Klemp believed it must have been that last phrase that did it. Von Doom must have rankled at Richard's nagging, but he wasn't stupid. He would have rechecked his work if it hadn't been for that last little bit of condescension: *Be careful.* Victor Von Doom hadn't gotten to where he was at that point in his life by being careful.

Stanislaw Klemp stared at the notation. He drank it in. He made it part of his soul. He *would* recheck the equations. He would re-create Victor Von Doom and Frank Forester's machine, only his version would work because he was smart enough to listen to Reed Richards when he'd said, "Be careful." Of course, he would never tell anyone that the machine hadn't, strictly speaking, been his idea, but that was what science was all about: building on other people's work, standing on the shoulders of giants.

He would make the machine work and then, oh, then . . .

Klemp felt the corners of his mouth start to inch up, but he resisted the pull and kept a straight face. He didn't rub his hands together or laugh maniacally, either. Only crazy people did things like that, and he wasn't crazy. Not even a little bit.

# 2

BEN GRIMM INHALED DEEPLY, EXPANDING HIS chest so wide that he heard the threads holding the buttons onto his dress shirt creak under the strain. Exhaling, he sighed deeply and threw in an expressive "Ahhhh!" at the end. He thought about saying, "It's good to be alive," but caught himself on the principle that the grumpy gods that seemingly ruled his fate would take such a sentiment as a gauntlet thrown in their collective faces. Instead, Ben merely grunted contentedly as the river of humanity parted and flowed around him.

The corner of 42nd Street and Park Avenue across from Grand Central was one of only a handful of places in the city where Ben could, if he held his breath and didn't move around too much, feel genuinely anonymous. He knew that this might only be because people confused him with a piece of public art, but the explanation he preferred—one that worked for him in both his most bighearted and most cynical moods—was that this was one of the spots where people were generally so overwhelmed by the spectacle known as the Big Apple that the sight of an oversized, rock-skinned palooka wasn't anything to get especially worked up over.

Early on a Friday morning was a particularly good time to be out. The tourists with their camera phones weren't up and about yet. The office jockeys and the retail monkeys were still taking their showers and shaking off the effects of whatever bad habits they'd indulged in on Thursday night. This time of day, mostly what you found out on the street were folks who had better things to do than stare: joggers, winos, and honest workaday slobs. Even the ones who stopped to take a look rarely gave Ben more than a second's notice. Anyone who passed this close to the Baxter Building more than two or three times in their life knew that they should expect to see odder sights now and again. Heck, most of them were probably grateful they weren't locking eyeballs with Dragon Man or Black Bolt or freakin' Galactus.

Ben had never been what anyone would call a morning person, though except for his stint in the service that hadn't been much of a problem. Most days—assuming he wasn't off helping to save the universe or babysitting or something equally strenuous—he rarely rolled out of bed much before ten and often closer to noon. Being the idol o' millions was intense labor and Mrs. Grimm's favorite son needed his beauty sleep. Every once in a while, though, if circumstances warranted it, Ben liked to hit the streets early and feel the city wake up around him. Today was one of those days.

Today was . . . "Ah, heck," he muttered to himself. "Gotta tempt the fates every once in a while." And, then, loud enough that a nearby plate glass window vibrated and everyone within twenty feet looked at him, Ben Grimm said, "It's good to be alive."

A pair of joggers jumped and some Mohawked young punk who looked like he hadn't found his way home to bed after a very long night on the town snorted derisively, but they were all quickly lost in the stream of humanity, leaving Ben with 99 percent of the happy glow he had been feeling. Turning to the southeast, he started down Park Avenue, taking his time, moving with the crowd, not feeling too out of place or even especially noticeable. Ben's dark gray suit was cut and sewn by some of the best tailors in the Garment District, and he liked the way the unbuttoned wings of his charcoal topcoat flapped around his legs in the light breeze. His shoes were custom-made and hand-sewn by craftsmen at Tanino

Crisci in Italy and dyed to complement his skin tone. Nice, well-fitted clothes and decent footgear were just a couple of the perks that defined being rich, but the main reason Ben Grimm was feeling especially pleased with himself was the *other* major perk of having ungodly amounts of money: giving it to people who actually needed it.

*Ben Grimm, Philanthropist.* He turned the phrase over in his head. While not a vain man in *any* sense of the word, Ben knew enough about how the world worked that he understood that in the event he died (and the world did not simultaneously go to the boneyard), someone somewhere would pull a mostly finished obituary out of a file and add the last line or two, maybe his last words, which he imagined would be something along the lines of "It's Clobbering . . . *ack!*" The first paragraph would mention his growing up on Yancy Street and then they'd get to the bit where he and Reed and Susie and the kid took a wrong turn on the way to Albuquerque and used the powers acquired thereby to fight the good fight and become the aforementioned Idol o' Millions. Probably the obituary writer would tactfully refer to the fact that he, Ben Grimm, would doubtless have taken first prize in any Ugliest Mug contest he cared to enter, and would close with a tasteful comment about the dozens of heartsick broads who were simultaneously mourning his passing. Hopefully, anyway; but, these days, the thought that pleased Ben even more was the pondering of how they'd talk about all the charitable crap he'd been up to since finding out he was a millionaire.

Later that morning—at ten A.M., to be precise—Ben would preside at the opening of the Benjamin J. Grimm Recreation Center on the corner of Yancy and Essex, not much more than a stone's throw away from his childhood home at 7135. Over the years, the Yancy Streeters had handed Ben more than his share of crap, but looking back on it now, even on his worst days, he had to admit he understood why they did it.

From the perspective of the Yancy Streeters, Ben had gone off and done what too many other mooks had over the years: He'd left the old neighborhood behind and seemingly never looked back. The fact that he lived atop a swanky skyscraper and was routinely seen around town surrounded by hot dames wearing skintight costumes was more than they could handle. As far as the guys from the Lower East Side were concerned, Ben Grimm had turned his back on his upbringing. Naturally, no one paid attention if you protested; no one wanted to know you thought about your old life nearly every single day and wished you could be more like the guy you were back then.

"Ahh," Ben said to no one in particular. "This ain't so bad, though. I guess I should stop my bellyachin'." He checked his watch and decided he was making good time. He hadn't eaten anything before leaving home that morning, not wanting to give Sue or Reed the chance to see him and wonder what was up with the spiffy duds. And if Johnny had found out what was going on, Ben knew there was no way he'd ever have gotten out of the building without getting into a tussle. It was bad enough they were all going to wonder why they weren't invited to the ribbon-cutting, but there were some things a guy wanted to do by himself without his teammates hanging around. Not that he wouldn't want them to come see the place . . . eventually . . . but there were times when you wanted to be a member of the Fantastic Four and there were even times when you wanted to be the Thing, but once in a while Ben Grimm just wanted to be Benny from the old neighborhood. He waved his hand in front of his face, shooing away these thoughts, frankly bored with even a shred of something that felt like self-examination.

His stomach growled. In his haste to get out while the getting was good, Ben had forgone his usual half-dozen eggs, side of bacon, four pieces of toast, and three grapefruits. He patted his pockets to check to see if he had one of Reed's special power bars on him, but no, he hadn't thought of that. He did have his wallet, and though he wasn't carrying any cash—the bulge ruined the lines of the suit—he had his plastic, which in 99 percent of NYC was all you really needed.

Ben had passed Union Square several blocks back and veered onto 4th a few minutes ago. He briefly considered detouring west to Greenwich Village to see if Mario was in his pizzeria, either still up from the night before or just getting into the kitchen, but decided it was too far out of his way. They were expecting him at the center in less than an hour and if that ponytailed, orange-clogged maniac started babbling about *Italia* Ben knew he'd never get where he needed to be on time. He consulted the detailed map he held in his brain of Manhattan below 14th Street and considered breakfast options. If he turned left onto Houston . . . Ben smiled. Gino's bakery. Cannoli and espresso. Perfecto.

Grinning, his stomach moaning so loud that he scared a little dog a sixteen-year-old girl was carrying around in her purse, Ben increased his pace and soon turned onto Suffolk. He hadn't realized how close the place was to the rec center (as Ben had begun to call it in his head). "Or I woulda asked them to cater the event," he muttered. Standing outside the tiny shop, Ben recalled why he hadn't been to the place in several years: As with most businesses in this part of town, its door was a remnant of earlier days when people were built on a smaller scale. It was a little narrow even for a normal-sized guy, let alone for a five-hundred-pound mook who was almost as wide as he was tall.

Ben considered tapping on the window to see if he

could get someone's attention, but the idea of making a fuss didn't sit well. The situation suddenly got weirder when a middle-aged lady carrying a bag of pastries and her kid while yakking on her cell phone pushed through the door and almost crashed into Ben's chest. "Yah!" she shouted, dropping the phone and the bag and almost the kid. Ben caught the bag, but didn't try to get the phone. The lady hopped backward and shouted again, managing to hit her head on the door when a man tried to exit from behind her.

"Hey, sorry, lady. Sorry," Ben said, reaching out to grab her, but she was so startled that she lurched backward again, knocking the cup of coffee out of the hand of the man behind her. "Ah, jeez," Ben said under his breath and then, having lived through this enough times before, he took a step backward and held his hands up. "C'mon, lady. Everything's cool."

Everything was sorted out in another minute or two. The lady calmed down and even had the decency to seem mildly embarrassed, and the guy who lost his coffee just walked back inside to get another cup without making too much fuss. The kid, naturally, started to cry, but Ben tried not to take it personally. As such encounters went, this one was about a six on a scale of zero to ten. Unfortunately, when it was all over, he still didn't have any breakfast, the clock was ticking, and the idea of trying to get someone's attention just seemed more trouble than it was worth. Ben was about to give up in sour frustration when he felt someone tugging the front of his jacket.

"Hey," the someone said. "Hey, mister. You're the Thing, ain'tcha?"

Ben looked down. The kid was the size of a ten- or eleven-year-old, but there was something about his attitude, the knowing way he grinned up at Ben, that made him wonder if the kid wasn't really a lot older. "Yeah," Ben answered, reaching down into the deepest recesses of his chest for a basso profundo note that would rattle the kid's molars. "Who wants to know?"

"Name's Julio, but everyone around here calls me Bender."

The way the kid looked at him, Ben got the feeling the nickname was supposed to mean something, but he had no idea what. He considered letting it pass by since curiosity had never done anyone any good, but the temptation was too much. " 'Bender'?"

"Like the robot, the smart-mouthed one." Julio fixed him with a stare that meant Ben's intelligence had been measured and found wanting. "On that cartoon about the dude who goes into the future."

Ben shook his head. "Sorry, kid. All the robots I know are either obnoxious or homicidal." He paused to consider and then mused, "Unless you count the Vision, but I don't think he's technically a robot." He brushed the thought away. "Never mind. What does a cartoon robot have to do with anything?"

"The robot's last name is Rodriguez, like mine."

"The cartoon robot has a last name?"

"Yeah. Same as mine: Rodriguez."

"So someone decided that you should be named after a robot?"

"My older brother, Marcus."

"Your older brother named you after a robot?" Ben was finding the discussion harder and harder to follow.

"Sure."

"He doesn't like you?"

"Of course he does. My brother thinks I'm *cool*. That's why he named me Bender."

"Bender is cool?"

"He's very cool."

"Huh," Ben said noncommittally. "Well, okay. But Bender is sorta close to my name—my real name—so how's about I call you Julio so there won't be any confusion?"

"That's cool, dude."

They considered each other in silence for a few seconds. Ben kept expecting the kid to ask another question—people usually had something in mind when they stopped you on the street, even if it was only a request for an autograph—but Julio apparently only wanted to know if he really was the Thing. Finally, sensing nothing else was going to happen, Ben said, "Well, you take it easy there, kid, but I gotta be moseying along . . ."

"Something you want?"

Ben groaned. He chalked the impatience welling up inside him to his rapidly falling blood sugar level. "Kid," he said wearily. "You're making my head hurt."

Julio pointed at Gino's door. "In there. You were looking at the door when that lady ran into you, but you're too big to go in, right? So, you want something? I'll go get whatever you want. Least I can do for the guy who paid for the center."

Ben almost inserted sardonically, "Not to mention saving the city all those times," but then realized that the kid was associating his name with the very act he had just been hoping people—at least people in this neighborhood—would best remember him for. So, instead, he said, "That would be swell, kid. Problem is I ain't got any cash."

"Got plastic?"

"Yeah."

"Gino takes plastic. Hand it over and I'll go get whatever you want."

Ben began to reach into his jacket pocket, but then he hesitated. He had to consider: What if this kid was conning him? What if he handed over his platinum card and little Julio "Bender" Rodriguez took off with it. What if . . . ? And then he stopped and asked himself another question: *So what?* So what if the kid took off? So Ben could run after him and might even catch him or he could throw something (small and nonlethal) and knock him down or, hey—here's a nutty idea—he could cancel the credit card before the kid could do anything with it. Ben Grimm felt ashamed: He was guilty of the same prejudice so many others had inflicted on *him* over the years, the assumption that being poor (though who knew if the kid really *was* poor?) was the same thing as having felonious intentions.

Ben handed over his plastic and gave his order: half a dozen cannoli and an extra-large Café Americano. Julio was back in three minutes with his order. Handing the paper sack and the coffee cup up to Ben, he said, "Gino says, 'Hey,' but he's too busy to come out to say anything else." Julio was holding his own paper cup and blowing through the slit in the plastic flip-top lid.

Holding the bag and cup in one hand, Ben waved at the window with the other, but couldn't see if anyone waved back through the tinted glass. Then, he reached carefully into the paper sack and pulled out one of the cannoli and popped the tube of sweet mascarpone and crunchy fried dough into his mouth. Munching contentedly, he popped the lid off his coffee and took a long sip.

Looking down, he saw that the kid was sipping from his cup and watching him carefully. "Must be hard to hold a paper cup with hands that big. How do you do that?"

Ben considered several answers, but settled on the simplest: "Practice."

Julio laughed, spraying his drink through his nose. Ben was relieved to see that it looked like the kid was drinking milk. "Hey," he said. "Watch the shoes." He ate another cannoli while the kid got himself under control. "Where's my plastic, kid?"

Julio reached into his pocket and handed it over.

"Receipt?"

"What"

"No receipt?"

"Nah. Gino's machine is broken."

Ben thought, *I bet. Well, so what. Kid might have given himself a little tip. How bad could it be?*

"Can I ask you a question?"

Ben nodded. "Knock yourself out."

"Are you planning to arrive at the center, y'know, fashionably late?"

Ben took a too-large gulp of hot coffee, then sputtered, "Aw, crap! What time is it?"

Julio pulled out a cell phone and checked the display. "Five of ten."

"Nuts!" He tossed the mostly empty bag at the kid and said, "Finish these! I gotta go." He took off and quickly reached full speed, though he did risk a quick look back over his shoulder to see Julio happily munching on a pastry. *Pretty good kid,* Ben reflected. *Better than I was at that age.* He had actually enjoyed their little conversation (if that's what you could call what they had been doing), and the best part of it was that the kid had treated him pretty much the same way Ben imagined he treated everyone: like a rube. He grinned and picked up his pace. Small cars parked at the curb bounced slightly as he passed. *There might be hope yet,* Ben Grimm thought, though whether he was thinking about himself or the rest of the human race, he did not know.

As he rounded the corner onto Essex and Yancy, Ben put on the brakes, but carefully. One of the little tips you picked up when you were in the super hero biz long enough was that if you stop too suddenly, you run the risk of tearing off the soles of your civvy shoes. Also, though he didn't perspire, Ben knew that when he exerted himself, the surface of his rocky plates heated up, and there was no point in showing up at the big event warm enough to toast a bagel. Slowing, he readjusted his tie and noted the crowd milling around out front of the center in the chaotic orbital pattern that meant "Press Corps."

Normally, Ben preferred not to mix it up too much with the Fourth Estate, but this wasn't a typical day. He figured Ms. Sullivan, the center's director, must have contacted the local news stations and papers. In New York, on a slow news day, that could mean pulling in ten or fifteen reporters and TV crews. Ben smoothed down the front of his shirt and assumed his jauntiest walk. *Might as well make a good entrance.*

Striding up to the crowd, Ben waved and grinned. A video crew fired up a light and camera flashes popped, leaving blue dots dancing in front of Ben's eyes. He thought he'd seen Ms. Sullivan over near the steps, and Ben did his best to keep the smile on his face while trying to navigate through the shifting bodies. Someone—probably one of the reporters—bumped up against him and Ben turned to his right to apologize. He heard a high-pitched voice call to him from his left and, thinking it must be Ms. Sullivan, spun back around. He felt something bang into his knee and in the next instant heard the entire crowd, as if sharing one prolonged breath, inhale and gasp. Everyone froze and then, a moment later, everyone sped up in crazed, agitated motion.

Someone was screaming shrilly and the cameras were flashing, flashing, flashing, and Ben was holding his hand up in front of his eyes. He immediately became annoyed with the reporters and wanted to growl at them, but managed to keep his temper. People were shouting; some—reporters probably—were asking questions and some were just *yelling*. Someone grabbed Ben's wrist in a firm grip and tugged at him, and though there weren't many people on the planet who could make the Thing move when he didn't want to, the sense of urgency pulled Ben along.

A moment later, he was climbing the four cement steps from the street and banging through the center's wide double doors. As soon as they were through, Ms. Sullivan put her back against the doors, blocking the plate glass windows.

"Hey!" Ben yelled, then felt every single person in the lobby freeze. "What the heck is going on?! What just happened?!"

Ms. Sullivan, a small, tidy woman of some indeterminate age between forty-five and seventy, took off her horn-rim glasses and bent over at the waist like she was trying to lower her blood pressure before she fainted. Her tightly wound bun of gray hair had come undone and strands were flying about wildly. After taking a couple deep breaths, she steadied herself and looked up at Ben. "You didn't see her?" she asked, and Ben didn't like the way that it sounded more like an accusation than a question.

"See who?"

"The girl! The little girl! You must have crashed into her!"

Reporters had climbed up the stairs behind them and were pounding at the doors. Cameras flashed. One of the camera crews lit up a flood and the lobby was suddenly brighter than an operating theatre.

"No," Ben whispered as the icy chill crept up his back. "I didn't see her. Is she okay?" He lurched toward the door. He had to get back outside and see if the girl was okay.

"I didn't see," Ms. Sullivan said, even as she was flinching away. "She fell down and I heard her scream." Ben remembered the scream and felt something inside him shrivel. "But you can't go back outside! Let me go and see what's happening, but we can't . . . The center . . . We can't . . ."

And Ben knew what it was Ms. Sullivan had barely stopped herself from saying: *"We can't risk you hurting anyone else."* She pointed at him, then gestured at the extra-wide door that led to the office the center officials had insisted they put together for him. Ben had known it was a silly idea. He'd never intended to come down here and even if he had, he wouldn't have wanted to sit in some stuffy office. He had imagined himself out in the gym, maybe showing the kids some of the moves he'd learned back in the day or out on the hoops court. Ben knew he couldn't really have played with anyone, but the idea . . . the dream . . . had been very appealing. He inhaled once and let the air out slowly.

With her back to the door, Ms. Sullivan was rewinding her hair into an acceptable style. The questions and calls outside were getting louder and more insistent. Ben heard a siren coming up the street—an ambulance or a paramedic, he hoped. Might be a cop, though. In New York, someone always calls a cop. Even on Yancy Street, if something bad enough happens, they call a cop.

Ben shuffled into his office, barely looking at the plate on the door: "Benjamin J. Grimm, Head Coach." He remembered asking Ms. Sullivan to make up the sign and how funny the idea had seemed at the time.

Just before he closed the door, Ben heard Ms. Sullivan call out to him, "Mr. Grimm?"

Ben turned his head to look back over his shoulder. Maybe something had happened. Maybe she had seen something through the doors and things weren't as bad as they had seemed. Maybe everything was going to be okay after all . . .

She was pointing at him. "Keep the door shut," she said. "And call your lawyer. You're probably going to need him."

Ben pushed the door shut behind him and stood with his hand pressed against it. Outside, he heard the reporters shoving their way into the lobby and, over the din, the sound of Ms. Sullivan trying to rein in the chaos. Ben grunted once, then said, "Hey, good luck with that, lady." He sighed, turned, and walked slowly around behind his desk. He stared at his chair—an extra-large, reinforced model that he'd had made and shipped down here a couple weeks ago— but didn't sit down. *Not much point,* he decided. *I ain't gonna be staying long.* He lightly, lovingly brushed the edge of the desk with his forefinger and said softly, "And it started out to be such a good day."

# 3

THE WORK WAS GOING BETTER THAN KLEMP
could have conceived even in his wildest fantasies.
The task that he had imagined would be the most
difficult—convincing his adviser that he was *finally*
sincerely engaged in a project—had been far simpler than he ever would have expected. It was almost
as if the old fool (well, the middle-aged fool, to be
completely truthful) had been eager to give Klemp
another chance. Maybe this was all he had ever been
looking for: some sense of investment or direction
or . . .

Klemp dismissed the thought. None of that mattered. The important point was that Klemp had been

granted access to one of the labs—a small lab, but one that was nestled snuggly up against one of the big labs, the kind that have high-energy equipment. And breaking into the computing systems, the big heavy-duty parallel processing rigs with petaflops of computing power? Not really a problem when you're a giant geek. As long as he worked in the wee hours of the morning—a schedule that pretty well agreed with Klemp—he had everything he needed to do his work. That was to say, his *real* work, not the nonsense he told his adviser he would be doing. In another month or so, someone would audit his logs, check his balances, balance his checks, and do whatever else the administrators fancied they were supposed to do— but the work would be finished long before then.

Almost everything he needed was in the lab notebooks, and the parts that weren't there—well, the gaps just seemed to smooth over in Klemp's mind as soon as he saw where they were. There were moments where he actually, physically felt like someone was studying the notebooks over his shoulder and pointing out the places where he needed to focus his attention, like a hand around his shoulder or on the back of his head, gently prodding and pushing. There was no work involved, no effort.

It all felt just like magic.

Susan Richards watched her brother fume. She had been watching her Johnny fume, one way or another, for most of her life. At a very early age—too early when you came down to it—after their mother had died and their father had retreated into the tiny, tightly controlled world of his laboratory, Sue had been forced to come to terms with the idea that she was the closest thing Johnny would ever have to a parent. It wasn't a job she had necessarily wanted, but even back then, as a child of three or four, Johnny Storm had been a hothead, and the truth was that sometimes the heat of his anger had frightened her. As much as anything, Sue had assumed the role of his monitor, because some part of her brain had told her that if she could convince her brother that he *needed* her, he couldn't hurt her.

Even now, all these years later, on days like today, on the (thankfully) infrequent days when a dark mood settled down over Johnny, she felt the urge to withdraw, to become (in a word) invisible. Fortunately, Sue also knew that when she felt this way, becoming transparent was the one thing she could not afford to do. Someone had to stand between the world and Johnny. Someone had to protect Johnny from himself.

Johnny was sitting on the couch in the living room, legs stretched out in front of him, slippered feet on the coffee table. There was an empty juice glass on the table (with no coaster underneath it, but Sue felt it was better to ignore this for the moment) and in his hand he held a gently boiling mug of coffee.

He was scowling and, well, *fuming*. Actually, it

was the couch that was fuming, but only barely since Reed had re-covered most of the communal furniture in cloth woven from unstable molecules. The price tag for this bit of home decorating was higher than the gross national product of several small nations, but Sue had shown him how much they had spent on replacing singed furniture over the years, and you could always depend on Reed to do the math in his head.

"Johnny," Sue called softly from the archway between the living room and the kitchen.

"Uh?" Johnny replied.

"Pull it back or the fire suppression system is going to go off."

"What?" Johnny shook himself awake and looked down at his coffee. "Oh. Nuts. Sorry, Sis." The coffee stopped boiling and the slight wisps of smoke that had been curling up from the top of his head were sucked away into the ventilation system. "Wool gathering."

Sue crossed the room and leaned against the back of the couch, arms folded over her chest. She needed to get to a meeting downstairs on the first floor, but she could afford to be a couple minutes late, especially if it meant making sure Johnny didn't set off the smoke alarms. "I'm not surprised," she said. "You must be tired. When did you get home last night?" She knew exactly when he'd gotten home—there wasn't much the Baxter Building's monitoring systems didn't track—but she didn't want to make Johnny think she was watching his every move. He was an adult (by strict legal definition) and though he sometimes acted like a spoiled brat, he was usually fairly responsible about coming and going at regular hours.

"Late," Johnny said.

"Good late or bad late?"

"Bad late," Johnny grunted. "Blowing off steam."

"Problem?"

"Broke up with Chrissy."

Sue searched the mental catalog of Johnny's various female friends. He hadn't been involved in a serious relationship for quite some time, but seemed to be keeping himself busy with a rotating cast of underwear models, actresses, and the occasional B-list super heroine. She hadn't been under the impression that any of them amounted to anything more than a fling, so Sue was uncertain of the reason for Johnny's funk. "The redhead who had been a semifinalist for Miss New Jersey?"

"No. That was Chrissy M. This was Chrissy S."

"Which one was she?"

"Fragrance counter at Macy's."

"Ah, yes. The one who made Val sneeze." This reminded Sue that she needed to mention her daughter's sensitivity to perfumes to Reed to see if he could do anything about it.

"Right."

"This does not strike me as a great loss," Sue said dryly.

"It's not," Johnny said. "Believe me."

"Then why the sulk?"

Johnny sighed and drank a sip of his almost-boiling coffee. Sue had long ago learned to not be alarmed by the temperature of liquids her brother could imbibe. "Because *she* dumped *me*."

Sue tried very hard not to laugh, but it was hard to always be the responsible, considerate one. She tried to cover up by finishing the guffaw with *"Really?"*

"Yeah, yeah," he said, the corner of his mouth quirking up slightly. "I know."

"Did she say why?"

"Yeah," Johnny said and the corners of his mouth turned down again. "That's the part that's kinda bugging me."

"So tell," Sue said. "I have a meeting with the tenants association in like three minutes and I'm not going to be able to focus if I don't get the whole story."

"Not much of a story," Johnny said. "She just said . . . well, basically she said that I was too good a guy."

"What?"

"You heard me."

Sue was confused. Any girl who would date her brother would, by definition, know that he was a good guy. More or less, it was his job description: Be a Good Guy. "What was she expecting?" Sue asked.

Johnny shook his head in mild bewilderment.

"Not sure. That's what I was doing until three: flying around trying to figure out what she meant. It got me to thinking . . ."

"About?"

"You know Logan from the X-Men?"

"Sure. Wolverine. The one who smells like a wet dog."

Johnny grinned. He always enjoyed it when Sue was snarky. "Right. You ever see how all the girls follow him with their eyes?"

"Honestly," Sue said, "no. I'll have to take your word for it."

"Or Daredevil. Back in the old days, when he made stupid jokes like Parker, he was practically a monk, but as soon as he got all broody and dark, he had to start beating the girls back with one of his billy clubs."

"I think you're exaggerating, Johnny."

"I mean, even *Ghost Rider,* for God's sake. He's a freaking skeleton and, let's face it, his powers are just a cheap rip-off of mine, and the babes can't get enough of him. Check the Internet! There are more Web sites—"

"You've really been thinking about this too much," Sue said. "What is it you're really saying? You want to be all dark and conflicted so you can attract girls?"

Johnny crossed his arms over his chest and frowned. "No," he said. "Not really." A thin wisp of smoke curled up from the tip of a stray strand of hair. "Okay, maybe."

"Johnny . . . ," Sue began, feeling herself slipping into lecture mode.

"And no lectures about the odd girl who wants the good guy, Little Miss Isn't-the-Sub-Mariner-Dreamy?"

*Should have seen that one coming,* Sue thought, but knew she couldn't give an inch. "I *married* the good guy," she said softly.

"Well, only because the dark and conflicted guy smelled like the ocean and you're allergic to shellfish."

Sue sighed. She could see that this discussion wasn't going anywhere productive, but she wasn't going to let her stupid little brother get the last word. "I like the smell of the ocean," she said, standing up and smoothing out her skirt, "and I'm not allergic to shellfish anymore. The guy I married gave me a pill and now I could eat lobster for breakfast, lunch, and supper."

"Of course he did," Johnny said, but Sue could tell from his tone of voice that he was out of ammo *and* feeling a little regretful about how he had been acting. He really *was* a good guy, she realized. Men like Namor or Logan or (for all she knew) the Ghost Rider would not have felt regret or anything even close to it, which was one of the reasons she had chosen a man like Reed and one of the main reasons she both liked and respected her brother.

"I have to go, Johnny. We can talk about this some more later if you want."

"Sure." He gulped the last bit of his coffee. "Whatever. I think I'm going to get dressed and head out. There must be something good and decent I can do out there somewhere in New York City."

"Maybe you can find Peter and commiserate with him. He's too nice for his own good too."

"My own sister—comparing me to Puny Parker," Johnny said with mock solemnity. "What has the world come to?" Before she left the room, he turned around and called to her, "Where's Ben?"

She pushed the button on her belt buckle that unlocked the security system and called the elevator to the thirty-first floor. "He went off early to that dedication thing for his rec center."

"The one he thought none of us knew about?"

"That's the one."

"Maybe I should fly by and say hell—"

"Don't you dare, Johnny Storm. If Ben had wanted us there, he would have said something."

"But . . ."

"No buts. Leave Ben alone."

Johnny subsided. "Yes, ma'am. Whatever you say."

"Because you're a nice guy."

"Because I'm a nice guy."

Even as the door was closing behind her, Sue heard her brother mutter, "I'm *tired* of being the nice guy."

Walter Brannigan had talked to Susan Richards exactly twice in the ten years he had been a tenant in the Baxter Building, once when he signed the lease and once the day after Doctor Doom and the Sub-Mariner had towed the building into space. When that particular adventure was over, she had been the one to find Walter hiding inside a supply closet. He had been surprised by how tiny she was—no more than five foot six and probably not weighing much more than a hundred ten pounds—but even back then in the early days, back when she was not much more than a girl, Susan Storm (as she was then) had had a way about her, a presence that fixed her in your mind. And, ever since that day, if they passed each other in the lobby or saw each other at a tenant meeting, she always smiled and nodded and said, "Mr. Brannigan. How are you?" Walter simply nodded and smiled in reply, but those occasions always left him with a spring in his step and the feeling that the daily grind of his little accounting business wasn't as dire as it often seemed.

Several months had passed since Walter had last seen Mrs. Richards. He had, of course, read the articles and seen the news on the TV about the Super-human Registration Act and knew that the Invisible Woman and Mr. Fantastic had been in conflict. He also knew (thanks to the Web site Costume Drama) that the couple had reconciled, but Walter wondered if he would perceive any change in her attitude since the last tenants meeting. They were rarely happy occasions—often as a result of the Fantastic Four's lawyers' having to explain why power had been cut or a wall was missing—but if you were a tenant in the Baxter Building long enough, you became accustomed to such things.

Walter looked around the conference room, counted the faces he recognized, and decided he had seen between half and three quarters of the men and women at previous meetings. The rest—kids in their twenties wearing jeans and sneakers—were likely from the offices on the twenty-fifth through thirtieth floors, the ones with businesses that turned over every year or two. Most of them were biotech or engineering start-ups, groups of highly specialized scientists that moved into the Baxter Building hoping to get Reed Richards' attention so he would be awed by whatever process or gizmo they had cooked up. Back in the old days, Richards had humored the start-ups, but as time passed he had obviously decided that there were only so many hours in a day and he wasn't going to spend them looking at inferior versions of inventions and processes he had already patented. Finally, in frustration, Richards had instituted the annual Baxter Building Science Fair, an event that now attracted guests from the biggest pharma and technology companies in the world and, for safety reasons, the New York City Fire Department. A good time was generally had by all, but it meant the whiz kids on the top floors were constantly in flux.

Brannigan nibbled on a poppy seed muffin (Mrs. Richards always hired the best caterers) and watched the door for their landlady. The representatives from Fantastic Four, Inc., had been circulating among the crowd and glad-handing for a half hour, but the tenants knew that nothing important would happen until one of the bosses arrived. Three minutes past the hour, Mrs. Richards pushed through the double doors and the corporate drones immediately swirled up to the front of the room and surrounded her, chatting, chatting, chatting away, all of them offering a folder or a pad or a cup of coffee. Most of the tenants—the old hands—settled down into their seats because they knew that Mrs. Richards didn't like to waste anyone's time with meaningless blather. She was courteous, but straightforward. The starstruck kids simply froze where they stood, coffee cups or pastries halfway to their mouths.

"Sorry I'm late, everyone," Mrs. Richards said, settling into the chair at the center of the long table at the front of the room. "We can discuss any topics you like at the end of the hour if we have time, but I want to get through the agenda items first." She glanced at the printed agenda, but then set it aside and leaned forward, addressing her audience with her usual candor. "Most of you already know why we called this meeting, so let's not be coy: We have to raise your rent."

Everyone in the room had received the same e-mail Walter Brannigan had, but despite that, half the tenants raised their voices in surprise or alarm.

Someone in the back row booed. Mrs. Richards waited patiently for the din to die down, though one or two of the corporate drones at the front table looked like they wanted to jump out of their seats and slap people's wrists. When the noise subsided, Mrs. Richards raised her hands in acknowledgment of the dissatisfaction. "I know, I know. You don't like hearing it and, honestly, I don't like telling you; however, bear in mind that rents haven't gone up in three years and we have a study here that shows that despite the green improvements we've made in the past five years we've actually been losing money on utilities." She pointed at a stack of folders on a table by the refreshments. Walter had picked one up while he had been waiting and paged through it now.

As was always the case with the Fantastic Four, the presentation of the facts was crystal clear. "Also, we did a survey of local businesses and found that your rents range between fifteen and twenty-two percent, less than any others of comparable size in a five-block radius." She pointed at a second set of folders near the door. "Of course, many of you have multi-year leases and Fantastic Four, Inc., will honor those, but as soon as the term expires, the annual fees will have to be raised." Mrs. Richards opened up a folder she had carried in and concluded, "For most of you, the increases will be in the nine percent zone." More groans and a couple more boos from the back row. Susan closed the folder and stood up. "Of course, you have the option to move out. We'll miss you, but that is your choice."

A middle-aged man wearing a bright plaid jacket stood up and said with mock politeness, "Ms. Richards . . ."

"*Mrs.* Richards," Susan corrected. "Good morning, Mr. Conway."

Thrown off his stride, Mr. Conway verbally stumbled for a moment and then continued, "Yes, of course. Mrs. Richards, I'm sure that everything you said is true. I'm sure that the math is right, if nothing else." He panned around the room waiting for an appreciative chuckle, but had to continue on empty-handed. "But no one in a five-block radius has to worry about the Inhumans dropping in while I'm meeting with a client—"

A deep voice behind Walter Brannigan said, "You got a client, Jack? Hey, congratulations!"

Mr. Conway dismissed the heckler with a wave of his hand and soldiered on. "And what about when the entire building shakes every time you and the rest of your gang take off in one of your Fantastic-mobiles . . ."

"Fantasticar." Everyone in the room was staring at Walter, and it took him a moment to realize that he was the one who had corrected Conway.

Mrs. Richards briefly made eye contact with Walter, and he was fairly certain he saw the corner of her mouth crook up. "Fantasticar. Thank you, Mr. Brannigan."

*"Whatever,"* Conway sputtered.

"With the shock wave suppression technology my husband has installed, you shouldn't be feeling anything at all," Mrs. Richards continued in honeyed tones. "If you do, you should contact our help desk. The phone number, in case you lost the magnet we sent to everyone, is 1–800–555-Fan4."

Walter heard several appreciative chuckles from various corners of the room. Conway was a well-known blowhard and generally disliked by the old-timers in the building, not the least because he managed a telemarketing firm that was under investigation for trafficking in suspicious subprime mortgages. But unfortunately, the man must have been speaking for at least a couple other tenants in the conference room, because other voices were now raised. "What about the Mole Man? Is there any chance he could undermine the foundation?" "Do you have dangerous weapons lying around? I read an article in the *Daily Bugle* where they said . . ." "What are we supposed to do if one of you goes crazy like that Avenger did and tries to blow up the building?"

The meeting was beginning to take on the air of an inquisition, with a handful of the loudest complainers up out of their seats, all of them raising their voices to be heard over the others. Several of the Fantastic Four, Inc., functionaries had jumped out of their seats and were holding up their file folders as if they might either use them to fend off the tenants or begin fanning the room to try to cool it off. Mrs. Richards closed her eyes and appeared to be trying to sort through the torrent of words; then Walter decided that, no, she was reining in her temper. A moment later, he felt an unexpected change in the room's air pressure, but it passed just that quickly. Mrs. Richards opened her eyes and said one word: "Enough." It sounded as if she were speaking right into Walter's ear, softly, but sincerely, and he could see from the startled expressions around him that everyone else heard her voice in exactly the same way.

Mrs. Richards continued, "I apologize for the theatrics, but I didn't want to have to try to shout over the din. I live with three men, a little boy, and a little girl, and it seems like I spend much of my time trying to get one or the other of them to listen to me, so you'll forgive me if I use some of the techniques on you that I have to resort to with them. And, I swear, the worst ones aren't the kids." She smiled grimly and scanned the room for the three or four friendly female faces. "Some of you women might know what I mean."

A woman in a business suit near the front said, "Amen, sister. Testify."

Mrs. Richards laughed and flipped her hair back over her shoulders. "I will," she said. "I thought I was doing my best to keep this on the level of business and simply explain your options. No one is making you stay here, though I guess I also thought we had all built up a decent level of trust. However, I'm hearing some anxiety in your voices, so there's another thing I want all of you to keep in mind, and it's this: You're all here in the Baxter Building for eight or ten hours a day." She leaned forward and enunciated each word very clearly: "I *live* here. My family and my friends *live* here. And most important, my *children* live here. My son, Franklin, and his sister, Valeria, are both upstairs right now, hopefully not getting into any serious trouble since I doubt my brother is watching them very carefully. We have a nanny and a couple of very doting aunts and uncles who also watch over them, but you must believe me when I say this: *No one* cares more about the safety and security of this building—their home—than my husband and me." Still leaning forward, hands flat on the table, she concluded, "And, as long as you are our tenants, we extend that courtesy to you. Am I making myself clear?"

This last question was phrased in such a way that only a person much more courageous than Walter Brannigan would have been able to say anything but, "Yes, ma'am."

Mrs. Richards scanned the room, looking to see if anyone had any more comments. No one stirred, but she had to have felt the lingering tension, and decided it needed to be released. "Or, you could take your chances and move into Avengers Tower." The corporate employees laughed with every show of genuine appreciation, but the joke had been weak at best and Mrs. Richards' sheepish expression made it clear that she knew it, too. Leaning back in her chair, she sighed, then looked at her watch. "We have enough time for a few more questions as long as you all promise not to bring up the Mole Man or the Silver Surfer or . . . I don't know . . . Paste Pot Pete."

This was greeted with something closer to sincere amusement (and a few questioning looks) and the meeting continued to a civil enough conclusion twenty minutes later. Without realizing what he was doing, Walter somehow made sure that he was standing near the door when Susan Richards left the room and was rewarded with a warm smile and a "Hello, Mr. Brannigan."

Walter smiled back and nodded, but something else was exchanged during the encounter. He saw, for a split second, a crease of worry in his landlady's otherwise flawless forehead and noticed the way she twisted her head to look expectantly toward the ceiling. *Here,* Walter thought, *is a woman who is waiting for the other shoe to drop.* And no matter how hard he resisted, several times over the course of the morning, he felt his eyes straying ceiling-ward, wondering sympathetically where the footwear was and just how big it was going to be.

# 4

KLEMP LOVED READING (AND REREADING AND rereading) the page in the lab notebook where Von Doom made his error and Richards wrote his note in the margin. He had briefly wondered whether Forester had showed the note to Von Doom, but then dismissed the thought. It wouldn't have mattered one way or another. Richards—the great big know-it-all—would have tracked down Von Doom and issued his warning personally. Still, there was no denying the man had formidable gray matter. Klemp could just barely follow Von Doom's reasoning and math, but Richards had walked past an open notebook, glanced at a set of equations for . . . what?

Two seconds? And from that, the man had seen that something wasn't quite right. Klemp knew it would be the height of arrogance not to doff his metaphorical cap to the man.

Still, Klemp had every intention of claiming his share of the credit when the moment came, and the moment, to use the phrase, was nigh. The apparatus that Von Doom had created was relatively simple, if mind-meltingly clever. Basically, it was a very precise tuning fork that could be adjusted to vibrate at an excruciatingly exact frequency. The vibration would reveal the lip of a dimensional layer which would then be very carefully pierced, allowing communication with intelligences from other dimensions.

The idea of parallel worlds was as old as the hills and had been mathematically and practically proven. Reed Richards himself had written extensively about his "discovery" of an "underverse" that he had dubbed (for some adolescent reason that defied comprehension) "the Negative Zone." Practically every college student in New York City had spent at least one night wandering around Greenwich Village looking for the home of the Sorcerer Supreme, Dr. Strange, who supposedly slipped into alternate dimensions as easily as a commuter driving through the Lincoln Tunnel. Klemp himself hadn't made the Strange Trek (as it was called), seeing as it was one of those activities one usually did either while inebriated (he didn't drink) or with friends (he didn't have any) or both, but he had heard the stories, though he'd also concluded that no one had ever really found the place. Odd, really, when you considered that there were photographs of the building from twenty years ago, but no one had any record of the places being demolished.

The only difference between Von Doom's communication device and Klemp's was size. According to Forester's notes, Von Doom had kludged together some kind of wacky giant helmet with retro earphones, a speaking device that sounded like it had come off a 1940s-era German U-boat, and (the only innovative touch) eyephones that would have felt at home in an early William Gibson novel. Klemp considered the idea of reproducing the whole retro cool thing, but decided against it, settling instead for the sleeker, more modern, and considerably cheaper options of recycling chunks of his roommate's discarded Xbox 360 and PSP.

He settled down in the padded leather chair (the one with the tear in the back that he had stolen from the chemistry office) and had a brief, pleasant moment of reflection. In a couple years, he decided, this chair would be in a museum, this apparatus would be studied or stored in display cases, and these notebooks (copied over in Klemp's hand) would be immortalized. He emptied his liter bottle of Diet Dr Pepper and started to toss it into the trash can, but then reconsidered, *No, maybe not.* Reverently setting the bottle on the corner of the desk, he thought, *Endorsement deal*.

Klemp plugged the intercom headset he had lifted from his roommate's Xbox into the console, then fired up the small HD monitor he had ordered with the last of his grant money. *If you're going to peer into another dimension,* he had decided, *you might as well see it clearly.* He checked his notes, fussed with the console settings, and made his final adjustments. Finally, he took a deep breath, let it out slowly, and pushed the ON button. The apparatus went *click,* and Klemp began to slowly turn the frequency adjuster, all the time listening carefully and watching the monitor for any signs of change.

He heard a faint pop and the monitor flared briefly, then went dark. Behind him, Klemp felt a shiver in the air, and a sensation crept up his spine that made him think of waking up in the middle of the night and knowing, just *knowing,* that someone had just opened your bedroom window, but not from the inside.

Reed Richards drummed his fingers on the corner of Tony Stark's gigantic teak desk and considered for the fourth time in twelve minutes whether maybe it might not be better for everyone involved that he just call it a day and go home. The meeting had been Tony's idea after all and though Reed had to concede that his friend's responsibilities as the director of S.H.I.E.L.D..

meant his time was precious, the man had been called out of the room six times in less than an hour.

Reed Richards drummed his fingers some more.

He had felt vaguely ridiculous wearing his F.F. uniform to the S.H.I.E.L.D. helicarrier, but Tony had made it a point in his invitation that Reed should "fly the colors," in order to boost morale, and otherwise reinforce the idea that the superhuman community was just one big happy family. Reed sighed. That idea—or, at least, the sometimes rigid manner in which Tony Stark chose to portray it—had almost cost him his marriage and the trust of his oldest friend. There was no question that Reed believed— no, *knew*—that the superhuman community needed to be reined in and made accountable for its activities, but he sometimes had second and even third thoughts about the long-term viability of some of the plans he and Tony had concocted. The law was the law—and the Superhuman Registration Act was *law*—but "law" did not always equal "justice" and Reed struggled with the idea of any law that made men like Peter Parker and Luke Cage fugitives.

The door to Tony's office slid open and a young, redheaded S.H.I.E.L.D. agent popped her head in and said, "I'm so sorry, Dr. Richards, but Mr. Stark asked if you could please wait another few minutes. He's been called away to . . ."

"Attend to a matter of national security," Reed finished for her. "Yes, I know. Thank you. The last one said the same thing . . ." As soon as the words were out of his mouth, Reed felt embarrassed by his churlishness. After all, it wasn't this young lady's fault that Tony was constantly being called away. "Sorry," he said. "I'm just . . . Could you . . . I need to call my wife. Could you ask the communications officer to adjust the scrambler so that I can get through? I gave them my frequency on the way up here." This request was, strictly speaking, unnecessary, as Reed had figured out how to reconfigure his communicator to punch through S.H.I.E.L.D.'s security system during the last long pause in the meeting. But, as Sue so often reminded him, courtesy counted.

"Certainly, Dr. Richards. Just give us a moment." She backed out of the office as if moving on rails and Reed briefly wondered if he had just been talking to one of the new-model Life Model Decoys, but then decided, no, it would be ridiculous for Tony to use such an expensive piece of equipment to act as a receptionist. On the other hand, now that he had an idea of the kinds of hours one of Tony's receptionists might need to work, maybe the idea made sense. The greeter at the reception desk in the Baxter Building was a hologram, after all . . .

"Dr. Richards?" said a cheerful voice from an unseen intercom. "We've cleared your frequency. Please go ahead with your call."

"Thank you," Reed said, looking up at no one spot in particular. He unclipped his belt buckle and brushed his hand over a smooth reverse face. Sensors registered his biometric signature and the interface lit up. Reed said, "Phone," and then a moment later, "Susan." The phone glyph appeared and blinked once, twice, three times before Sue's face appeared on the screen.

She seemed relieved to see him, but then caught something in his expression that made her frown. "I know that look," Sue said. "How much longer are you going to be?"

"Good question," Reed said. "Another question we might want to ask is 'How many times can Tony Stark leave a room in an hour before you begin to wonder if your antiperspirant isn't working?'"

"It would be a better question if you actually perspired. You don't anymore, do you?"

"No, and I've been trying to factor that into my calculations, but so far I'm not getting much traction."

"That must be frustrating." Sue actually smiled, and Reed counted this as a spectacular victory. But he could see the lines of tension in her forehead and she was hunching her shoulders, which she only did when she was very tired or aggravated.

"You have no idea."

"So the meeting isn't going the way you had hoped."

"No, but about how I expected. Tony has too many irons in the fire."

Sue groaned. "You've been waiting to say that all day, haven't you?"

"I thought of it during the second interruption. Please tell Johnny and Ben that I actually made a joke."

"They'll be thrilled." Sue inhaled and let the breath out slowly. "Will you be home soon? It's been a hard day and I could use a neck rub."

Reed sighed. "I think we're over Kansas now, so if I called it a day now, I could be back in New York in an hour or so . . ."

"But . . . ," Sue said leading him.

"But we've barely finished the first item on our agenda."

"Not your fault."

Reed knew he was headed into a bad place. To agree with his wife meant he had to concede. To deny meant he would have to lie, and Susan always knew when he was lying. It was the superpower most of the public didn't know the Invisible Woman possessed, but the one Reed both feared and respected the most. Sensing the pause was getting too long, he finally said, "No. Not my fault. I'll just leave him a note and tell him that—"

"Even if you left now, you wouldn't be home in time to say good night to the kids, so don't worry about it."

Reed checked the chrono on the display. "Right," he said. "I'll make them breakfast."

"I think that's an acceptable compromise," Sue said. "Promise you'll make some noise when you come home. I hate it when you try to be quiet."

"I promise," Reed said. "Tell the kids I love them."

"I will," Sue said. "And I love you. See you soon."

"Good night," Reed said and started to push the DISCONNECT button. "No, wait. How did Ben's thing go . . . ?" But it was too late. Susan had hung up. *Oh, well,* Reed decided. *I'll find out in the morning.*

Klemp looked over his shoulder, but saw nothing that hadn't been there two minutes earlier. He turned back to the blank monitor and began to turn the frequency knob again, but the feeling that someone was standing behind him and staring at the back of his head was so strong that his scalp itched. This time, he pulled off his headset, spun the chair around, and squinted into the gloom. The lab was so small that he could see every square inch from where he sat. Could someone have installed one of those microcameras? But why would they? Klemp had been so careful about pulling together his resources: Some things were old, a few things were new, a few were borrowed, and . . . well, there was nothing blue, but a few things had been . . . what was the term? Liberated. Yes, he had liberated a few items from unappreciative owners, items he had every intention of returning and/or making restitution for when the opportunity arose. He had nothing to feel guilty about and no reason to feel like someone was watching him.

Klemp turned back to his console. A single blood-shot, red-pupiled eye was staring up at him from the monitor. He shouted, "Holy mackerel!" and pushed himself away from the console so quickly that the cord went taut and yanked off the headset, pulling his glasses with them. The office chair crashed against the wall and Klemp rolled onto the floor. Effectively blind without his glasses, he groped around on the floor until he felt the earpiece. Pushing them back onto his face, he crab-walked toward the door, but felt compelled to check the monitor to see if the eye was following his progress. It was not. In fact, the eye was gone.

Sagging against the door, Klemp smoothed down the hair on the back of his head and successfully suppressed the urge to open the lab door to see if someone was standing there. "Okay," he said when his breathing evened out. "What the hell was that?"

*Good question,* came the reply. *I know what I saw, but what about you?*

Klemp actually felt his knees quiver and all the liquid in his lower abdomen simultaneously ask if it could please, pretty please, be allowed to leave by the most expedient means possible. He managed to issue a strong denial to the liquids, but couldn't help but sink to the floor, his back flat against the door. He let several seconds tick past to see if there were any other unexpected sounds, but Klemp heard nothing. *Maybe I hit my head,* he thought.

*Maybe you did,* the voice said. It was a fairly pleasant voice: deep, sonorous, even comforting in a manly sort of way . . . except for the fact that it was coming from out of thin air.

"Wait a second," Klemp said. "It heard me when I was thinking."

*You were thinking very loudly,* the voice said. *It was hard to ignore.*

Klemp pushed himself up into a half-standing/half-leaning position. He looked from left to right, up and down, scanning the room for the speaker. He even felt his head again to make sure part of the headset wasn't attached to his ear.

"So . . . wait. Help me understand. You can read my mind?"

*Oh, no,* the voice replied, and Klemp was pretty sure that this was followed by something that sounded a lot like an amused chuckle. *No, no, no. That would be rude. Intrusive. And besides, not something I would have any interest in doing. Rather like taking a vacation to Schenectady. I mean, you could go, but why bother?*

"I . . . I grew up in Schenectady," Klemp said.

*Yes,* the voice said. *I know. I know everything about you. Didn't take too long. A rather brief, uninspiring tale, all in all. Not much worth remarking on except for the part right there at the end . . .*

Klemp felt the liquids making their insistent demands again and did his best to lock his knees so he wouldn't move closer to the floor. The need to flee was becoming overwhelming. He knew he should try to figure out what was happening, make some sense of events, maybe even just calmly sit down in the chair again and put the headset back on, but the impulse to respond to the voice was just about irresistible. "At the end? What part at the end?"

*The part where we meet,* the voice said. *The point where we join forces.*

"Join forces?" Klemp asked. This sounded less threatening than what he had been imagining. "You mean, like form a pact? Make a deal?"

Klemp "heard" a noise like someone taking a deep breath and exhaling slowly, as if the owner of the voice was deeply considering a difficult question. *Not exactly,* the voice finally said. The pressure in Klemp's bowels came on again very strongly. The voice asked, *Would you like to use the lavatory?*

An ancient memory suddenly flooded through Klemp's mind. He remembered his first day of kindergarten and his teacher telling the class to line up so they could all go to the lavatory. Even at the age of five, Klemp had been fascinated by the image of the scientist that he had seen in sci-fi monster movies: tall, commanding men with neatly trimmed hair and white lab coats. Most of them smoked pipes and possessed resonant, booming voices not much different (now that he thought about it) from the one that had apparently taken up residence inside his brain. He remembered how he had excitedly told all his classmates about how interesting it would be when they got to the lavatory, how they would pour chemicals back and forth between test tubes and look at the wavy lines on the oscilloscope (a word Klemp had heard at a young age and stuck to like a best friend). All the way down the hall, holding hands with his partner, Klemp had felt an unusual bounce in his step, secure in the knowledge that he knew something about where they were going that none of the other kids could know. For that pitifully brief span of minutes, young Stanislaw Klemp had felt *special*.

Imagine his disappointment when they finally reached their destination. Not even the novelty of the water fountain that you could control with the foot pedal could lift the gloom that descended on him. He could never hear the word "lavatory" without thinking of that moment, that gloom, that sense of disappointment.

He clawed at the door, finally managed to twist the knob, and tore it open. Racing as fast as he could down the empty hall, Klemp rounded the corner and skidded to a stop in front of the heavy door that had been stenciled with the word "MEN." He yanked it open and quick-stepped inside, but it was late and the lights were turned off. For several frantic seconds Klemp swiped futilely at the spot next to the door where light switches usually were, then finally

magaged to clip it with the side of his hand. The fluorescents flickered and popped, blinding Klemp with
their glare.

When his vision cleared, he realized that he was
standing very still in front of the large mirror, his arms
and legs spread wide and the urge that had propelled
him hither completely evaporated. Klemp studied the
mirror—his too-large hands, sunken chest, scrawny
legs, and pipe cleaner arms—and he knew, absolutely
*knew* that it wasn't really him that was letting those
seconds tick past in careful study. Someone—some-
*thing*—was examining him through his own eyes.
Finally, the voice made a *tsk-tsk* sound and said, *This
will really not do. Not at all. Not one tiny bit.*

Finally, the feeling that someone was staring at the
back of Klemp's skull ceased and turned into the sensation of someone pulling open the back of Klemp's
skull. He wanted to scream, but took too long to
inhale and by the time the breath was sucked in it
didn't belong to him anymore. The new tenant had
moved in and started to renovate.

Years earlier, only a short time after he and his teammates had been transformed by the cosmic ray storm,
Reed Richards had discovered that while he rarely
*required* food, the psychological desire to eat had never
disappeared. It was a pleasure that he never wanted to
give up and, he had learned, one of the few avenues
open to him for dispelling stress.

Ten minutes after concluding his call with his wife, Reed started thinking about a turkey sandwich on rye with Swiss cheese, lettuce, tomato, and a bit of brown mustard. Never the yellow kind. Reed hated yellow mustard. Five minutes later, he left Tony's office, asked the receptionist (he was now almost positive that she was an L.M.D.) for directions to the galley, and headed off in search of food. Tony could come find *him* when he was ready.

Security agents posted at key intersections watched Reed curiously as he passed, but no one attempted to stop him. The pass clipped to his jacket gave him clearance to all but the most secure areas and the big, blue "4" on his shirt guaranteed a certain amount of cooperation. The galley was found, a cook of no small skill—a middle-aged woman named Rachel Tyson—was in attendance, and she said she would be happy to construct a sandwich that matched Dr. Richards' specifications. As the rye bread toasted and the turkey was sliced, the young cook asked Reed polite and interesting but unobtrusive questions about his work on the helicarrier and his adventures with his teammates. The sandwich was perfection and came with a garlic dill. Reed had intended to take his food back to Tony's office and eat there, but he found himself enjoying Rachel's company so much that he settled down at the long counter and they talked while he ate.

Reed found out that Rachel had been with S.H.I.E.L.D. since she was in her early twenties, had been on several missions with both Captain America and Nick Fury, but had settled into the somewhat quieter life of a cook after she had been injured on a mission. Rachel was unmarried and had no family; S.H.I.E.L.D. was her life, so she decided the best thing to do was gracefully accept the change. "And," she said, "I'm a good cook. Some of the younger agents have even started calling me Mom. I threatened to smack the first couple, but then I decided, *What the hell.* There are worse things."

Reed laughed. All in all, the encounter was almost making up for Tony's behavior.

While he was telling Rachel a story about one of his first encounters with Nick Fury, Reed noticed a sudden change in her demeanor. One moment she had been leaning forward, elbows on the counter, hand on her chin, nodding and smiling, and the next she was still looking at him, still smiling, but with her back straightened and her hands flat on the counter. Every ten seconds or so, her eyes would flick upward and look over his left shoulder. Finally, Reed had to turn around to see what was so distracting.

Above the door, four lights flashed in a sequence: green, yellow, orange, yellow. When he had been walking down the corridors, Reed had seen the same lights, but then they had blinked green, yellow, green, green. He turned back toward Rachel. "What's happening?"

"I don't know," she said. "Something unexpected, but whatever it is, we haven't gone to battle stations."

Reed stood up and brushed the crumbs off his lap. "Point me toward the bridge."

"Dr. Richards . . . I'm not permitted . . . I'm not sure if you have clearance for the bridge under these circ—"

"Agent," Reed said, pitching his voice low and subtly lengthening his spine so that he would appear taller and broader. "If I really want to get to the bridge, do you honestly think there's any way you could stop me?"

"I . . . ," Rachel began. "No, sir, I don't." She stood up straight, lifted her chin, and reached around behind her back to untie the apron she had been wearing. Bunching the apron up into a ball, she laid it down on the countertop and said, "But I would be obliged to try."

Feeling slightly ashamed, Reed contracted his spine and exhaled slowly. "Would it be breaking the rules if you escorted me?"

The corner of Rachel's mouth twitched and she cocked her head to the side, considering her options. "That," she concluded, "would be more like *stretching* the rules."

"A condition I feel perfectly comfortable with," Reed stated.

"As do I," Rachel said. "Let me get my weapons."

Minutes later, Reed and his escort strode through the bridge's main doors, paused only briefly for the guards to clear them, and then ascended the wide stairs to the sensor control area. Tony Stark was standing between the oversized chairs bolted to the floor before the two primary scanning stations, his arms flung around the headrests on either side. Both officers on duty were wearing the helmets and control gauntlets that gave them complete control over the helicarrier's sensor rigs and, as much as possible, immersed them in the incoming data.

If he had had to judge by the sharp creases in Tony's shirt and slacks, Reed would have been inclined to believe that the director of S.H.I.E.L.D. had risen and dressed less than an hour ago, but he also knew that looks were always deceiving where Mr. Stark was concerned. Stark glanced at Reed and then refocused his laserlike attention on the scanner displays. "What kept you?"

"I had to finish my sandwich," Reed said, studying the display. "What's happening? That's Manhattan, isn't it?"

"Answer to the second question: yes. Answer to the first question: We're not sure. We're not picking up anything on our scanners. No energy spikes. No weapons being discharged. No sightings of any unusual superhuman activity."

"Then why the alert?"

"The psychics started twitching." Tony had a fairly low regard for S.H.I.E.L.D.'s Psi Division, citing (once a businessman, always a businessman) its low rate of return on investment, but Reed also knew that there were documented incidents where the psychics had alerted the director to disasters no other source had discovered. Pointing at the screen, Tony continued, "And then this popped out of nowhere."

Reed studied the display and quickly interpreted the data. "Extra-dimensional incursion," he said and then asked, "Can you overlay a street map?" The sensor officer tapped a key on his control interface and the streets of the Upper West Side appeared. "It's Empire State."

"Right."

"Whatever it is, it's fairly localized."

"So far."

"What are you going to do?"

"I was going to send a S.H.I.E.L.D. team in, though I expect the mayor to be on the phone about twenty seconds after they touch down. He's been on edge lately."

"May I suggest another idea?"

"You want to take a look?"

"I was supposed to be having a meeting with the director of S.H.I.E.L.D."

Tony faked a grimace. "Right. Sorry about that." He looked over his shoulder and glanced at Rachel. "Agent Tyson," he said. "Thank you for looking after Dr. Richards."

"My pleasure, Director," she said with a smile before withdrawing to the sentry position near the door.

"So, what are you suggesting, Reed?"

"I think I know someone who could be convinced to take a look and has some experience with extra-dimensional beings."

Tony nodded. "I think I see where you're going. Okay. Just be sure to tell Mr. Storm to call if he runs into something bigger than himself."

At that very moment, in the men's lavatory down the hall from Stanislaw Klemp's lab, something grabbed the chrome door handle and it immediately began to melt and run in its grip. The being that had briefly lived inside Klemp's mind, but that had now taken up residence in every other bit of him, too, removed its hand and watched the liquid metal boil and bubble as it ran down over the palm. *Well,* it said in a voice that echoed like a cracked bell tolling in a sewer tunnel, *I'll have to get* that *under control if I'm going to get anything accomplished.* He concentrated for a moment, then reached out and touched the door with one fingertip. The paint blistered ever so slightly, the pungent odor of charred oil-based paint filling the room. "Better," he said and grinned, the skin around his lips cracking ever so slightly. "I think I'm going to like it here."

**5**

FROM SPACE, EVEN USING THEIR MOST SOPHISTI-
cated scanning technology, S.H.I.E.L.D. could only
barely detect the wave of spectral energy that slithered and shimmied out of the hole Stanislaw Klemp
had poked in the firmament. From two hundred feet
above the street, with only the naked eye, the effect
was completely invisible.

Johnny Storm hovered in the late evening sky, the
orange-yellow flames that licked over his body vivid
against the lowering sky. Watching the students, professors, and other academic-looking types who criss-
crossed the campus, he let his mind wander back to
that handful of months when he had taken classes at

Empire State. *This is where I met Wyatt,* he mused, and tried to remember the last time he had talked to his former roommate. Though he knew Wyatt Wingfoot had enjoyed the months he had spent as an adjunct member of the F.F., Johnny had always known his friend would return to his reservation and take on the responsibilities of adult life. *Unlike me,* Johnny thought ruefully. *I've been too busy being "a good guy."*

Even after the heart-to-heart with Sue—usually a cure for almost anything that ailed him—Johnny had continued to fume about the breakup. Though most people believed he possessed a level of self-confidence that bordered on arrogance, the truth was Johnny didn't handle rejection very well, mostly because he didn't have a lot of experience with it. Chrissy's words had burrowed into his psyche, carved out a little cancerous niche, and set to festering.

When Reed had called, the promise of action had temporarily roused Johnny from his torpor, but now, watching campus life unfold beneath him, the Human Torch sank once more into his funk. *Coeds,* he thought, *are much, much cuter when you're a few years older.* He sighed. *Great. Now not only am I boring, but I'm old. What's next? A paunch? Bald spot? Fallen arches?*

The commlink on his belt vibrated: Reed checking on him. He willed the flame around his belt and on his hand to disappear and tapped RECEIVE. Johnny didn't say hello and didn't wait for his brother-in-law to speak. "Wild-goose chase, Reed," he snapped. "Nothing here."

"Move two hundred meters to the northwest, Johnny. There's a building with a dome on the southeast corner. Do you see it?"

"It's dark down here, Reed, and I don't have infrared vision. Hang on." Johnny knew he was sounding surly, but didn't care. Just because Reed had lost track of time and didn't know night had fallen . . . "I see it. I'm dropping down to the roof." He cut his flame a couple meters from the rooftop in case there were smoke alarms nearby. Over the years, Johnny had learned not to fly too close to public buildings. Having been a fireman himself for a few months, he knew how much the FDNY hated to be called out on false alarms. "I'm on the roof." Johnny stomped his foot down hard a couple times. "Seems stable. No dimensional rifts detected."

"It might be inside, Son."

Johnny rolled his eyes. *Son?* "Yes, okay, *Dad.* I'll take a look." Why was Reed being so condescending? Because he was up there hanging out with a bunch of S.H.I.E.L.D. bigwigs? Okay, maybe not a fair question: Reed was condescending *most* days, but for some reason it was really poking a finger in Johnny's eye today. How did Sue deal with this? And Ben . . . How had two guys as different as Reed and Ben ever become such close friends? Johnny remembered about the dedication of Ben's rec center for the first time since the conversation with Sue and was taken slightly off guard by the wellspring of resentment that suddenly rose up in him. *How is it that I can get crap for being a "nice guy" when a big grouch like Ben gets a recreation center named after him?* Johnny knew perfectly well that the answer to his question was that Ben had *paid* for the rec center, but, still, the idea aggravated him. A wisp of smoke curled up off the back of his hand and Johnny had to suppress the urge to set the comm on fire and toss it across the quad.

"Whenever you feel you have the time, Johnny."

*Great. Sarcasm from "Mr. Fantastic."* Johnny heaved a mighty sigh and dropped down into the narrow lane between two buildings by simply warming up the air beneath him just enough to slow his fall. Something darted away behind a Dumpster as he touched down and Johnny almost reignited and went aloft. He hated rats.

Disoriented now that he was on the ground, Johnny looked to the right and left, searching for a door. Did they lock up these buildings after dark? He hadn't ever had the chance to find out when he was a student, but figured that the science buildings, most of them chock-full of expensive equipment and chemicals, had to be locked. Of course, college students being college students, there had to be a door propped open with a wood block or a lock taped over with duct tape somewhere nearby. He walked slowly up the alley toward the quad, scanning the shadows for scuttle creatures.

Just past the next Dumpster, Johnny found a fire door. He tugged on the handle experimentally, but it was locked. Just as Johnny was wondering how much trouble he would get into if he softened up the jamb (he could always fix it again later), the door flew open, barely missing his outstretched hand. A small, bespectacled woman wearing a baggy sweatshirt and sweatpants stared at him, her eyes wide and wild and her short-cropped hair literally standing on end all over her head. She took a half step back, then shrieked, gathered her strength, and sprung forward, shoving Johnny in the chest with surprising strength and sprinting past him.

Johnny Storm had had years of experience exploring strange environments, but this unexpected encounter left him utterly flummoxed. Staring into the dark hallway, he felt his heart racing and struggled not to follow the young woman into the night. Nothing before him moved, but Johnny had the unshakable feeling that something waited inside the door, something that knew how to sit in a pool of shadow and remain perfectly still.

His commlink vibrated in his hand, and Johnny gave a strangled cry. When he felt he had his voice under control, he answered, "I'm busy, Reed."

"This is Tony Stark, John." *John.* You had to appreciate that about Tony: He knew how to make a guy feel like an adult. Maybe he should make Reed, Sue, and Ben call him John from now on. "Reed's busy with the sensors—which, just so you know, say you're pretty much standing on top of whatever it is that's happening. Anything to report?"

"I'm not sure," Johnny replied, trying to muster some of the old bravado. "I'm staring into what looks like a dark stairwell and I've got the heebee-jeebies, like the Hulk just asked me if I'd like to go square dancing. Also, a college girl just ran out of the building a minute ago, and she shrieked when she saw me."

"By 'shrieked,' I'm assuming you mean 'shriek of terror'?"

"Right."

"Not what you're used to, is it?"

Johnny appreciated the ego-stroking. "Not really," he said, feeling some of the old cockiness returning.

"What about the hallway? Does anything about it feel familiar? Could it be some kind of gas? Maybe a psionic?"

Johnny shook his head. "Not a gas. I'd recognize that. Psionic . . . Maybe, though not a Charles Xavier type. Those kinds of guys always feel kind of soothing so that whatever crazy thing they ask you to do, it feels like a great idea. *Nothing* about this feels like a great idea."

"Like something is trying to keep you out."

"Exactly." There came a long pause, and Johnny began to wonder if the signal had been cut. The feeling of dread was growing stronger, and Johnny took a step back from the door. He shook the commlink and held it close to his mouth so he could speak softly. "Tony?"

"Hold your position, John. Something is happening."

*Something is happening.* Not exactly the words Johnny wanted to hear. Nor was he happy to hear the blood pounding behind his eardrums. "The hell with this," Johnny said to no one in particular. Igniting his left hand, he flicked a small, slow-moving, but very bright ball of flame through the doorway, into the murky hall, sending long, erratic shadows squiggling up the walls. Nothing terribly dangerous or unexpected lurked inside: The hallway looked like just about every institutional hallway Johnny had ever seen, with alternating doors and lockers. When his fireball blinked out halfway down the hall, the difference hit him: *No lights.* Not a single office light was lit. He looked around at the rest of the campus to see if there had been a power failure, but no, only this hallway was dark. Even the emergency lights were shut off. Trying to sound jaunty, he quoted a line from *Jaws:* "I think he ate the light." Unfortunately, instead of sounding cool, Johnny heard his voice crack slightly.

Without thinking about it, Johnny ignited (except for the hand holding the commlink) and lifted off to hover six inches above the ground. The crackle of his flame comforted him and kept the feeling of dread at bay. His phone buzzed again, and he lifted it to his ear. "Johnny?" Reed was back. Despite Johnny's earlier annoyance, he felt reassured to hear Reed's voice again.

"Still here. Still waiting."

"What are you seeing?"

"Darkness. Where there shouldn't be any. What are Tony's fancy sensors seeing?"

"Something we don't understand. That's why I need you to give us some context."

"The feeling I had earlier has gotten stronger. It's like the darkness is looking at me, that whole 'Stare not into the abyss . . .' thing."

At the far end of the narrow lane, Johnny heard the screech and sharp pop of a car colliding with something solid. Farther away, there came the wail of sirens, many sirens, all heading in different directions. A large rat, either emboldened with some stranger lust or blind with fear, skittered beneath Johnny's hovering form, unafraid of his flaming feet. "Reed," he said. "Something really bad is starting to happen down here."

"I see it. The sensor readings just spiked. Stand by."

Johnny parted his lips to reply, but before he could say a word, he felt his gut twist, abruptly aware that the thing in the darkness was focusing its undivided regard on him. He tried to tear away, to blast straight up into the sky, but felt like someone had dumped a mountain of wet sand over him. He couldn't move, couldn't take a breath, and his eyes and ears were sealed shut. Something clutched his throat and dragged him forward. A distant part of his mind marveled at the idea that anything could touch him when he was aflame, and that thought—the memory of fire—gave Johnny strength.

Johnny Storm thought, *Burn,* and gave himself over to the fire. The inhibitions built up over most of his life stopped him from going nova, but no one for blocks around missed the flare that momentarily changed the sky from black to gold.

Johnny sagged to the ground, only dimly aware of the steaming concrete and smoking walls. The garbage in the nearby Dumpster had been vaporized and the smell of incinerated plastic hung heavy in the air. A voice spoke in his ear: *Not bad, kid,* it said. *But fire ain't gonna do it.* The darkness found its grip and hefted Johnny up into the air, bouncing him lightly or a second or two the way a kid docs with a ball when he's looking for the right grip before a long, hard heave. His head whipped back and forth and a moment later, Johnny Storm was airborne. He knew the sensation should have frightened him—his flame was snuffed out, after all—but the only thing he could think about was how glad he was to be out of reach of the darkness. The rushing wind was delightfully cool on his face and Johnny let his eyes slip shut. *Only for a moment,* he thought. *And then I'll be ready to go again . . .*

*That went better than I could have hoped for,* thought the shadow that swallowed Stanislaw Klemp. The process of gathering together substance and knitting it to Klemp's form had been easier than it had expected, though it had let its mind wander a bit while putting together the final product, which had come out looking a little more *theatrical* than he would have liked. *Could have been worse,* it reflected, flexing its oversized hands and feeling the muscles ripple in its arms and chest. Clearly, some nightmare or fantasy image of Klemp's had crept into the mix, resulting in a blend of mythological archetype and a morphology that the creature knew (obviously another remnant of Klemp's mind) as "super villain."

It ducked low and stepped back through the doorway into the dark hall, its horns gouging furrows in the ceiling tiles. *These could be inconvenient,* it thought and briefly considered snapping them off, but then decided they made a useful statement. Fear was important. If the rulers of this dimension could afford to use a creature as powerful as the flaming one as a scout, the shadow would need to move slowly and exercise caution. Fear and the resulting chaos were its best weapons.

Reaching out with its mind, the shadow that ate Klemp touched the pinprick-sized portal to its dimension and peeled back the edges. The force that had created the bubble of anxiety in and around the building spilled out and surged across the landscape like a tsunami. The energy cascaded over him, caressing his back like a lover's kiss. The mild sense of mingled dread and anxiety that had been oozing out of its home suddenly became swollen, distended, and then burst like a gangrenous wound. The shadow closed its glowing red eyes, listened intently with its very sensitive ears (pointed, it noted), and waited for the screaming to begin.

"Dr. Richards!" the sensor officer shouted. "You have to see this!"

Though he typically avoided elongating his limbs around "civilians," Reed was so startled by the S.H.I.E.L.D. agent's tone that he stretched his neck across the length of the bridge to see what was wrong. The rest of his body followed a moment later, arching over the crew and then snapping back into shape in much less time than it would have taken him to run across the bridge. Reed did not bother to ask what had alarmed the agent; the wave of energy that they could just barely discern a few minutes ago was now pulsing like a strobe light on the sensor display.

"What the hell is it?" the sensor officer gasped.

Reed didn't reply, but began to rapidly flip through the different scan modes, looking for additional data. The sensor officer stepped aside and let him work, probably because he knew Reed had contributed to most of the scanner technology, but just as likely because he was too stunned by what he was seeing to protest. "Nothing showing up on the visible spectra,"

Reed noted. "No one on the ground will notice anything unusual . . ."

"Until it's way too late," Rachel said. She had quietly and calmly slipped past the sensor officer and was now standing beside Reed. "Do those readings mean what I think they mean?" she asked. "It looks like everything the energy wave is touching is losing coherence."

Reed shook his head. "Not losing coherence, but being overlaid with another stronger dimensional frequency."

"Like the way one loud, out-of-tune voice can overwhelm a whole choir," Rachel said. "You can't hear the good music for the bad."

"Your metaphor is a bit . . . labored, but, yes, that's essentially correct."

Rachel closely studied the displays. "And no sign of the Torch."

"None. He disappeared right after his last communication. We need someone on-site immediately." Reed was still holding his phone and briefly considered calling Susan, but decided to wait. He would catch hell for this later, but decided that was the least of his worries at the moment. Given the recent altercations with the Inhumans, Susan didn't have the luxury of teleporting Franklin and Val to Attilan for safety, so her only choice would be to take the children with her if she wanted to search for Johnny. Reed sighed. S.H.I.E.L.D. might be able to get an

Initiative team on-site, but he already knew that the Avengers, Stark's primary New York–based group, was dealing with a problem in near Earth orbit. *Maybe Ben . . .*

"What are those?" Rachel asked, pointing at the ring of tiny lights that had suddenly appeared on the sensor grid.

"Yes," Reed said. "What are those?"

"Director Stark didn't tell you?" asked the sensor officer, who had regained his composure and was seating himself at the control panel.

"That wasn't the question, Ensign," Rachel said sharply. Twenty-five—no, thirty pinpricks of light glowed a bright purple and then pairs of dotted lines began to radiate out at forty-five-degree angles, enclosing the southern half of midtown and lower Manhattan.

"Those are the force field generators," the sensor officer said, and Reed caught the slight hiccup of anxiety in his voice. "I'm guessing by your expression," he gulped, "that this means you didn't build them."

Emma Johnston hunkered down behind the mattress she had tipped up on end against the wall of her dorm room farthest from the door. She had tried to shove the desk in front of the door, but dorm furniture was massive, and probably bolted to the ground anyway. The only reason she had been able to move the bed was because she and her roommate, Cho, had removed the heavy metal bed frames and constructed bunk beds from lumber they'd paid for out of their own pockets. Housekeeping didn't mind, especially if it meant having beds they could use somewhere else.

Right after Emma had decided the two girls who lived in the suite next door had become zombies, she'd found the tools and used the leftover nails to seal the door shut. The certainty that the girls next door—Serena and Tiffany—were now shuffling, undead zombies had settled over Emma an hour earlier, and she was sort of proud of the reasonable manner in which she'd made preparations to survive the impending apocalypse. First, she had checked to make sure there was plenty of water and diet cola in the mini-fridge, then she'd tested the batteries in her emergency radio and double-checked to make sure Cho still had the pail under her bed, the one she kept around in case she got sick after a night of partying. Emma wasn't planning to vomit, but she knew she wasn't going to try to cross the hall to the community restroom anytime soon, either.

She cranked up the emergency radio and listened to the campus station, but nothing had changed since the last time she'd checked. The DJ—a guy named Brad she knew for a fact was from Brooklyn—had flaked out half an hour ago and now was just muttering and blubbering to his mother, telling her how he hated her *and* loved her. Emma didn't really want to listen to any more, but the idea of not being able to drown out the noises she had heard coming from outside bothered her worse.

She took a tiny sip of diet soda, fully aware that cola was a diuretic and would only hasten the inevitable moment when she would need to use the restroom, but Emma also wanted to stay alert and the caffeine helped. After switching off the radio, she listened carefully for noises around her. The zombies next door were doing their best to keep quiet. Why wouldn't they? As long as they couldn't get anything—anyone—to eat, what was the point of wasting energy? Outside in the quad, she heard the occasional scream or wail of panic as another poor soul suddenly realized that the zombie apocalypse had finally come.

The screams faded and Emma curled up in a ball in the nest of sheets, blankets, and comforters she had thrown onto the floor behind the mattress. She heard the weak banging against the door and listened as Cho begged to be let in. Her voice was getting weaker and hoarser all the time. Emma hadn't been able to figure out how a tiny thing like Cho could make so much noise at first, but she decided the zombie virus must give its victims some sort of burst of energy when they first catch it. A few hours had passed now and Emma figured zombie Cho was running out of gas. Maybe when the noise stopped completely, Emma would risk popping out the nails and taking a look outside. She was going to need more supplies someday and she knew she should consider finding a gun or a club or something. Couldn't be too hard, she figured. After all, this was New York. There were plenty of guns to be found, and zombies couldn't use them.

Could they?

Peter Parker hung upside down by a silken thread twenty stories over Park Avenue and scanned the ground for the next idiot who was going to run out into traffic. Forty-five minutes ago, his spider sense had started to pound so discordantly that he'd had trouble seeing through the jangling haze inside his head. Every ninety seconds or so, the jangle would spike and he would have to swing down and pluck another terrified soul off the street before an enraged cabbie would run him or her down. Peter kept wondering if he was simply having a nightmare, but decided no, he knew what nightmares felt like and he was never this tired in a nightmare. Also, he had his pants on. Suddenly Peter realized that he hadn't bothered to change into his work clothes, hadn't even bothered to pull on his mask. Oddly, none of the petrified civilians he was saving from certain doom seemed to be paying this fact any attention either. This vaguely troubled him, so he swung to a wall, clung for a second, and quickly checked his pockets. No mask. Damn.

His spider sense rattled against the inside of his skull. A middle-aged woman dragging a small dog on a lead was darting out into mid-town traffic. Seven cabbies hit the gas and headed for her at eighty miles an hour. A weak voice in the back of his mind told him that there had to be a better way to handle the situation, but there was no time to listen to this extremely reasonable voice.

Peter leaped and shot out a web line. This one was going to be close.

Matt Murdoch jumped from the edge of the brownstone and bounced off the wall of the narrow alley, grabbed the TV cable strung across the gap and spun around it, once, twice, three times, then landed. The three thirteen-year-old girls who had been about to dismember the sixteen-year-old drug pusher who had been working the alleyway for the past three weeks froze. Matt's radar sense told him that each of the girls was holding a serrated bread knife, and the coppery scent of blood that hung in the air told him the pusher had already been slashed a couple times. From the sound of the guy's heart, Matt knew the pusher's wounds were superficial, but his accelerated respiration revealed they were extremely painful. These girls, whoever they were, knew what they were doing.

He decided he didn't really care that much. Matt had been planning to terrify the punk himself as soon as the opportunity presented itself; the girls were just saving him the trouble, though their enthusiasm was a little disturbing. The waves of fear he sensed rolling off the pusher—the stink of his toxic sweat, the rapid drumming of his pulse—seemed disproportionate to the threat the girls presented, but who was Matt Murdoch to comment on how others used fear to make their point?

Though he had touched down only a few feet behind the young women, none of the trio seemed to have registered his presence, though judging by his suddenly spiking heartbeat their victim clearly had. "Girls," Matt called, trying to sound both authoritative and kindly, "I think he's had enough. Why don't you let me take it from here." For the first time, it registered on Matt that the girls' pulses were practically normal, even a little sluggish. None of them turned or changed their rate of advance. Each of them lifted her bread knife a little higher into the air. "Hey," Matt said and stepped forward to grab the wrist of the hindmost girl. "Listen to me: I said—"

As soon as he had grabbed the girl's wrist, the two on either side of her spun around, moving like they were on clockwork gears, pivoting and slashing in identical arcs. Matt barely stepped back in time to avoid being eviscerated. Tumbling backward, he tucked, rolled, and came up on his feet a safe five feet away from the closest girl. The lead girl, the one nearest the pusher, had never turned around and was still slowly advancing. Matt tossed his billy club overhand, bounced it off the wall, and knocked the lead girl's knife from her hand. Almost anyone, let alone a thirteen-year-old girl, would have grasped their hand then and shouted in pain, but the kid didn't even break stride. An involuntary groan rose up in Matt's throat. "Great," he growled. "Weirdness. I don't need weirdness."

The two who had turned on him leaped forward, startling Matt by their speed. He barely dodged their slashing attacks, but quickly recovered and stabbed each one in the big nerve cluster at the back of the neck. Both collapsed in heaps, and it was the work of only a second before he had the third down, too, though not before she opened another wound on the pusher's cheek, this time with her nails. Now the punk lay on his back, cycling back and forth between hysterical laughter and hysterical tears, oblivious to Matt's presence.

Something odd about the girls' faces had registered while he had been fighting them, so, with the pusher oblivious to his surroundings, Matt slipped off his glove and touched one of their faces. What he found made him catch his breath in wonder and mild disgust: The girl's mouth and jaw were huge, three times wider and much heavier than a normal human's. He carefully ran his fingertip over her teeth to confirm his initial impression: They were tapered like a viper's, needle-sharp, and as near as he could tell, there were dozens of them.

Laying the girl's head back on the ground, Matt knelt down over the pusher and grabbed him by the lapels of his jacket. "Who are they?" he asked, using the low menacing tone he knew could make bone reverberate. "Where did they come from? Tell me."

"I don't know, man," the pusher moaned. "I've seen them before . . . or thought I did. Did you see their mouths? What the hell is *that* about? I never seen nothing like that before in my life. You gotta protect me, man."

"Why should I?" Matt asked, then realized he wasn't just trying to intimidate the man. Some part of him was weighing the idea of leaving the pusher here to wait for the girls to regain consciousness. *A different kind of justice,* a voice said.

"They'll kill me when they wake up," the pusher moaned. "And if not them, something else will. Something worse. They's worse things out there, man. I just know it. I can feel it."

Matt released the weeping man and stood up. Tilting his head, he let his enhanced senses reach out across Hell's Kitchen and was startled by what he found. Many dreadful things were happening out there tonight, all across the city. He could feel the center of the disturbance up north and slightly east, well out of his usual patrol area. Daredevil would tend to his home first and then, when things were sorted out here, he would see what he could do for the rest of the world.

Matt retrieved his billy club, then went over and knelt by the pusher. "I don't have time to deal with you right now," he hissed. "And they'll be awake soon. I don't think you want to be here when that happens, do you?"

The man shook his head, his pulse rate soaring again.

"Then I strongly urge you to stagger down the street to the precinct house and turn yourself in. Tell them the Devil sent you."

The pusher nodded his head and made a squeaking sound deep in the back of his throat. Matt grinned and stood to consider his next move. He didn't bother to check where the man went after he staggered out of the alley. The pusher would do what he was told; he understood the consequences if he didn't. Better the devil he knew . . .

# 6

THE POLICE AND EMTS CALLED TO THE REC center acted as decently and considerately as they could without actually sweeping the incident under the rug. Amelia Sullivan understood that and understood also that some sort of report had to be filed. After all, two camera crews had caught the accident on tape and every one of the twenty-four-hour news channels would run some version of the story in regular seven-minute cycles until a newer, fresher atrocity turned up. She didn't even want to think about what the scandal rags would say. "Thing Crushes Child" might be unnecessarily inflammatory (and flagrantly untrue), but there was no denying it would catch your attention.

Just as the sun began to sink behind the skyline, the remaining TV crews flicked off their bright lights and settled in to see if they could get a shot of Mr. Grimm slinking out of the building (if Mr. Grimm could slink). The fact that their quarry hadn't shown his face since the incident several hours earlier or the fact that his best friend likely could whip together a teleportation device out of tinfoil and a couple of paper clips did not dissuade them.

Standing in the unlit lobby with her ear pressed to the window, Ms. Sullivan listened to the journalists discuss the story. Mr. Grimm's lawyers had already contacted the little girl's family and offered to pay all the medical expenses. On one hand, they agreed, this was a good move: It showed concern. On the other, it was a tacit admission of responsibility, if not out-and-out criminal guilt. The good news was that the emergency room doctor had released a statement saying the injury was only a fracture, though when you're five, mused Ms. Sullivan, even a fracture can be terrifying, especially if it's inflicted by a huge, orange, rocky . . .

Ms. Sullivan sighed and let the word slip away unvoiced, even mentally. She knew she had to go to Mr. Grimm and help the poor man try to figure out how to get home. Sadly, the teleportation device had not materialized, and all the back entrances were being covered by zealous young things, and, pitifully, when last she had been in the office the waves of guilt rolling off him were so intense as to be disquieting. Self-pity was never attractive and even less so when it was unwarranted. Ben Grimm had saved the city—saved the world—more times than anyone could count. Didn't the fact that he had put life and limb on the line innumerable times mean *something*? Ms. Sullivan sighed and leaned against the window. She knew the answer to her question: Of course it didn't.

Though he had lost his balance for only a scant second, Ben Grimm, the Thing, had stepped on a little girl's foot. Almost anyone else in the world and the result would have been a simple "Excuse me" or an "Are you all right?" and everything would have been fine. At the worst, an application of lollypop might have been required. But no, Ben Grimm was incredible wealthy, and Ben Grimm was . . .

There was the word, almost spoken, again.

Ms. Sullivan shook her head, troubled by the thought. True, Mr. Grimm's appearance was a little startling when you first met him, but it hadn't taken more than a few minutes—well, a few hours—before you simply forgot what he looked like, especially if he was dressed in one of his three-thousand-dollar, custom-tailored suits. And his appearance wasn't his fault. It had been an accident, a terrible, terrible accident that had scarred him . . .

She had to shake herself again. Mr. Grimm hadn't been scarred. He had been transformed. Inside, underneath the rocky shell, he was still the same man that he had been before, a man who had grown up on these very streets and gone on to make something better of himself. He had been a pilot, practically an astronaut before the accident. He couldn't help how he looked or how people sometimes reacted when they saw him. Children couldn't stop themselves, couldn't edit their reactions, so it wasn't their fault, either, if they sometimes took a step back when Mr. Grimm came in through the front door. It was just that he had a "bigger than life" presence. And he smelled so nice if you stood near him, especially if it was warm outside.

Ms. Sullivan crossed the lobby and looked through the floor-to-ceiling windows that divided the reception area from the first of the three gyms. A four-foot-tall statue of Mr. Grimm by the sculptress Alicia Masters stood on a low table at the center of the wall. In the statue, Mr. Grimm was grinning in that lopsided way he did when he was particularly pleased with something, his right arm raised, his bicep flexed playfully. The artist had succeeded in capturing the spirit of mischief the man exuded in his best moments. Ms. Sullivan had felt slight trepidation when Ms. Masters had delivered the statue, worried that some might look at it and believe Mr. Grimm was teasing them, making fun: "Kid, you'll never have muscles like me no matter how much you work out." Clearly, no one else had felt this way. The children loved the statue and few of the patrons could resist patting Mr. Grimm on the head as they passed. In fact, Ms. Sullivan had been contemplating purchasing bronze posts and velvet ropes to protect the statue from sticky fingers. Nothing said "Stay back" like velvet ropes.

She stared into the gym, illuminated by only the blue-tinted work lights. On the evenings when she stayed until closing, Ms. Sullivan had always avoided going into the giant, echoey room, finding the stillness vaguely sad. Tonight, gazing into the cobalt-tinged shadows, she found the room more ominous than sad. If the worst happened, if the media decided to make a meal of Mr. Grimm's misfortune, this might be the last night Ms. Sullivan would ever be here. The thought made blood rush into her face. She didn't care that it was his name on the door or that he had paid for every brick, every dab of mortar, and every pane of glass in the place—the recreation center was every bit as much hers as it was his. How dare the man continue to sulk?

She marched across the lobby, the heels of her shoes tick-tocking sharply on the wood floor. Ms. Sullivan lifted her hand, ready to knock, but then stopped herself. *No,* she decided. *He won't respond. He'll pretend he doesn't hear.* So instead, she twisted the knob and pushed. Stepping inside, she was surprised by how faint the light was, a single diminutive desk lamp casting only a minuscule circle of illumination.

Ms. Sullivan was ready to speak, ready to say

everything that she had been thinking about while she'd been calming down the little girl's parents and making explanations to the press and trying to keep the gawkers and tourists from dismantling the center. She was ready to argue if need be, to persuade and cajole, to yell, but every word that she had rehearsed flew out of her mind when the monster stepped forward from the room's most stygian corner.

It didn't say anything. It didn't growl or snarl or even snuffle the way big animals at the zoo sometimes did. It just stood there, all crags and shadowy ridges. Ms. Sullivan was certain it was about to reach out and envelop her in its gigantic arms, pull her toward its chest and crush her. She couldn't release the breath trapped in her chest, and the pressure was threatening to burst her lungs as if they were a couple of moldy old paper bags. Her knees went weak and she began to topple backward, but Ms. Sullivan found that the doorknob, her old friend the doorknob, was still in her hand, and she managed to stay upright. In relief, she released the breath, but it came out all wrong, as a shriek. The sound of her own voice, so high and wild, frightened her almost as much as the monster did—almost, but not quite.

She took one step backward, then two. And then she was spinning around, flinging herself toward the glass double doors that would take her to the street. Had she locked the door? Yes, of course she had. She remembered doing it, but Ms. Sullivan also remembered leaving the key in the lock and she could remember that you had to turn it a quarter-turn clockwise before you turned it counterclockwise and she was doing it, turning the key, and the door banged open and she was free, out on the street under the gloomy sky, and the TV crews were gone, though their trucks were still there for some reason. Free; she was free. She looked around to see which might be the best way to run, but there were more monsters in the shadows. Monsters in every shadow.

Ms. Sullivan picked the direction that had the fewest shadows and ran.

With the sound of Ms. Sullivan's clacking heels disappearing into the distance, Ben Grimm carefully poked his head out the rec center doors, expecting to see a mob of reporters or maybe just some curious Yancy Streeters, but he found none of those things. Over the past several interminable hours, Ben had reflected on how his world went a little crazy from time to time. He had just reached the point where he had decided that sometimes it went crazy in a good way and sometimes in a bad way and that a person just had to be willing to accept both. Sometimes, you just had to man up, roll up your sleeves or otherwise suck it up, head back outside, and deal with what had to be dealt with. Usually, the world cooperated to some degree. Today, though, not so much.

As if on cue, as soon as Ben stepped outside, people emerged from the shadows, most of them running, some away from something and a few definitely *toward* something.

A tall, gangly business-suit type charged around the corner, pursued by a squat runty guy wearing a Yankees cap who had to take two steps for every one the tall guy took. The pursued was taking swipes at the little guy with an overloaded briefcase while he ran, just barely keeping his balance, an almost comical sight except for the fact that the little guy had blood smeared all over his face and mouth. As the pair passed, Ben grabbed the little guy by the back of his shirt and hauled him up into the air. He started to say, "Hey, pal, what the heck is goin' on here?" but he couldn't get out more than "Hey" before the little guy reached out and started to claw at Ben's eyes with jagged nails.

Ben Grimm had been the Thing long enough to get used to being practically invulnerable, but he also knew his weak spots, and his eyes were one of them. He had spent more than one sleepless night miserably contemplating what would become of him if he ever went blind. Not that blindness in and of itself was a curse: His sometimes girlfriend Alicia Masters was proof of that, but Alicia moved through the world as gracefully as a rose petal on a breeze. If he was blinded, he would be trapped inside his monolithic body, afraid to move for fear of crushing everything in his path. The memory of hurting the little girl that very morning flashed through his mind; his reaction was instinctive and instantaneous: He tossed the little guy away.

It wasn't a hard toss, barely more than a flick of the wrist, but, as Ben well knew, people were fragile and easily broken, especially when they hit stuff like posts or brick walls. The little guy bounced off a parked car, and Ben expected to see him crumble to the ground. Instead, he *literally* bounced off the parked car, hit the ground with a roll, and leaped back to his feet. Ben watched as the surface of the car rippled like it was made of gelatin. The little guy hissed at him and headed back down the street, baying at the heels of the tall guy.

Ben stood stunned, his arms still held out in front of himself the way they had been when he'd grabbed his little adversary. Staring out into the dark, now empty street, he muttered, "What the heck . . . ?" and then stepped forward to tap the side of the car, which, just as it had the moment before, bounced and jiggled. "Okay," he concluded. "This has now officially entered the realm of 'too strange for me.'" He pulled out his cell phone and punched out the speed dial and then the number one. Lifting the oversized phone to his ear, Ben Grimm muttered, "Better bring in the big guns."

"No," Reed Richards said. "No one told me anything about the force fields." He clamped his hand down on the sensor officer's shoulder, and though he knew he was putting much too much pressure into his grip, Reed didn't care. "Maybe *you* should tell me."

"Maybe you should let me do that, Reed," a voice said from the doorway of the sensor bridge. "And please release my agent's arm. They're a lot more fragile than you or me." Reed turned to see Tony Stark, now wearing his Iron Man armor, except for the helmet, which he held under his arm. He finished, "Especially me." Reed was impressed by how much quieter the new Extremis armor was compared with the older suits. "Come into my office, Reed."

"I think I've spent enough time in your office today, Tony. Tell me what's going on. What are these force fields? Who authorized them and why wasn't I told?"

Tony's mouth became a thin, impatient line under his neatly trimmed mustache. "I have to tell you this, Reed: I'm getting really tired of always being the sinister jerk these days."

"Then maybe you should . . . ," but Reed stopped himself before the entire sentence came out. "Forget that. Just tell me."

"The force field generators were installed after the Battle of Times Square. The first thought was that if something like the Civil War ever happens again, I wanted to be able to shield civilians. Since then, I've thought of another dozen good reasons to have them, including the fact that one of my oldest friends and closest allies insists on keeping a portal to another dimension, a *hostile* dimension, in his living room."

"We've been over this, Tony. The Negative Zone Portal is *safe*. Nothing can penetrate the shields I've installed around it."

"Just like the way Logan couldn't break in and steal your inventions?"

"You know this isn't the same sort of thing," Reed said. "And besides, you had me create gateways to the Negative Zone in most every state of the union so that your Initiative teams could take prisoners directly to the prison. How is that any different?!"

"The Initiative gates *aren't* in the middle of the largest metropolitan area in the country . . ."

"That's a spurious argument, Tony. You're avoiding the point! What about the force fields?"

Tony sighed and brushed an imaginary strand of displaced hair back into line. "Right. Sorry. According to the sensor logs, there's been a dimensional incursion: Something bad broke through at Empire State. The force fields are designed to hold whatever it is inside until we can get there."

"And what about the civilians who are inside the fields?"

"The shields are calibrated so that only certain morphotypes can pass. Humans can, but anything that comes through the dimensional gate will be trapped."

Reed felt the tension leave his neck and shoulders.

"Actually," he said, "that's rather clever. I should have thought of that."

"You aren't the only genius in the world, Reed," Tony said. "But the truth is I based the design on a paper you published a couple years ago."

Reed searched his memory. He published erratically, but prodigiously. Sometimes he submitted papers to journals only to be told that they had published an identical item two or three years earlier. "If you say so, then your force field generators are coupled with a DNA scanner?"

"Correct."

"What about variants like mutants and most of the superhuman population?"

"If they're in the database, they can pass. If not, we try to keep them in, though we recognize that there are certain individuals who can work their way past a force field generator. If the Rhino approaches, we let him through."

Reed searched for other loopholes in the concept, but he found it largely sound, at least as a method to try to protect civilians. Finally, he concluded, "I can only think of one problem . . ."

The sensor officer waved his hand and called out, "Sir? Director Stark?"

"Yes?" Tony said.

"I have a high res camera over Manhattan. We're getting video from the perimeter."

"Good."

"No, sir."

"What?"

"Not good," the officer said, and his voice sounded uncomfortably shrill to Reed's ears. "Very bad." He punched a sequence on the keyboard, and the big screen over his console lit up. It showed a computer-enhanced shot of a Manhattan street. Reed checked the time stamp in the frame and realized that the sun had set, so the image was also being repainted in "day for night"–like tones.

Dozens of people were standing on either side of an invisible line looking at each other, some trying to talk calmly and others wildly gesticulating. The camera zoomed in and Reed discerned men and women trying to push their way through the force field from either side, but being shoved back. Parents beckoned to their children; lovers struggled to touch each other. A throng of teenagers inside the wall scattered when a large man wearing a tattered shirt ran at them. They fled like gazelles fleeing a cheetah, crossing paths, running parallel, then separating.

"Why is this happening?" Reed asked. "Why can't they get through the shield?"

"I don't know," the sensor officer said. "We're scanning, but we're not finding—"

"Hold on," Tony said, and Reed turned to see that his friend had his eyes tightly shut. "I'll have it in a second." Tony was communicating with the machines, mentally interfacing with them in a way that

Reed barely understood and sometimes found alarming. When Tony opened his eyes, he said, "There. See?"

And Reed did see. The sensor officer studied the new output. "The people inside the force field have been altered. Not significantly . . ."

"But just enough that they can't pass," Tony finished.

"Widen the scan," Reed said. The sensor officer complied and a moment later they were looking at a map of Manhattan overlaid with shaded concentric circles whose center was the Empire State campus. The intersection they had been studying was more than ten blocks away, but already the effect of the dimensional rift had altered the genetic code of individuals inside the perimeter. Reed studied the scans and concluded that the modification was slight compared with what he and his team had experienced, but obviously significant enough for the DNA scanners to flag them.

Then, Reed's gaze locked onto the intersection of Madison Avenue and 42nd Street. Taking a long, single stride away from the sensor pit, he unclipped his phone and punched the speed dial for his wife.

Sue answered a moment later. "I was about to call you," she said. "We just started receiving reports of disturbances nearby. The police superintendent—"

"Raise the force fields around the Baxter Building."

"What? Are you sure? People will be trapped—"

"There isn't much time. If you don't . . ."

She didn't answer and the line was silent for several seconds. Then, she was back, saying, "It's done. As if our tenants aren't angry enough with us."

"They'll thank us later. S.H.I.E.L.D. will be sending in agents as soon as possible, but until then you need to sit tight."

"Like I have a choice now. Do you want me to contact Johnny and Ben?"

"Johnny is already involved. I called him an hour ago to do some reconnaissance work for us, but we've lost touch. If you hear from him, tell him to call me. Ben was down on Yancy Street, wasn't he?"

"This morning, yes, but he might not be anymore."

Reed considered the time line of the event. "Then Ben's probably already in the thick of it. If you have a moment, yes, try to contact him, if only to let him know the extent of the event."

"Which is what?"

"By our usual standards," Reed said, "still manageable, but I can see how it might quickly get out of control."

"Are you going to be able to make it home soon?" Sue asked. "If things are going to get worse, I'll need help with the children and whoever's left in the building. At this hour, probably no one in the lower levels, but a lot of the professionals in the middle floors work late."

"I'll be there as soon as I can, Sue. S.H.I.E.L.D. has erected force fields around part of the city to try to contain the problem."

"Do you think that was a good idea?"

Reed sighed. "I'm not sure. It's a long story . . . Wait . . . something's happening . . . Sue? Can you hear me?"

But Sue was gone. The commlink had died. Reed considered the possibilities and concluded that the signal couldn't pierce the double layer of the field around the Baxter Building and the one S.H.I.E.L.D. must have just erected. Sue would have to rely on her own resources for a short time, though Reed knew there was no one more capable. In the interim, he would see what he could do to help here. Then he'd head for home as quickly as possible.

When he returned to the sensor console, Tony was leaning forward, intently staring at the big screen. Rachel stood beside him, her arms crossed tightly over her chest. "What's wrong?" Reed asked.

"Things," Rachel reported, "just got worse."

"How much worse?"

"Much worse. 'Going to hell' worse."

"The dimensional rift," Tony said, pointing at what, moments before, had been a black fissure at the center of swirling colors. The fissure had torn open and was now an ebon maw. "Something tore it open. If we don't do something quick, Manhattan is going to fall inside and then pull the rest of the world after it."

*     *     *

The shadow that had eaten Stanislaw Klemp stood on the roof of the science building and considered the events unfolding before its feet. The energies emanating from its home dimension were beginning to have an effect on this new world. Humans were fleeing in terror from the figments that lived inside their minds; others were *becoming* the figments inside their minds. Such beautiful symmetry was rare and the shadow was determined to enjoy the spectacle for as long as possible. With the pace of change accelerating, it was free to move around the city with moderate anonymity, to observe, collect information, and make more plans.

But what to do about the invisible fences it sensed? From the memories sucked out of Klemp's mind, the shadow understood that one of the superhuman or mystical beings that called this world home was probably responsible, but which one? Even from this distance, it could sense that the machines generating the fields would be difficult to reach. Someone had put some thought into the project. It pondered the question: The shield generators were shielded, but what about the ones who *controlled* the shield generators? Where were they?

The creature cast out his senses and turned in a slow circle, searching the cityscape. There. To the south, no more than a few miles away, it sensed another force field, somehow different from the first one, much stronger and surrounding only a single building. This would be the control center for the generators, though his opponent's strategy eluded him. Why place the control center *inside* the shields? Klemp's memories explained it: The building belonged to one or more of the city's primary protectors. They weren't only defenders, but citizens, too.

The shadow shrugged, then grinned. *Fine. It makes them that much more vulnerable.* It cast out its thoughts again and found minds willing to serve. Several hundred of the humans had already been infected enough that he could control them directly, and the contagion was spreading faster every minute. Among the minds, the creature touched a handful of the special ones, men and women Klemp called "super villains." Though they had not fallen under his direct control—their minds or their egos were too strong— they could be influenced.

*Excellent.* Borrowing the imagery from Klemp's mind, it thought, *My pawns are in hand. They will breach my foe's defenses so that their king may enter and take the prize.*

**LUKE CAGE VERY BADLY WANTED TO GET HOME TO** his wife and daughter. He knew that Jessica and Danielle were as safe inside their temporary headquarters in Dr. Strange's mansion as they could be anywhere in the tortured and twisted hell that Manhattan was becoming, but he also knew that they would be safest with his steel-hard hide standing between them and whatever might be able to break through the sorcerer's magical defenses. Cage had been uptown in Harlem showing pictures of his baby daughter to friends and acquaintances, folks who had known him back in the day when everything had started to go crazy. Jake's Bar was more or less empty, and Luke had been showing his stack of four-by-six prints to Marge (the only bartender he still knew) when this weasellylooking dude slipped inside, scurried behind the bar, and tried to crack open the cash drawer. No gun. No threats. Just a blatant attempt at a snatch-and-grab.

With Luke Cage standing three feet away.

Marge looked at Luke with this expression like, "Aren't you going to do something about this?" but Luke had not been able to stir for a couple seconds. *This,* he thought, *displays an unacceptable level of disrespect.* What had happened to his rep? Sure, it had been years since he had lived in Harlem, but, *Christmas.* He patted Marge's wrist, took the stack of pictures from her and slipped them into his jacket pocket, and then cracked his knuckles as loudly as he could. The weaselly guy had just damaged his day, and now Luke Cage was going to have to damage something of his.

"Hey, pal," Luke said, stretching his arm over the bar and grabbing the guy's shoulder. "Are you out of your mind?" Without warning, the weaselly guy spun around, slapped away Luke's hand, and launched himself over the bar so fast that Luke didn't have time to dodge or block. Caught off guard, Luke stumbled backward and tried to catch himself on the edge of a small table, but Jake's cheap furniture wasn't sturdy enough to steady his four-hundred-plus-pound bulk. The table was crushed into kindling and Luke landed flat on his back. Before he could move, the weaselly guy was on him.

Jake's Bar was, even on its best days, a pit, and almost as dark as one, so Luke couldn't be sure whether what he saw next really happened or was a trick of the light. Luke *thought* that what he saw was the weaselly guy tilt his head back and open his mouth so wide that it looked like his lower jaw detached. Then, the guy's eyes went jet black, like the pupil had swallowed the rest of the eye, and every tooth in his head became as sharp as a needle and six inches long. Half a second later, the guy attempted to chomp Luke's neck, a snuffling and growling sound in the back of his throat.

If Luke Cage had been anyone other than Luke Cage, that might have been the end of it all—ticket punched, thank you very much, ma'am. As it was, even considering the durability of his hide, the bite *hurt,* though considering the shriek the weaselly guy let loose and the sound of shattering bone, Luke suspected he had come out somewhat the better.

The guy jumped away, his hands over his mouth and thin streams of blood seeping out between his fingers. He spat a curse that might have contained a very bad word, but sounded much more like a wet hiss. Luke rolled up onto his knees and tried to grab his attacker's ankle, but the guy slithered away and was out the door before Luke could get to his feet.

He looked back at Marge, who hadn't budged an inch. "Did you see that?" Luke asked, rubbing his neck and wincing. His skin might have been steel-hard, but that didn't mean he didn't feel pain. "Dude tried to rip my throat out." Luke was suddenly aware that Marge was wearing an expression he'd never before seen on her face: fear. "Marge?" he asked. "What's with you? I didn't do—"

"Get out," Marge shrieked and reached down under the bar for the place where Luke knew she kept the sawed-off. The pellets wouldn't do any more damage than the guy's teeth had, but he didn't want to exacerbate the situation.

"Sure," he said, backing away with raised hands and stepping through the shards of the guy's teeth, which made a sound like toothpicks cracking. "I'm leaving. You just take care of yourself and I'll go see if I can figure out what that was—"

"Get out! Now!" Marge pulled the trigger just as Luke shoved through the dingy, leather-backed door, most of the pellets striking the wall to his left.

Outside, people were racing up and down the street like every house and shop was on fire, though none were as far as Luke could tell. People were *scared,* though he couldn't see why. Then, studying the scene more carefully, Luke realized that only *most* of the people were scared. The rest, maybe one out of every dozen, were enjoying everyone else's fear and doing whatever they could to make it worse.

An old man wearing a ratty porkpie hat shuffled past waving around an old revolver and screaming at the top of his lungs. Luke grabbed the old guy, snatched the gun out of his hand, snapped open the cylinder, and broke it off. Dropping the cylinder onto the ground, Luke turned away, expecting the old man to continue walking, but instead he started smacking Luke with his manky hat. Fending him off, Luke shouted "What the hell is going on here?!" and turned south toward Greenwich Village. He badly wanted to find Jessica and Danielle. It was times like these that Luke most missed all the technological gadgetry that Tony Stark had provided. Back in the old, pre–Civil War days, one touch of a button and, *boom!* Captain America, Iron Man, and Spider-Man would be on their way. With the way things were now and relying on his little band of misfit Avengers, the best he could do was try to get someone on a cell phone, and half the team didn't even own one of those.

The thought of Spider-Man made Luke look skyward, half-expecting to see the costumed clown bouncing off buildings, but what he saw was much weirder and a lot more distressing: The Human Torch was falling out of the sky.

Luke had worked with the Fantastic Four enough times to recognize the peculiar, flickering outline and to know it was a half-extinguished, likely unconscious Johnny Storm. Comprehending he had only seconds to act, Luke assessed his options. He considered tearing a fire hydrant off the base and hoping the geyser would cushion the kid's fall, but dismissed the idea as ridiculous, the kind of thing someone would do in a Saturday morning cartoon. With the resources at hand, only one alternative made any sense.

"Aw, crap," Luke said. This was going to hurt. People didn't understand that just because he was pretty much invulnerable didn't mean he didn't feel pain. In all likelihood, the kid would be crippled, but he didn't have any other choices. Spider-Man or Wolverine might be able to survive a fall of several hundred feet, but Luke seriously doubted that Johnny Storm could.

He set his feet, spread his arms, and found himself suddenly thinking of a high school gym teacher who had taken a sadistic delight in putting Luke in the outfield despite his obvious skills as an infielder. "Eye on the ball, eye on the ball," Luke muttered. He squared his shoulders, lowered his center of gravity, and waited for the crunch.

The crunch never came.

Luke opened his eyes and saw the kid's feet dangling in midair three feet in front of him. A voice spoke inside his head. "Luke," it said. "You have to come home. Jessica is worried about you."

Despite having been in the super hero business for several years, Luke had not grown accustomed to the whole telepathy thing and had a difficult time matching a voice to a persona without a face to help him along, but this was a voice he had heard enough times to take a stab. "Doc?" he asked.

"Yes. And please do not be long. Jessica can be most insistent, and I am a bit busy with other things at the moment."

Luke watched as the limp form slowly dropped to the pavement at his feet. "Did you just catch Johnny Human Torch here?" he asked.

"Yes. Fortunately, I had the spell ready and saw what was happening when I made contact with your mind. You were right, by the way: The fall would have killed him."

"Uh, okay," Luke said, still having trouble with the whole "talking to air" thing. Jessica said that when Strange contacted her, she could "see" him in her head, but that had never worked for Luke. "Can you always see what I'm looking at when we talk this way?"

"Yes."

"Then never do this when Spider-Woman is in costume."

"I understand perfectly."

"Should I bring the kid with me?"

"No," Strange said. "Oh, and please hold your arms out."

Luke did as he was asked without thinking. As far back as his days with the Defenders, he had learned to do whatever Strange asked without commentary. The spell that had held Storm in the air dispelled and Luke caught the limp form in his outstretched arms. "Any idea why he was falling out of the sky?"

"Likely something to do with why lower Manhattan has gone mad," Strange replied. "You should hurry, Luke. Initiative forces will move into the area soon, and you do not wish to be found holding the unconscious form of a registered hero." With that, Luke felt the magician's presence dissipate. Storm appeared to have awakened, so Luke gently lowered him to the ground. The kid moaned, eyes fluttering, and began to thrash his arms like he was trying to fend off a nightmare.

Despite the urgency of Strange's entreaties, Luke didn't feel right leaving the kid on the street, so he knelt down next to him and shook him by the shoulders. "Storm. Torch. Hey, you okay?"

The Torch's eyes snapped open, and Luke would have sworn he saw a light flare at the center of each pupil. He tried to sit up, but Luke held him down with one hand. "What's going on?" Storm barked. "Where am I?"

"You fell out of the sky," Luke replied, trying to keep his voice calm. "And you're in Harlem. What's the last thing you remember? You feel okay?"

"The last thing I remember," Storm said, a note of uncertainty in his voice. "I remember . . . I remember." And then, much to Luke's surprise, the kid shuddered. While the Torch had always been a bit of a blowhard, in all their encounters, either in team-ups or during the big battles that seemed to roll around every few years, Luke couldn't remember ever seeing the kid look frightened. Just the opposite, in fact. During battles when he probably should have showed a little discretion, Storm would launch himself into any fight without anything that resembled forethought.

"What?" Luke asked, laying a steadying hand on the kid's shoulder as he sat up. "What did you see?"

"I saw . . . nothing. Nothing. Just another baddie looking to get his butt kicked." He brushed Luke's hand away and pushed himself up onto his knees. "I was at Empire State. There's something there. It grabbed me while I wasn't looking, tossed me." While Storm rambled, Luke checked the street and was surprised to find that they were alone. Everyone had either cleared off or was staying in the shadows.

"I have to get going, kid. Some people are waiting for me, and if everything's hitting the fan, I want to make sure they're okay before I—"

"Save it," Storm snarled. "You do what you need to do." He grabbed a street sign and pulled himself up, but not without a brief wobble. "I'm going to . . . I'm going to go back to college and educate this guy." His words sounded like the usual kind of bluster, but Luke caught the slight flutter in the kid's voice. "Stand back," he warned, and Luke did as he was told. "Flame on!"

The flash made Luke duck and turn his head away. The heat seared the side of his face and he smelled burning leather. When he looked up, the Torch was five hundred feet in the air, leaving behind only a charred patch of pavement. The kid's flame trail looked different than Luke had ever seen it before: wilder, roiling, almost out of control. "Hey," he yelled up at the fading trail. "You're welcome." He patted the front of his still smoking jacket. "Damn, Jess gave me this." And, with that, he started moving at a steady trot. It was over a hundred blocks to Greenwich Village, and who knew what kind of hell he was going to have to face on the way.

Johnny flew southeast toward the Baxter Building, a wide flame trail in his wake. Whatever was going on, Sue or Reed would be clued in by now, and all Johnny wanted was to be told who he should throw fireballs at and for how long. His phone was gone, which meant that he had lost it when whoever-it-was had clocked him. How many phones was this now? Three? Four? However many, it meant a lecture from Reed or Sue, an idea that made Johnny want to curse.

The entire day had been nothing but one aggravation after another. First, there had been the scene with Chrissy. Then, Sue had lectured him. After that, a complete newbie, some jerk with scary eyes and a bag of parlor effects, got lucky and tossed him across town so that he could be saved by freakin' Luke Cage. And now, joy of joys, Johnny knew he could expect a twenty-minute lecture about being an irresponsible kid! The idea made him so mad, he could feel his blood boiling. The kid; the negligent brat—that's how his family saw him! But everyone else—especially the ladies!—thought of Johnny as the good boy, the hero. The safe one! It wasn't *fair*! It wasn't bloody fair!

The Human Torch clenched his fists in frustration and a bright orange ball of fire popped out from between his fingers, fell away, and exploded below him like a flashbulb. The detonation was so unexpected that Johnny halted in midair and studied his hand in wonder. His gaze drifted up and he saw his reflection in the windows of a midtown skyscraper, a sight that both shocked and delighted him. Wild tongues of blue-hot flame licked around his head and shoulders. Yellow-orange waves and troughs of black shadows rippled up and down the length of his body. A scalding shudder rose up from Johnny Storm's core and emerged as a wide grin. Who was this dangerous-looking individual?

Five stories below him, Johnny heard a woman scream in terror, though there was no way to know whether it was because she was looking at him or something else. Johnny considered flying down to street level to see what was up, but the thought annoyed him. He decided to compromise and dropped a fireball, shouting, "Hey! Cool it down there!"

The screaming stopped. Another job well done.

It dawned on the Torch that the idea of going home so Reed and Sue could yell at him was really stupid. Staying in the city and looking for trouble seemed like a much better idea. He studied his reflection for another half minute and then decided Ben might like his new look. That was the play: The two of them could stay out late and have fun.

The Torch turned to the west, enjoying the sight of the sun sinking below the horizon. He failed to notice that his flame trail was much longer than usual and that balls of hot plasma were falling to the ground, setting afire trash cans, treetops, and awnings. As the flames spread, coils of black smoke climbed into the sky and blotted out the stars. Johnny didn't pay any attention. He had other things on his mind.

Ben shook his cell phone and punched the buttons a third time. He understood that there might not be any living, breathing people back home to pick up, but why no robots or call-waiting? He tried the direct lines for Reed, Sue, and the kid one more time, but again, no answer. Batteries and systems checked out and the signal strength was fine, so the problem had to be . . .

The problem had to be . . .

Ben flipped the phone shut. *Crap.* It could be a thousand different things. He considered calling his chauffeur, but decided that Biggs would probably be safer wherever he was, and besides, it wasn't the Grimm style to put employees in the line of danger.

He stood under the street lamp and pondered his options. Go back into the rec center and see if the phone inside worked? Start back up across midtown to the Baxter Building? Avengers Tower was closer, but Ben hadn't much patience with Stark and his crowd these days. The other option, the one that actually appealed to Ben, was to stay on Yancy and see what kind of help he might offer. If the Big Apple was currently under siege, the locals might think more kindly of Ben if he hung around and pounded on whatever idiot Skrull or Kree or Creatures from the Id had been foolish enough to wander into the neighborhood.

Lost as he was in his musings, it took Ben a couple minutes to notice the old lady standing on the stoop of the brownstone across the street. A thick wool shawl wrapped around her neck, she leaned on her cane and stared intently at Ben. It kind of gave him the creeps. "Hey," Ben said, waving his hand slightly. "Hey, lady. You should go back inside where it's safe. There's some rough customers out here." The old lady didn't respond, except to pull her shawl more tightly around her shoulders. Ben noticed that there was a metal can by her feet, one of those gallon containers of olive oil Sue kept around the kitchen. "Lady?" he called again, the word hanging in the air. An unnatural silence descended and Ben found he was standing extremely still.

Finally, the old woman opened her mouth, and a single word creaked out: "Monster."

Ben hesitated, but finally decided that any answer was better than no answer at all. "You mean in your apartment? You want me to come and take a look? I'm . . . I'm pretty good when it comes to monsters."

"Monster," she said again, and this time there was this low-down tone of menace in her voice that made Ben flinch.

"Inside?" he asked again, but felt pretty sure he knew that this wasn't the point.

"Monster," the old lady said, raising her hand and pointing a bony finger at Ben. "Here. Right here."

Ben sighed. "Oooo-kay," he said. "I don't like where this is goin'." He heard a soft shuffling susurration to his left and was completely unsurprised when he saw an old man waiting with a heavy metal container in his hand. *Probably kerosene,* Ben thought. *Bunch of these folks have kerosene heaters to keep the heating bills down.* He glanced to his right and, yes, just as expected, there were two more old gents, both with their own kerosene cans. One particularly innovative soul was wrapping an old kitchen towel around a barbecue spatula and setting it on fire. *Makeshift torch. Great.*

More front doors opened. More people holding cans and cheap plastic lighters stepped out.

Pretty much in unison, the whole lot of them moaned, "Monster."

Ben groaned. "Is this day *never* going to end?"

The first call came in less than three minutes after Sue turned on the shield generators. She considered letting the answering service take it—she wanted to find the children—but decided she was being overly protective and needed to tend to whoever might still be left in the building. Explanatory messages had gone out via e-mail and phone as soon as the shields had gone up, but Sue knew that few people listened to their messages after suddenly discovering their front door was blocked by an energy field.

Thankfully, the first call came from Mr. Brannigan, one of the most understanding and levelheaded of the tenants. "Could you tell me what's happening, Mrs. Richards?" he asked as soon as the visi-screen lit up. Mr. Brannigan was also one of the few tenants who seemed to actually understand how a visi-screen operated and knew not to get too close to the monitor. "There are only a couple others on my floor: Mr. Schwartz and Lois Floyd from the law firm next door. They're both in my office right now, in a bit of a state. Is this a test or is there a problem?"

"The latter, I'm afraid, Mr. Brannigan."

"Super villains?" Mr. Brannigan asked with only a slight note of concern. "Atlanteans? Alien invasion?" The man really was a longtime New Yorker.

"I don't know. Not Atlanteans, in any case; Namor promised he wouldn't do that again. I received some calls from the police about disturbances nearby, and then Dr. Richards recommended we put the shields up. He also said that S.H.I.E.L.D. has erected some kind of barricades around the city. Unfortunately, we were cut off before he could tell me much more."

"So he's not in the building?"

"No, he's away on business."

"Are your teammates here?"

"No, just the children and me for now." Other lines started to ring as more tenants began to discover that the elevators were locked down or that the lobby door was sealed. "Mr. Brannigan, I have to clear the line. Could you tell the others on your floor to remain calm until we've had a chance to assess the danger?"

"I'll be glad to, Mrs. Richards."

"Thank you."

"And Mrs. Richards . . . ?"

"Yes, Mr. Brannigan."

"You're all right there by yourself? I mean, of course you're all right, but if you start to feel anxious or need some help with the children . . ."

Sue smiled, genuinely touched by the offer. "You're the first one I would call, Mr. Brannigan."

She closed the circuit and punched a control sequence into her computer console that activated the wide-scale communications system. The conversation with Mr. Brannigan made Sue realize she still didn't know much about the threat they were facing, and before she tried to answer more calls, she felt she needed to know more about what was happening. After quickly recording a brief message to respond to the incoming calls, she turned the phone lines over to the reception program and focused her attention on the news feeds.

The double layer of force fields around the Baxter Building was interfering with cell phone, radio, and TV broadcasts, but a special service created by Reed and Tony Stark to keep the Initiative teams informed had dumped a lot of data into sensor buffers before going down. The picture they painted was not pretty. Panick-fueled riots were breaking out everywhere. No one could find an airborne agent, so the next most likely agent was some kind of psionic attack, and unfortunately, psionic attacks were notoriously difficult to pinpoint unless you had a powerful psychic on your side.

Sue fed all the incident reports into the evaluation software and instructed the program to strongly weight the responses toward supernatural or extra-dimensional causes. The response was quick and disturbing: Space/time around the Upper West Side was beginning to warp under the influence of some as-yet-unidentified influence. Physical laws were being subverted; architecture was morphing and people were being transformed. Soon, midtown would begin to experience the same effects.

Sue knew she needed to consult with an expert, but who? Stephen Strange was the best candidate, though he was notoriously difficult to contact and would likely be quite busy. She recalled meeting an Avenger named Dr. Druid, but hadn't seen him in years. Times like these Sue truly missed having Agatha Harkness as a nanny.

No sooner did Sue shut down the threat analysis software than the automated reception system requested her undivided attention. Sue entered the password and said, "Report."

"Threat level amber," said the holographic receptionist, all trace of the algorithmically programmed pleasantness gone from her voice.

"Exterior monitors," Sue said, reaching back and tying her hair into a knot. Amber was bad. Not the worst: not Galactus bad or even Doctor Doom bad, but Frightful Four or Diablo bad. Diablo. She hadn't considered him as the source of the threat; this kind of magic didn't seem to fit his profile.

A video camera mounted midway up the Baxter Building showed a view from the northwest. The streets were swarming with figures. Not well-organized, but not a mob, either. They were all more or less headed in one direction: toward the Baxter Building.

The receptionist signaled again. The program had more to tell. Sue said, "Continue."

"Report from the lobby: Individuals are massing outside the main doors. Magnetic locks are currently holding, but sensors indicate superhumans with power ratings between ten and twenty in vicinity."

"Can you give me names?"

"Negative. Seventy-two percent of sensors have

been disabled. Will continue to report as long as possible."

There wasn't enough evidence yet to form a definite opinion about the attackers. Was this a random encounter or part of some larger plan? Would they head for the top floors and ignore the tenants or be methodical and gather hostages? In some ways, the most terrifying option was that these were simple killers who didn't know or care that the Baxter Building was the headquarters of the Fantastic Four.

Activating the building's public-address system, Sue said, "Attention, all tenants, this is Susan Richards. Please get to the thirty-fifth floor as quickly as possible. If you must use an elevator, use the blue—I repeat, the blue—elevators. I will be waiting for you in the receiving area." She set the message to repeat every two minutes for the next quarter hour.

Exiting the communications center, she found Franklin and Valeria waiting for her. The baby stood very quietly beside her brother, thumb in her mouth, a wet trickle running out of her nose. Franklin said, "Val doesn't feel good, Mommy."

Sue bent down to pick up her daughter and felt her forehead. The child flinched slightly and made a scared little gurgle in the back of her throat. "You're not warm," Sue said.

"Not that kind of sick, Mommy. She says she feels just bad."

"Franklin, honey, Val is only sixteen months old. She doesn't have that many words yet."

"I know," Franklin said in that very blunt, matter-of-fact way he had. "She didn't 'tell me' tell me. She just told me."

Sue sighed. The connection these two had sometimes worried her. Was this evidence of Franklin's repressed powers manifesting or was he simply being the intuitive big brother? She remembered saying precisely these kinds of things to her father about Johnny when they had been small. "All right, dear. She's probably just tired. And when was the last time either of you ate?"

"H.E.R.B.I.E. gave us some cereal a little while ago, but now Val says she wants popcorn."

"Really?" Sue asked. "Val says."

"Uh-huh," Franklin replied and headed for the stairs that led up to the kitchen.

"Well, go tell H.E.R.B.I.E. I said you—I mean Val—could have some popcorn. In fact, tell him to make a lot. We're going to have guests."

"Okay. How many guests? Is it going to be Peter and Mary Jane and Aunt May?"

"Not this time, dear. Friends from the building."

"Oh, okay." Franklin started up the stairs, but then stopped and looked back over his shoulder. "Mommy, will Val and I have to go to the moon?"

"No, dear. Aunt Crystal . . . we're still not sure about when she's going to be able to babysit again."

"Are we still mad at her?"

"We were never mad at her, dear. But Medusa and Black Bolt . . ."

"They were mad at us, weren't they?"

"Yes, dear."

Franklin nodded and continued back up the stairs. "That's okay. We didn't really like going there. It was too echoey."

*Echoey?* Sue thought in wonder. *What an amazing boy.* Val snuffled, whined a little, and put her head down on Sue's shoulder. "All right, love. Hang on. Let's go see about the people and then I'll get you ready for bed." Val whined again, gave a little kick with her sharp little toes, but then settled. Sue sighed again. It was going to be a long night.

# 8

As Reed Richards and Tony Stark fast-walked down a wide corridor that led from the heli-carrier bridge to the hangar deck, the soles of Stark's boots made sharp *tick-tack* noises against the deck. "You have to lower the force field, Tony," Reed said. "Just for a second. You have to let me get back into New York."

"No, Reed," Stark said. "In fact, I don't. I think it would be a very bad idea to crack open that field, and if you weren't worried about your wife and children you would see that."

Startled, Reed skidded to a stop, and when Stark didn't stop too, he took two elongated steps to get back in synch with the director's stride. "I'm not thinking about my wife and children," Reed said and then realized what he was saying. "Which is to say, of course I'm thinking about Sue and the kids, but I'm also thinking about how to solve the larger problem."

"You think you know how to solve the larger problem?"

"Yes," Reed said. "Of course. We have to seal the dimensional tear at Empire State. If we can do that, the rest of the problem—"

"The rest of the problem is that approximately two hundred thousand people have been affected by the energy emanating from the rift and can't exit the danger zone. Of those, we're estimating about ten to fifteen thousand are acting very strangely, one might even say *aggressively,* and many of those are amassing at the perimeter of the force shield. If we should lower the force shield even for a second, I'm pretty sure some of those would slip past, and the Initiative teams aren't in position—"

"I know all this, Tony," Reed said sharply, grabbing Stark by his shoulder to slow their headlong pace. "Tell me something I *don't* already know."

Tony ground to a halt, his boots screeching on the deck. When he wasn't wearing his armor, he and Reed Richards could look each other squarely in the eye, but Tony was currently half a head taller and so could stare angrily down his nose. "Something you don't know? All right, Reed, here's something you don't seem to know: *I'm in charge here.* This isn't Galactus we're facing or Annihilus or even Doctor Doom. This is several thousand New Yorkers, most of whom are functionally within the definition of 'innocent bystanders.' There may be a central cause or source of this problem, but here at S.H.I.E.L.D. we have a basic philosophy about such things. We're not super heroes and we're definitely not 'imaginauts,' whatever the hell that is. We're cops and that means first, we save the innocent bystanders. Then, after they're secure, we go in and start punching the bad guys. *Am I making myself clear?*"

Reed successfully held Tony's stare, but only barely. He wondered if the effects of the dimensional rift could be reaching as high as the helicarrier or if Tony Stark was simply overtaxed by the responsibilities of command. After a moment's consideration, he let his attention refocus on Tony and said simply, "Yes, you are."

Tony inhaled deeply and then let the breath out slowly. "All right. Thank you. I need to go check on the status of the Initiative teams forming up around the perimeter of the field. For some reason the Nevada team is having a hell of a time with their portal. Do you want to come along?"

"No. I'm going back to the bridge to see if I can help with the sensors or comm systems. I'd like to try to recontact Sue."

"You shouldn't worry about her, Reed," Tony said. "Of all of us, the least of all her." Reed knew that this comment was Tony's way of opening up for some kind of rapprochement, but he didn't feel like responding. Before he could walk away, though, Reed felt an armored gauntlet fall heavily on his shoulder. "I'm sorry, Reed. I know you mean well, but not every problem can be solved by pulling some kind of technological rabbit out of a hat."

Reed considered this statement for a moment and then replied, "That's a rather strange sentiment, coming from you."

Tony chuckled, then replied, "It is, isn't it? I guess it's this job."

"Maybe you should take a vacation when this is over."

"Maybe," Tony said, but then he lifted the helmet that he had been carrying under his arm and settled it onto his head. Reed heard the thin *whoosh* of an airlock seal and the rapid whir and click of connections locking into place. *"But not likely,"* Iron Man said, his voice shaded with the characteristic electronic blur, the eye holes in his helmet glowing an unearthly gold. Iron Man turned and entered the elevator. When the door slid closed, Reed turned and found Rachel Tyson waiting for him.

"Dr. Richards? I wanted you to see some new data we've received from Manhattan." She handed him an active palmtop computer without further comment, and Reed silently studied the images and text for several seconds.

"If I'm reading this right, the target is moving at only about fifteen klicks per hour. Can you confirm that?"

"Yes."

"And the secondary blips?"

"Superhumans. We can't get a fix on their exact IDs through the force fields, but we think they're all in the force-ten-to-twenty range."

Reed keyed coordinates into the handheld and then gave it back to Rachel. "If you can, please log this flight plan for me and get me airspace clearance. If you can't, well, don't worry. The Fantasticar is still faster than anything S.H.I.E.L.D. flies."

Rachel glanced at the coordinates, then glanced up at Reed with an uneasy expression. "You're sure this is where you want to go?"

"I'm sure. I need to get to New York, and if Director Stark won't let me in the front door, then I'll have to find another way." Reed nodded at the elevator. "Will this take me to the hangar deck?"

"Yes. You'll need clearance to take off, so give me five minutes to get back to the bridge."

"That should be fine. I have to warm up the Fantasticar's engines anyway."

"Really? Warm them up?"

"If I don't, she tends to get balky when she hits mach four."

"Ah," Rachel said. "Well, that would be bad."

Reed took the stylus from the palmtop and quickly

sketched out a design on the screen. "Here," he said, handing back the device. "I was working on a design for a portable force field generator that Director Stark might find useful," he said. "Nothing he couldn't have devised himself, but he's been so busy . . ." Reed decided to keep his thoughts to himself. Then, he held out his hand and said, "Thank you for your help, Agent Tyson. It's been a pleasure to meet you."

"And you, sir."

"You know, you're probably going to get in a lot of trouble for helping me."

"I know," Rachel said. She held up the palmtop. "This might mitigate the situation somewhat. Also, I'm of the opinion that this might be one of those problems that could be better solved old-school."

"You mean, with some forethought and planning?"

"Yes, sir. Followed by liberal application of punching and kicking."

Richards chuckled. "I can imagine you and Nick got along quite well."

Rachel grinned. "We had our moments. Good luck, Dr. Richards."

Five minutes later, the Fantasticar lifted off from the helicarrier flight deck and rapidly rose into a suborbital flight path. Then, after watching the world spin beneath him for several seconds, Reed tipped the nose of the vehicle down and dropped into a steep dive toward central Europe.

\*   \*   \*

The shadow that had made itself at home inside Stanislaw Klemp noted with pleasure that it was dragging the effects of the dimensional bleeding behind it as it moved, like an ever-widening trail of slime behind a gigantic snail. Buildings dripped and oozed; men and women metamorphosed, some very subtly and others more profoundly.

It found the so-called superhumans it encountered particularly fascinating, especially the ones who considered themselves "villains." The first half dozen it came across were nothing more than enterprising thugs with little or no interest in committing any act more evil than robbery and the occasional accompanying assault. One or two had a mild streak of sadism in them, but they lacked the raw power to be useful.

When it crossed paths with one of the heroes, the creature would provoke panic among the gullible masses and then move on. It seemed that the more overwhelming the heroes' sense of guilt and responsibility, the harder they found it to shake free from the creature's influence. That one poor, benighted fool, the one who swung on webs and stuck to walls, would continue to dive down into traffic and snatch idiots from the path of cars until he died of exhaustion. And the other, the one who dressed like a devil, would keep skulking in back alleys looking for shadows that only he could see until he finally succumbed to his own inner darkness.

All in all, the creature decided, New York was its kind of town.

Only now, standing outside the building protected by the force field, the one Klemp called the Baxter Building, did the creature decide to reveal itself completely. The quartet who had heeded his subtle call—Hydro-Man, Electro, Vapor, and Chemistro—had gathered without knowing precisely why they were assembled and assumed that the creature was one of them, a super villain. The fact that they could think clearly in the creature's presence was remarkable, though this might be attributable to their strange physiologies, and to the fact that they might already be amoral monsters. In particular, the one called Electro appeared to be about as close to a demon as anything the creature had ever seen in its home dimension.

The shadow's first problem was convincing the villains that it was the one responsible for the bedlam in the city, but that argument was settled when it focused its will on a weak-minded man who had been cowering in a nearby car and forced him to bash his brains out on its simulated leather-upholstered dashboard. Electro pretended not to be impressed, but the creature could sense his simmering resentment.

"But you're planning on taking on the Fantastic Four," Chemistro said. "That's quite another thing."

The creature already had some knowledge of this Fantastic Four, courtesy of Klemp's memories, and knew it would be foolish to get into a protracted engagement with them. Its only goal was to lower the force screens so the effect of the hellwave would be felt outside the city. After that, when the wave's influence had grown, it would decide how to confront this Fantastic Four. Indeed, if as it suspected the flaming one had been one of the Four, there might not be any need to defeat them in battle. Depending on the condition of their souls and whatever dark desires they might be suppressing, they could very well fall under his sway.

"You have nothing to fear from the Fantastic Four," the creature said. "One has already been defeated and the others will no doubt be occupied. Our goal is not their immediate destruction, but simply to remove the walls that contain my forces. Afterward, you'll be free to loot and pillage to your dark hearts' content."

The four exchanged glances. The creature could almost read their thoughts: The risk would be high, but the rewards would be great. None of them wished to face the legendary Four, but they saw the logic of the creature's words and were willing to be persuaded that this might never happen. One by one they nodded, then Electro spoke for the quartet. "Okay," he said. "We're in. As long as you take point, we'll watch your back. I've faced the Thing, and he can be shocked just like anyone else."

"And I've taken out the Torch more than once," Hydro-Man said. "I hate that stupid punk."

The other two held their silence, and the creature decided they were probably the most intelligent of the quartet.

"There's just one problem," Electro said.

"And that is?"

"We don't know who you are. What's your name? You have to have a name."

"Why?" the creature asked.

"What if we get into a fight with the Invisible Woman?" Electro asked. "I want to be able to say, 'Hey, whatever your name is—here comes the Invisible Woman.'"

"Except you wouldn't be able to say that," Vapor said. "Since she'd be invisible."

"You *know* what I mean."

"Call me whatever you wish," the creature said, wishing to get under way. This turned out to be a mistake.

"We could call you Hellion," Vapor said. "Because you're big and red and have horns."

"No," Chemistro said. "There's already a Hellion. Some mutant kid."

"Okay, then what about Devil-Man?"

"There's one of those, too. Japanese *manga*."

"What are you talking about?" Electro sneered. "Are you *twelve* or something? How do you even know this?"

"Hey, I take this business very seriously," Chemistro snapped back. "I try to keep current."

"With a name like Chemistro," Electro retorted, "you cannot claim to be taking this business seriously."

"Oh, right, *Electro,*" Hydro-Man scoffed.

"Hey, the name is a *classic,*" Electro shouted. "I've been around since back in the *day*. When I started, we put some thought into what we were doing."

"And *Electro* was the best you could come up with?" Hydro-Man asked.

"That does it," Electro hissed, sparks flying from his eyes. "Team dissolved. Let's go . . ."

"How about Hell-Man?" Vapor suggested, oblivious to Electro's ranting, still engaged by the original question.

The creature was considering leaving to find other villains when Chemistro said, "Hellspawn would be better."

Both Hydro-Man and Electro turned toward Chemistro, relaxed their fighting stances, and considered him with something that looked like admiration. "If you could think of *that,*" Electro asked, "then why was Chemistro the best you could do for yourself?"

"Bite me," Chemistro said, polishing the barrel of his alchemy gun. "Now, can we get on with this? I'd like to make my stake before the heroes get the city back under control."

"Yes," said the newly christened Hellspawn. "Let us get on with it."

Everyone must have been really impressed with the guy who had wrapped the flaming kitchen towel around his spatula, because half his neighbors disappeared inside their houses and reappeared a couple minutes later holding imitations.

"Great day," Ben muttered as he shuffled backward toward the rec center. "Really. I'm having so much fun today. Nice to be back in the ol' neighborhood, seeing all you folks."

The neighbors shuffled down the steps from their houses either carrying kerosene cans or hefting baseball bats. One or two were clumsily loading small-caliber handguns.

"Monster," the mob murmured again, getting into the whole "speaking in unison" thing.

"Really, folks," Ben said in his friendliest tone, "this is a bad idea. First of all, there ain't one of ya that could really put a dent in me."

As one, half the mob set down their kerosene cans and kicked them over, sending out streams of oily liquid that seemed to magically pool around Ben's now scuffed Tanino Criscis. The fumes tickled Ben's nose and made him feel a bit woozy. Long-buried memories of the kerosense stove his dad had kept by his ratty old easy chair in the living room at 7135 Yancy Street bubbled up to the surface. His mother had always fretted about the idea of the old man falling asleep and letting his drink slip out of his hand into the heater. The way she repeated that story, night after night, gave Ben the feeling that she didn't so much dread the thought as believe the repetition of the nightmare would bring about the reality.

"Second of all," Ben continued, "it's not like I'm going to stand here and let you set me on fire." He heard the sound of a couple more cans tipping over behind him. Risking a quick look over his shoulder, Ben saw that a few of the old ladies had dumped their cans over against the rec center steps, which were stone and probably wouldn't burn very easily—but that didn't mean the flames couldn't reach the front doors. One of the ladies feinted at Ben with her torch and he flinched away. Probably the saner option would have been to give her a flick on the side of the head with one of his fingers, but a lady that old had to have a noggin thinner than an eggshell. "Wouldn't that look great on the front page of the *Bugle*? 'Thing Crushes Old Lady's Skull.'" He tugged down on the knot in his tie and whipped it off over his head. "Livin' the dream here, folks. Livin' the dream."

The old lady who seemed to be in charge hobbled down a couple steps shouting at Ben, "Silence, Monster!" Lifting her cane, she pointed at Ben and screamed, "Burn!" A half dozen of her geriatric cohorts touched their torches to the pools of kerosene, which went up with a smoky black *whoosh*.

Most of the geriatrics were just barely spry enough to stagger away from the flames, all except one old lady whose robe hem caught on fire, provoking screams of terror. Ben dashed forward through the blaze and tried to pat out the fire with his hands, but the flame quickly spread up the threadbare flannel, so his only option was to twirl the old girl around and strip the robe off. In the act of flinging the robe to the ground, Ben spun in the wrong direction and found himself standing in the middle of a flaming pool of kerosene.

All around him, he heard the old folks cackling and braying. The old woman began to chant, "Burn, monster, burn! Burn, monster, burn!" and this was gleefully taken up by the mob. Ben bounded out of the pool, stripped off his now flaming suit coat, and threw it into the gutter. Feeling his temper beginning to boil over, Ben knew that if he didn't get himself under control quickly, there were going to be broken dentures skittering across the pavement.

*I could just clap my hands together,* he thought. *One good pop and the flames are out and I can head home and have my supper.* Of course, the old people would be out too, with concussions and burst eardrums all around. Right at that moment, however, Ben was finding he didn't care. He felt an old, familiar rage churning up from the pit of his stomach, an acid-tinged wrath that he hadn't tasted since his earliest days of being trapped inside the rocky prison he called a body.

Out of the corner of his eye, Ben saw that one of the old men had tottered up the steps to the rec center and had doused the front door with his kerosene. Now he was wobbling back down as fast as he could, his arms raised in triumph like a kid who'd just hit a home run or tugged on a little girl's pigtails. The varnish in the door was fresh and started to smoke immediately, a black stripe rippling up to the window frame. The heat found a fault in the tempered glass, which cracked with a fine tracery of lines.

The old woman, the ringleader, dared to dance through the flames, cracked Ben on the side of his head with her cane, and screeched, "Die, monster!"

The Thing gritted his teeth, which were vibrating with the echo of the aluminum cane. *Monster?* he thought. *So they want to see a monster?* He pressed the tips of his fingers down into the surface of the blacktop, fissures radiating out from the points of impact. *I won't even have to tear up the street,* he decided. *Just shake things around a little. If anyone asks, I'll tell them I was looking for a water main to put out the fire.*

His back tickled and Ben knew that his dress shirt had begun to smolder. *I really liked this shirt,* he thought and dug his fingers in a little more deeply. *What jury in the world would convict me, the idol of millions?* He wiggled the tips of his fingers experimentally, just to see what it would be like, and more fissures rippled out from the first.

Ben sensed movement behind him and turned to see that a new player had sauntered onstage. A tall figure dressed in a heavy Army surplus camo coat with the hood pulled up was waving a red can back and forth before the rec center's front door. "Okay, pal," Ben growled. "You're first." Standing, he tore a fist-sized chunk of paving out of the street, uncertain whether he would flick it at the arsonist's gas can or his head.

The guy turned around to look at Ben, his hood flopped back. He was, Ben saw, another monster, this one even worse than the sharp-toothed little guy who had run past a little while ago. The monster had a mis-shapen, hairless, bullet-shaped skull, slitted holes for eye sockets, and formless lumps where his ears should have been. A thin, white smoke curled around his feet and Ben was convinced he smelled brimstone. All in an instant, the cause of the day's accumulated difficulties became clear. "Demon," he muttered and bent down to pick up a much larger chunk of concrete. The Thing had dealt with just enough supernatural menaces to know they could take a surprising amount of damage.

"Hey, that would be really uncool," a familiar voice chided.

Ben looked back over his shoulder and saw that the kid he had talked to in front of the bakery was standing there with a fire extinguisher, casually putting out the kerosene fire and shooing away the old folks with freezing-cold foam.

Ben searched his memory and was annoyed that he couldn't remember the kid's real name, but only the ridiculous nickname: "Bender."

"Only my friends get to call me that and you're no friend if you're going to be insulting my brother like that."

The same feeling of confusion that had crept over

Ben when he had first talked to the kid began to seep back into his brain. He heard another whooshing sound and glanced back over at the creature that had been fanning the flames in front of the rec center door. The fire was out, doused by the "demon" and his fire extinguisher. "What's his problem?" the figure on the steps asked.

"Nuthin', Marcus," the kid said. "He's just bein' a fool like most everyone else around here today."

*Marcus,* Ben thought, and that name rang a bell. *The kid's brother.* Ben realized he was still holding the chunk of paving, and let it slip from his hand. Marcus loped stiffly down the steps, walked over to his brother, and helped him to snuff out the last patches of burning kerosene. The old folks had scattered and the street was now deserted except for Ben and the two brothers, Marcus and . . .

"Julio," Ben said. "Now I remember. Julio."

"You don't get to call me that, either, pal. You call me Mister Rodriguez until I tell you otherwise. We don't need you comin' down here to our neighborhood and insulting us, you rich piece of—"

The kid had started to bop back and forth from foot to foot in a threatening little dance until Marcus laid a hand on his little brother's shoulder. "Be cool, Bender," Marcus said, but the words came out a little slurred, like his lips wouldn't flex quite the way he wanted. "You said it youself: Everyone's actin' kinda weird tonight. Why should he be any different?"

*Why should I be any different?* Ben asked himself and felt the shame well up inside him. *Because I'm supposed to be different.* He stared down at his hands and the holes in the street. Then he looked at Marcus's face and said only, "You in the service?"

"Not anymore, man," Marcus said and stood a little straighter. "I got discharged after . . ." He awkwardly pointed at his face and Ben saw that the fire had gotten one of his hands, too. His two smallest fingers were curled up together into a claw. "Transport got hit by an RPG."

"Sorry to hear that, kid," Ben said. "Tough break."

Marcus shrugged. "Coulda been worse, man. Coulda died."

Ben didn't have any reply to that, so he just nodded and pointed at the extinguisher and said, "Thanks for putting out the fire."

"Thanks for building the rec center. Me and Bender come down here most days and he helps me with rehab."

"Rehab?" Ben asked. "Really? We do that here?"

"Sure. Lotta guys from this area come home and need some help. We got the V.A. over in Queens, but, hey, this is a lot nicer."

Ben shook his head. He thought back and tried to remember whether Ms. Sullivan had mentioned anything about rehab, but couldn't recall. All he had ever thought about was the kids playing basketball or doing gymnastics and creating other happy little pictures.

"So, you got any idea why people been actin' so nuts?" Julio asked. Seeing his brother and Ben treating each other so courteously had calmed the kid down.

"No," Ben said. "But I'm going to do my best to find out, now that you've finished kicking some sense into me."

"He's good at that," Marcus said.

"Damn straight," Julio said, leaning toward Ben, but he was smiling now. "And I'll do it again if—"

The kid didn't get to finish. Twin columns of flame flashed down out of the sky and blocked Julio's path. He threw himself back against his big brother, who let out a high, nasal cry of shock and alarm. *He can't like fire,* Ben thought and considered what it must have cost Marcus to walk up to the burning door.

The Human Torch dropped like a meteorite out of the sky between Ben and the brothers, hot coals flying every which way. Marcus regained his composure and pulled Julio inside the protection of his oversized coat while Ben frantically waved off his teammate. "Be careful, flame brain! You tryin' to bring down the whole neighborhood?"

"Looks to me like someone was already working on it," Johnny shouted back. He pointed a finger and a red needle of flame flickered off and landed squarely on Marcus's chest. Ben saw the older brother flinch and wondered whether Johnny could see the man's burn scars. *Maybe he can,* Ben thought. *And that's what's bothering me.*

"Back off, kid," Ben shouted. "These two didn't have anything to do with it. They saved me from . . . Well, they helped put out the fire."

"I saw what they were doing," Johnny taunted. "The high-and-mighty Thing needed some help against a rampaging mob of geriatrics."

The impulse to grab one of the kerosene cans and toss it at Johnny was almost overwhelming, but Ben was beginning to understand what was happening on Yancy Street that night. The whatever-it-was, the demons or invisible rays or nanobots, didn't actually make you evil, but it could make you act out on your anger. He wasn't sure exactly what was going on with Johnny, but he knew he had to keep himself under control.

Before he could explain any of this to anyone else, Julio turned his fire extinguisher on Johnny, shouting, "Cool off, sucker!" The chemical foam never stood a chance against the Torch's intense blaze, but it did have one effect: It made the Torch mad.

Johnny clenched his fist in a gesture Ben had seen a thousand times. When he opened it again, he was holding a white-hot fireball and there was a murderous gleam in his eye. "Kid," he said with a wicked grin, "you are *so* going to regret that."

# 9

"HOW MANY ARE THERE, H.E.R.B.I.E.?" SUE asked. The reception area had filled up much more quickly than she had expected and the crowd was overflowing into the kitchen and living quarters.

"Thirty-five and counting, Mrs. Richards," the pint-sized robot said. Hovering impassively beside Sue, his large gold eyes reflected the light cast by the monitor screens. Reed had created H.E.R.B.I.E. to perform routine maintenance in his lab and around their quarters, but then Franklin had taken a shine to the little 'bot, so now he served as the Fantastic Four's majordomo and occasional child-care fallback.

Most of the tenants were clustered around the

forty-six-inch plasma screen HDTV in the living room, watching the events of the day unfold. Most appeared calm, though Sue attributed some of that to the fact that Franklin was regularly passing through all the rooms and handing out refreshments. *It's hard to panic,* Sue reflected, *when an eight-year-old boy is calmly handing you popcorn and juice.*

"Can we tell how many more are in the building?"

"Not precisely," H.E.R.B.I.E. said, "but I estimate another six to nine. The security program can only account for persons moving through the halls, elevators, or stairwells. If someone chooses to stay in their office or suite . . ."

"We don't know they're there," Sue finished for him. "Right." Reed had been obliged to be courteous when he had installed the security system. Not everyone warmed to the idea of the landlord having cameras in their offices.

"Any suggestions?"

"I could go from door to door and attempt to assess whether anyone is within."

Sue considered the option and tried to imagine the reception H.E.R.B.I.E. would receive if anyone actually did answer the knock on their door. Franklin might consider the robot "cute," but Franklin's mother doubted if anyone else would. "Let's hold off on that for now," she said. "If one of us has to go out looking for stragglers, it might be better if I do it."

"Understood, Mrs. Richards, though I have concerns about what Valeria would do if you left. She is not feeling well."

Sue stared at the robot in amazement, which, she knew, meant nothing to him. "What makes you say that?" she asked. "I mean, I agree, but on what basis did you form your opinion?"

H.E.R.B.I.E. tilted his body toward Sue as if he was leaning in toward her. "She is being moody, if you don't mind my saying so. Usually, Valeria is very pleased to have company and enjoys interacting with strangers, but she is more withdrawn than usual." Sue had noticed all this too. Usually when they had guests, her daughter would walk from person to person and find some way to engage their attention. Tonight, she was sitting in her room holding her bunny, watching a *Dora the Explorer* DVD and likely sucking her finger. "Also," the robot concluded, "she appears somewhat flushed. I believe her temperature is slightly elevated."

"Coming down with a cold," Sue said. "I should get her cleaned up and into bed."

"You are probably correct, Mrs. Richards," H.E.R.B.I.E. replied. "As is often the case, 'Mother knows best.' However, I would like you to keep in mind that the force field around the Baxter Building may not be completely filtering out the pernicious effects of whatever is affecting the rest of Manhattan."

Sue looked around the reception area. "Everyone

else seems to be doing all right," she observed. "Especially compared with what we're seeing on TV."

"But Valeria is a very young child," H.E.R.B.I.E. said. "And one who feels very deeply."

Sue gave the little robot a sidelong glance. He was right, of course. "I'm beginning to wonder if you might know more about my daughter than I do."

"Nonsense," H.E.R.B.I.E. said huffily. "I cannot, by definition, know anything that you or Dr. Richards do not. The algorithms that govern my electronic brain—"

"Have obviously learned something about tact," Sue said. "Maybe you could work on passing that on to Franklin."

"I have tried," H.E.R.B.I.E. said and drifted off in the general direction of Franklin, "but I'm only a robot, ma'am, and not a miracle worker."

Several of the tenants clustered around the television gasped, and Sue began to wonder about the wisdom of leaving the set on. No one looked at her as she approached, their gazes fixed on the flickering images. They were watching grainy video shot from outside S.H.I.E.L.D.'s force fields. Men and women were lunging at the invisible fence with ever-increasing frenzy, many of them crying out in frustration or rage when the repulsers pushed them back. The cameraman zoomed in on a figure climbing out of a second-story window and watched as the paunchy, fortyish man leaped from the ledge at where he must have imagined the top of the fence was. As Sue expected, the man became enmeshed in the energy matrix and slowly slid toward the ground as if he were slipping down a wall made of molasses. When his feet hit the ground, the man crumbled into a ball, his nervous system temporarily overloaded.

Sue could see on the faces of her guests that many were thinking about what other sorts of insanity people might be attempting in order to escape the city. She had no idea why S.H.I.E.L.D. had erected the barriers, though she appreciated the fact that the fields were meant to be nonlethal. The camera began to pull away from the scene, but then something altogether unexpected occurred, something that made Sue stand bolt-upright and search for Franklin to make sure he wasn't watching the screen.

As everyone watched in abject horror, a hunched figure dressed in an expensive-looking overcoat entered the frame, pulled the paunchy man to his feet, and then pressed him against the force field. The hunched figure threw back his head and the camera zoomed in on his mouth so that all the viewers at home could see his needle-sharp teeth. When he snapped his head down on the paunchy man's throat, the cameraman fortunately lost track of his shot, but there wasn't any doubt in anyone's mind about what had just happened.

Several of the tenants screamed and Sue heard someone being ill. When she didn't see Franklin in the main room, she ran into the kitchen and was relieved to find her son in deep, serious conversation with H.E.R.B.I.E. The little robot seemed to know precisely what had just occurred on the TV and was doing his best to keep her son occupied.

Racing back to the reception area, Sue found that most of the tenants were still clustered around the monitors, though several men and women were huddled together near the windows, conversing in shrill, rapid whispers. At this hour on a normal day, Sue would have seen the bright panoply of lights that was midtown New York swirling below her, but tonight she saw alarming swatches of darkness punctuated by undulating towers of orange-red and acidic flashes of yellow and green.

One of her guests, a middle-aged, fashionably dressed woman who sat kneading her Versace scarf in both hands, turned to Sue and demanded stridently, "What's going on out there? Isn't there anything you can do?"

Sue pointed at the TV. "I know as much as you do . . . ," she began, but then saw that her interrogator was not really looking for answers, but rather for an opportunity to vent her frustration.

"But you're super heroes! Don't you have some way to find out what's happening?" Several other expectant faces turned toward them. The tension level in the room was rising, and Sue wasn't sure what she would do if the tenants began to panic.

Normally, the F.F. had access to special resources, but the double whammy of two layers of force fields had disabled most of them. In fact, Sue wondered how much longer they would have cable TV, but decided not to voice this fear. Instead, she tried logic. "It's possible that what you just saw has *nothing* to do with the force fields. There are a lot of unusual individuals in Manhattan. Maybe this event has just flushed them out."

A tall African-American man wearing a T-shirt advertising the fitness center on the first floor pointed at the TV. "I don't think so, Mrs. Richards. Something else is happening." As they watched, a wave of dark figures emerged from the shadows and raced toward the men and women clustered near the force field. It may have been a trick of the light, but the dark figures appeared to be skimming along several inches above the ground. As soon as the first shadow reached a man, it unfolded and swiftly enveloped the unsuspecting individual like a black silk sheet fired from a cannon. The captured man tumbled over backward, completely immobilized, and when the shadow unraveled a moment later, he was gone.

The crowd turned into a frightened mob and tried to flee, but the shadows were all over them. Several of the tenants shrieked and one man wept uncontrollably. Just as Sue started to think that now was the time to shut off the television, the news feed went dead and they were all left staring at flickering gray fuzz. The woman in the Versace scarf turned toward Sue, her eyes wide with panic. One by one, everyone else in the room turned to stare at Sue and she knew she had to find something reassuring to say. Oddly, she found herself thinking that she was wearing the same outfit as she had on during the tenants meeting that morning and how inappropriate it felt. *I should get my costume on,* she thought. She was the authority figure, and authority figures did not wear BCBG Max suits.

But before Sue could say a word, H.E.R.B.I.E. flitted into the room and bobbed to a halt. "Ma'am," he chirped. "Please come with me. We have a slight problem."

"Is it Franklin?" Sue asked, torn between the need to reassure the guests and fear for her son.

"It *includes* Franklin," H.E.R.B.I.E. said meaningfully.

"Where?"

"Valeria's bedroom."

"I'll be right there," she said and then realized that she was about to leave the tenants to their own devices. "You stay here with the guests." As she raced for the living quarters, she heard H.E.R.B.I.E. trying to organize a game of Pictionary. He tended to go with the old standbys when situations became grim.

When Sue reached her daughter's room, she found the little girl curled up on her bed, her knees drawn up tight, her arms wrapped around her bunny, and her eyes scrunched tightly shut. Franklin was in the corner farthest from the television, his eyes wide but fixed on the screen. The monitors in the kids' rooms were wired so that they could only watch programs from their copious online library.

A quick glance at the screen showed that Franklin had manipulated the monitor so he could see what was happening through the security system cameras. Obviously, he had decided to show off his ability to his sister. Sue momentarily wondered how long the boy had been doing this, but when she saw what was happening on the screen, she instinctively concealed it behind an invisible bubble. Sue scooped up her trembling son and deposited him on the bed next to Val so she could wrap her arms around both of them simultaneously. Scolding would come later; her primary task of the moment was to give comfort and assess damage.

She hummed a low, wandering tune for several minutes until she felt her children relax. Franklin began to sob very softly, though his mother recognized it as the good kind of crying, tears of relief and release rather than suffering. Val just clutched her bunny in one arm and her mother's arm with the other. When her daughter finally relaxed, Sue realized that the little girl had fallen asleep.

*Good. Let her sleep.* It would make speaking with Franklin a little simpler. "What happened, sweetie?" she asked in her calmest, yet firmest voice.

Franklin needed a few seconds to collect his thoughts, but once again Sue was reminded how brave and self-assured her son could be. He began to speak in his "Here's what I did with H.E.R.B.I.E. today" voice: "Val was worried about Blondie." Several months ago, Val and Franklin had heard Ben call the holographic reception program in the lobby "Blondie," and the name had stuck. Sue was fairly sure Val considered Blondie to be a real person, which, considering the number of unusual characters who paraded through her life, shouldn't really have come as a surprise.

"So you rewired the monitor to look at the lobby."

"It wasn't hard, Mommy."

*Of course it wasn't,* Sue thought. *Not for you.* When he got home, she was going to have to talk to Reed about better Franklin-proofing. The boy was starting to show dangerous signs of being much too smart for his own good. "Okay. And what did you see?"

"We saw the men outside the force wall Daddy put up."

"Okay. Did they scare you?"

"Not at first," Franklin said. "They were all just standing there, row upon row of them. All of them were staring at the camera and I started to get the feeling they were looking back at me. And then one of them smiled and he had really, really big teeth."

"That must have been scary."

Unexpectedly, Franklin displayed one of his

flashes of world-weary eight-year-old pique. He sighed, rolled his eyes, and said, "Don't be silly, Mommy. I've seen big teeth before." He shook his head. "The scary thing was what happened next. He held up his hand and we saw he was holding a bunny, one just like Val's."

*What?* Sue thought, but she didn't interrupt.

"And then the man opened his mouth and stuck the bunny's head in his mouth and he bit down . . ."

Sue could only imagine what this cruel magic trick must have done to Val, but she wasn't sure why Franklin had been so shaken.

"And then the bunny started to kick and shake his arms and we could hear him screaming and screaming." Franklin huddled in close to Sue, but he kept talking in the same tone. "And then the man twisted the bunny's body and the head came off and the bunny stopped screaming, but there was blood on the man's mouth . . ."

*Holy God,* Sue thought and clutched her son to her breast. "It was just a trick, Franklin. You know that, don't you, that it was just a trick?"

"I know, Mommy. I know, but . . . but Val was scared and I didn't know what to do so I called H.E.R.B.I.E. and told him to come get you and while he was gone, while Val wasn't looking, something else happened."

"What was it, love? What happened?"

"The men, all of them, raised their hands and

pointed at the camera. They smiled and showed me their teeth and then they started to walk forward and push against the invisible wall. I could see it sparking and glowing red. It was getting hotter and hotter and then the men started to burn, but they wouldn't stop smiling and they wouldn't stop pushing and I didn't know what was going to happen so I just backed up into the corner because I could feel them looking at me and I wanted to find someplace to hide, but all I could find was this corner . . ." Franklin closed his eyes and pushed his face into Sue's belly, burrowing for warmth and safety.

"Don't worry, love," Sue whispered reassuringly. "I won't let them get in. You know I won't. You know I can stop them. You know I can keep back anyone or anything, no matter how big their teeth are."

"I know, Mommy. I know. It's just that—"

But Sue never got the chance to hear what Franklin was going to say next. His words were drowned out by the security system alarm. "Warning, warning," it droned. "Shields are down. Repeat, shields are done. This is *not* a drill. There are hostiles in the building and they are approaching the elevators and stairs."

Sue dropped the invisible bubble she had cast in front of the monitor, and was shocked by what she saw. As Franklin had described, there were several rows of men with their hands up in the air, standing where the force shield had been not a minute before.

All of them were indeed smiling, but there was neither pleasure nor joy in their faces. In point of fact, none of them had faces anymore. Their smiles were the grimaces of the dead. Somehow, they had pushed through Reed's force shield, overloading it, and as a result the collapsing field had apparently stripped away their flesh. None of this made sense to Sue; for one thing, Reed's force shields didn't work that way. No one could burn themselves pushing against one and, furthermore, simple physical pressure couldn't bring one down. Clearly, other forces were at work, a hand that wished to conceal its existence behind Halloween tricks. Sue understood all this, understood the nature of the threat if not its goals or intentions, and she was confident she could outthink it as long as she kept a cool head.

But there was the problem: keeping a cool head. Without warning, she felt a thin shiver of panic slide down her back. Sue Richards found that she could not take her eyes off the monitor and the row of empty, grinning, bony faces.

And she could not shake off the feeling that every one of them was staring back at her.

The Emperor reclined before his hearth and stared into the banked coals, a mug of mulled wine cooling on the wide arm of his iron chair. He rarely drank, but the mingled aroma of wine and spices reminded him of his youth and quieter times. The room where he sat and watched the flickering lights would be considered by many to be tiny, even cramped, but the Emperor had grown up in small rooms and found comfort in confined spaces.

He swirled the wine in the mug and held it to his nose, inhaled the rich scent of cloves and coriander, then set it back on the chair's arm. The Emperor knew there were unworldly forces at play somewhere in the universe—he could feel them like an itch on the nape of his neck—and though it vexed him that he could not put a name to the energies, he also trusted his finely honed senses. He had come to this room, this quiet, unostentatious room, to calm his mind, to marshal his resources, to reflect and to plan.

Something was coming. He could feel it: A door had been opened and soon the Emperor would need to confront whoever or whatever stood on the threshold—perhaps battle it, or perhaps persuade it to form an alliance. He knew that most of the world considered him a violent man, a figure of dread, the epitome of conflict, but the Emperor paid no heed to that kind of dim-witted prattle. The truth was he preferred to be left in peace, though he insisted that the peace be one that he himself defined.

Holding his hands up before his eyes, he formed a triangle with two forefingers and overlapping thumbs and stared into the middle distance. The crude face of the universe receded and his inner eye began to emerge. The scent of the cloves triggered a memory, a rare clear winter morning when his smiling mother had sat with him before a fire and showed him how to make ornaments from dried fruit, ribbon, and whole cloves. How they had enjoyed themselves, and how long the smells had lingered on their fingers.

Someone knocked at the door.

The Emperor lowered his hands and thought of a curse he had heard his uncle use once, but he had long ago concluded that the use of such language was for lesser men. His servants understood what it meant to disturb him when he was meditating, and while he had little faith in their wit, he trusted he had instilled an appropriate level of fear in them. So, though he felt a mild temptation to simply obliterate whoever walked through the door, the Emperor knew this would be a useless waste of energy and time. Besides, he could always obliterate whoever it was *after* he delivered the message.

"Enter," the Emperor said.

Captain Rudi, the master of the Emperor's personal guard, entered and stood at attention. "Sire," he said and waited to be acknowledged.

"Captain," the Emperor said, composing himself. He was pleased to find that he had done the correct thing by suppressing his earlier impulse. Rudi was a valuable member of his staff and would not interrupt unless it was absolutely essential. "Report."

"Our sovereign airspace will be breached in less than three minutes. We shall, of course, obliterate the intruder unless you give the order to permit him to proceed."

The Emperor, a man who was rarely surprised, felt his left eyebrow rise in mild consternation. "Why," he asked, "would I do such a thing? I believe my orders on such matters were perfectly clear."

Captain Rudi inhaled deeply and let his breath out slowly. "Perfectly, sire." He paused and then continued. "In every instance except one."

The Emperor felt the hairs on the back of his neck bristle. "Richards," he said.

"Yes, sire."

"With an escort?"

"Alone, sire. He radioed ahead to ask for clearance. And he . . . he requested an audience."

The Emperor considered this unprecedented turn of events and then flicked his right finger and said, "News feed."

A moment later a blue sphere rose from a hidden niche in the floor. A light flickered in its depths and images began to quickly play on its surface. The Emperor touched the orb and began to quickly shuffle icons and images across the sphere. Two minutes later he said, "Ah. I see that New York is once again in peril."

"Indeed?" Captain Rudi asked. It was a slightly impertinent response, but the Emperor permitted it. He was too intrigued by what he was reading.

"His wife and children must be in peril," the Emperor said. "It's the only sequence of events that fits."

He considered the images for another moment or two and then commanded the orb to return to its niche. "Distance?"

"Seven hundred klicks, sire. He is dropping from low orbit."

"What is his rate of speed?"

Rudi consulted a handheld computer. "Approximately mach five, sire."

The response elicited a chuckle. "So he has no intention of stopping if I say no."

Captain Rudi performed the math in his head. "Apparently not, sire."

"Then it would be foolish to say otherwise. By all means, give Dr. Richards clearance to land. Tell him to use the south landing field. I doubt he will obey, but let us at least follow some kind of protocol."

"Very well, sire."

"And tell cook to prepare a meal. I daresay Mr. Fantastic will be hungry."

"I will, sire."

After Rudi exited, Victor Von Doom raised his hands again and attempted to reconstruct the picture that had been forming earlier, but the circumstances had changed and the memory of his mother that had seemed so vivid, so immediate only minutes earlier now felt exhausted and unreal. *Richards was coming.* The thought excited him and, naturally, angered him. What could the fool be thinking? What stratagem, what game was unfolding?

Then, unexpectedly, Von Doom found himself recalling one of the few interactions he and Richards had shared back in their university days that had not been about science or research. Richards had been playing chess in one of the common areas and Von Doom had decided on a whim that it was time to show the fool who was master. Richards had accepted, probably thinking that this was the opportunity to get Von Doom to "open up" and let his mind be picked. The idea, of course, had been ridiculous.

Surprisingly, within three moves, Von Doom had recognized that Richards had obviously studied the Immortal Game and understood its intricacies. Within seven moves, Von Doom saw that if he did not bring the full weight of his intelligence to the game, he might lose. And then, as he was forming his strategy and planning his next five moves, Richards began to talk. Von Doom could not recall the man's exact words, but the subject had been something along the lines of a film he was thinking of seeing that weekend or some minor bit of research he had been doing. Von Doom looked up from the chessboard and saw that Richards was staring out the window and, half-smiling, watching a yellow and black bird perched on the branch of a nearby tree.

Von Doom had risen then and left. Richards attempted to call him back, to find out what was wrong, even to apologize (though the fool had no idea why he was apologizing), but Von Doom refused to acknowledge his pathetic mewing. If a man could not be trusted to bring his full attention to a game . . .

The Emperor shook his head and was mildly annoyed to discover he had no idea why this memory had surfaced. He picked up his mug of mulled wine and inhaled deeply, but the wine had cooled and the smell of the spices had faded. The familiar rage rose within his breast and Von Doom tipped the mug off the arm of his chair, watching it fall like a tumbling pawn. He listened to it shatter on the stone floor and then, moments later, forgot it had ever existed.

## 10

ONCE UPON A TIME, JOHNNY HAD TRIED TO convince Reed that the Baxter Building needed a Danger Room, a place where they could practice using their powers, either as a team or individually, but Sue always nixed the idea. One reason, she said, was that the insurance company would never let them get away with such a thing. Second, she said, he and Ben already got as much practice fighting as they could possibly ever want, usually against each other.

At the time, Ben had thought this statement was not entirely fair. For one thing, he and Johnny rarely got into the kind of knock-down-drag-outs they had indulged in back in the early days, largely because

Ben wasn't as angry as he had been back in the day. Also, though Ben would never admit this to the kid's face, Johnny wasn't the same annoying punk he had once been.

So, Ben thought, all those times, all those scuffles, all those romps around, over, and through the Baxter Building . . . they were the practice runs and now here he was facing the real deal. Judging by the waves of heat rolling off the Torch, the insanity that had gotten its hooks into so many was affecting Johnny, too. Ben knew that if he didn't do something in three seconds or less, the Human Torch would flash-fry an eleven-year-old kid and never look back.

The problem was that Ben was pretty sure he couldn't beat Johnny. The Torch was fast, agile, and normally too smart to let a brawler like the Thing get in range. Ben's rocky hide was pretty thick, but all Johnny had to do was let go with a nova blast and everything within a quarter-mile radius would be toast.

Back when they were both younger and dumber, Ben knew how to taunt the kid and make him give up his advantages, but he was smarter than that now . . . normally. *The key word,* Ben concluded, *is "normally." Whatever we're seeing here tonight ain't normal.* That slight tactical advantage would have to do.

Ben inserted himself in front of Julio and Marcus with his back to the Torch. Glancing over his shoulder, he did his best to sound contemptuous and sneering, "Don't get your asbestos knickers all in a twist, flame brain. These two were just helping me out, and damn if they weren't more useful than you would've been against a bunch of geriatrics." Scorn was his best weapon now, and Ben knew he didn't dare look back to see what Johnny was doing. Instead, he whispered as softly as he could to Julio, "What's he doing?"

Julio peered up over Ben's shoulder, gave the slightest of shrugs, and replied, "Nuthin'. Floating. Looking like a big flaming dork."

Ben closed his eyes, hoping against hope that the Torch hadn't heard. He didn't know what he could say to Julio to get the kid to chill, but then he saw that he didn't need to worry. Marcus laid a hand on his brother's shoulder and, barely moving his lips, said, "Cool it, Bender. Can't you see what the big man is trying to do?"

Mentally saying a quick thankful prayer, Ben muttered, "When I say, 'Run . . .'" Marcus gave him a barely perceptible nod.

"What are you up to, Ben?" the Torch asked, his voice tinged with fury. "I came all the way down here to your old neighborhood despite the smell and was all ready to lend a hand, but I can see my generosity isn't really being appreciated." Ben felt a burst of blast-furnace heat on his back. Johnny was trying to get his attention.

No longer concealing his intentions, Ben said to Marcus, "Give me that extinguisher." Marcus handed it to him. "When I turn around . . ."

Marcus tightened his grip on his brother's shoulder, and Ben saw the corners of his mouth tighten in what might have been a sardonic grin. "We're gone." He raised a hand in salute. "Good luck."

Ben tried to think of something clever or cool to say, but his mind was a blank. All he was thinking about was how hard he could throw the extinguisher so that he wouldn't kill his clearly deranged teammate—on the very slim chance he connected. *Like there's even a chance,* he thought and whirled.

The extinguisher was a half-dozen feet away from him before Johnny vaporized it.

Johnny didn't understand precisely why Ben was being such a jerk, but then he decided that he didn't really need to know. *Good guy, good teammate, good friend—I don't need any of that.* Despite the thickness of Ben's skull, the day's craziness had apparently seeped into his mind. *I have no patience for this,* Johnny thought, watching Ben's clumsy attempt at a sneak attack. He casually flicked a fireball and the extinguisher dissolved in midair. The burst of vaporized gas was spectacular—fireworks on Yancy Street—and Johnny was momentarily dazzled.

And the distraction did what Ben had expected: It gave him a chance to catch the Torch off guard. Bounding upward, he smashed into Johnny and bounced him off the rec center wall. It wasn't a move he used very often—Ben didn't like the idea looking like a second-string Hulk—but how else was he supposed to engage an airborne opponent?

Johnny saw the jump coming and didn't resist, thereby lessening the impact. The bounce hurt, but he could tell that Ben hadn't given it his all, unlike Johnny, who used any contact as an opportunity to crank up the heat. The Thing bellowed, his shoulder plates cracking and hissing like wet clay under a blowtorch. Johnny was surprised by how much he enjoyed Ben's grimace and decided he didn't want the look to disappear too quickly. Previous experience had taught him that he couldn't carry the Thing's weight for more than a few seconds, so he put the spurs to it and rocketed straight up. Three hundred feet above the ground, his grip gave out and Ben slipped away. Johnny was another two thousand feet up before he could turn around, so he missed seeing the crunch, but heard the crash. Looking back, he saw the hole in the roof of the rec center but no signs of movement. The Torch wasn't fooled: Ben had survived much worse falls. At this point in the game, he was likely just really mad. *Good,* Johnny thought. *He's dumber when he's mad.* Folding his arms to his sides, he dove back down, his trail of fire hanging in the air for many seconds after he disappeared into the hole.

Ben hated falling, and not because of the sudden crunching stop at the end. The worst part was the gut-churning sensation of free fall, a feeling no pilot enjoyed. The roof offered little resistance and a second later Ben was lying spread-eagle at center court of the rec center's main gym. *Aw, man,* he thought as he listened to the floorboards crackle and squeak beneath him. *No way the janitor's gonna be able to buff these cracks out of the floor.* His eyes focused and saw far above him, through the jagged hole he had just made, a tiny yellow dot that was rapidly getting larger. Ben heard his high school football coach's voice in his head: *Shake it off, big guy. Shake it off, shake it off, shake it off.*

Ben did as he was told: He shook it off and took a look around. *Wood floor, wood bleachers. Bad place to fight a guy who shoots fire.* He made a decision and dug his fingers down into the floorboards, then tore up two huge chunks of the finest polished pine money could buy and lobbed them both straight up, with barely any juice behind them. Though neither would connect, he knew both would explode into puffs of superheated debris when they got close enough, hopefully making the kid flinch.

Johnny blinked, and when he opened his eyes again, Ben was gone. The gym was cavernous and seemed to swallow the light from the Torch's flame. He flicked a spark off the tip of his finger and it dropped like a magnesium flare, revealing a large hole in the floor where Ben had been lying. Had it collapsed under him or had the Thing burrowed down under like the hard-headed little mole he was? The Torch approached cautiously, then tossed down another flare and, a moment later, a couple fireballs for good measure. The light flickered and died what seemed like only a few yards down. Johnny cursed and fumed. The idea that Ben might escape his spanking infuriated him, but he had seen too many times just exactly what happened to bad guys who made the mistake of trying to take on the Thing in a narrow space.

And then the thought hit him: *Bad guys?* Johnny stared at his flaming hands. *Am I the bad guy here?* He shook his head. Of course not. The problem was that Ben had been overtaken by the same craziness that was getting everyone else. Johnny had to get him under control, stop him, before the Thing hurt anyone. If he needed to use a little more force than usual to do that, then so be it. If Ben ever completely lost it, he would be a monster. Johnny nodded. *Right. Ben could be a monster. It's up to me to stop him.*

Besides, it felt good to cut loose. If he could push Ben back out into the open, maybe someone would catch the final confrontation on YouTube and then Chrissy would see that the Human Torch wasn't quite as *nice* as she thought. Grinning again, firm in his resolve, Johnny floated down into the hole.

As soon as he passed through the opening, the Torch boosted his flame output. If the Thing was close by, the wave of heat would push him back. It also lit up the space enough that Johnny could see where he was. Performing a quick three-hundred-sixty degree spin, Johnny made sure Ben wasn't coming up behind him and then dropped to the ground. He had been burning his flame for longer and much hotter than he customarily did and felt gravity snap up at him when he lost his lift.

Johnny leaned against one of the metal crossbeams that supported the gym floor, lit up his hand, and studied his environment. The space was almost, but not quite, high enough for him to stand upright. Crossbeams and struts cluttered the area, making it difficult to get a clear view, but the space had to be at least as big as the gym, say thirty meters in every direction. Ben could be hiding anywhere. Johnny knew he should throw a flare and light up the entire space, but he suddenly felt exhausted. How long had he been on the go today? His memories of the past several hours were fuzzy and indistinct. The only two things that seemed really real were the need to pursue Ben and the large red guy who had tossed him . . .

Wait. What *about* the large red guy? He had been talking to Reed and then there had been the shadow in the hall and then . . . What had happened? Nothing was hanging together. Memories were disjointed and incomplete. The way he felt reminded him of the couple times the Puppet Master had gotten him on a string. Was that what was going on? Could Alicia's father be behind—

Suddenly he heard a crash and a screeching sound.

Ben was punching through or pulling apart some-thing. Johnny shouted, "Flame on!" and tossed a fireball in the general direction of the sound, but it slapped harmlessly against a crossbeam no more than three meters away. "Dammit!" Flying in such tight quarters was dangerous, so instead Johnny charged toward the sound, his feet baking the moisture out of the damp earth with each step.

A hole was torn in the wall of reinforced concrete. Johnny shot a flare into the gap and was surprised to see another wide space on the other side. Ben must have waited here as long as he could and then, when he'd seen that Johnny wasn't giving up the chase, had taken a chance that there would be an exit on the other side of the wall. "Lucky, lucky," Johnny mut-tered. He cranked up the heat and stepped through.

To his surprise, he dropped a couple meters before his instincts kicked in, and then he found himself hovering only a few inches above a shallow stream of murky water. Johnny couldn't smell anything when he was in his fiery state (his flame incinerated most of the chemicals that carried scent before they could reach him), but he knew that if he flamed off, the odor of sewer would be overwhelming. He shouted, "Ben! This is a new low, even for you!" He fell si-lent and listened intently. If Ben was moving, Johnny would hear him splashing through the water.

Nothing.

"Or maybe you belong down here! A couple more

hundred feet down and you'll probably find a tunnel that will take you to the Mole Man! Go hang out on Monster Island with all the other *freaks*!" He listened again, but heard only the snap and crackle of his flame. Looking down at his hands, he was surprised to see that the edges of the fire were no longer the blue-white they had been.

*Dammit.*

He might not be able to smell anything, but Johnny knew that the air down here was probably not good for him or for combustion. If he hit some kind of gas pocket, he might bring the sewer tunnel down over his ears, but the idea of giving up the chase nagged at him. He eased forward a few meters, moving carefully, worried about the way the edges of his flame guttered and popped. Reaching a T-shaped junction, Johnny listened to the sound of flowing water and decided it sounded deeper and faster-moving.

Feeling like the air was fresher here, he risked shooting off two tiny flares in each direction to see if Ben was trying to hide in the shadows again, but saw nothing. "Well," he said aloud, "pick a direction." Downstream felt logical, so the Torch stretched out into flight position and then eased along down the tunnel, gaining confidence with every second, picking up speed. He would check out this section of tunnel for a few hundred meters and if he didn't find anything, he'd turn around and head back the other way.

Ben wouldn't get far.

\*        \*        \*

It was hard to keep his eyes open under water knowing what was probably *in* the water, but Ben told himself that most of what was washing over him was nothing more than good old-fashioned New York City runoff. Nothing too toxic, right? They kept the sewer water separate from the stuff that came out of the men's room at Madison Square Garden, didn't they? Of course they did.

The only good news was that Ben didn't need to keep his eyes open any more than a slit, Johnny being pretty much the only thing that *could* be seen in the gloom. When the bright blob appeared at the junction, Ben knew that all he had to do was hold his breath and look like the floor of a storm sewer, which fortunately, for him, wasn't all that hard.

The blob hovered in place for a few seconds, then started to get bigger and brighter. Ben flexed his muscles and tried to stay loose, though he knew the burn on his shoulder was going to give him trouble for a while. Johnny appeared to pick up speed, so Ben opened his eyes wide. He knew he would get only one shot at this. If he missed . . . Well, that really wasn't an option, was it?

The kid never saw it coming.

Chemistro and Hydro-Man stood across the street from the Baxter Building munching on chestnuts they'd looted from an abandoned pushcart and watched the zombies bang on the lobby doors. "This," said Hydro-Man, "has got to be the strangest gig I've ever had."

"This? Really? Weren't you in on that Sinister Twelve thing a few months ago?"

"Sure, but this is much weirder." He finished peeling a chestnut, popped the nut meat into his mouth, and dropped the shell on the ground. Pointing across the street, he said, "C'mon: zombies."

"Not really zombies, though," Chemistro observed. "Wouldn't they be after us if they were?"

"Are you worried?"

"No. I can turn into water. If I were *you* I'd be worried."

"I'll just use the alchemy gun and turn them into glass or wood or something."

"So, I guess we're not worried, are we?"

"No." Chemistro tossed away a burned chestnut. They stood and watched the zombies (or whatever they were) as they continued to pound on the windows. "Think we should help them with that?"

"Hellspawn said not to bother," Hydro-Man replied. "Part of the plan, I guess."

"Any thoughts about this plan?"

"Well, I think I like the idea of Electro and Vapor being the first ones to go up. The F.F. aren't pushovers. I've fought the Torch, and that was no fun."

"Big Red . . ."

"You shouldn't call him that. Give the man his

due. Besides, you're the one who came up with the name."

"Okay, okay. *Hellspawn* said that he thinks there's only one or two of them up there. Probably the Invisible Woman and maybe her husband."

"Mr. Fantastic."

"Right." Chemistro rolled his eyes. "Now there's a name a ten-year-old must have thought up."

"Can you imagine what it must be like when she's mad at him? 'Get your butt in here and wash these dishes, *Mr. Fantastic.*'"

Chemistro pondered the idea in silence for a few seconds. Then he nodded toward the alleyway where Hellspawn, Vapor, and Electro had disappeared and asked, "What do you think of him?"

"Who? Hellspawn?"

"Yeah."

"He seems to have a plan," Hydro-Man said. "He's serious about what he's doing, but he's not one of those 'Nyah-hah-hah! Now I'll make them pay!' nut jobs. I figure I'd let him call the shots for now. If things get too weird, I'll be down the drain, man, and won't look back."

"No loot that way," Chemistro observed.

"But no jail time, either. I've been out on the Raft, man. Don't care to go back."

"Can't argue with that, but that's not exactly what I meant. What I meant is do you think Hellspawn's what he, y'know, says he is."

"What? You mean, like a demon from Hell?"

"Yeah."

Hydro-Man turned his hands semiliquid and he flicked his fingers, dispersing specks of chestnut shell that were clinging to them. "Everyone has to be from somewhere," he said reasonably. "I mean, the way I see it, what difference does it make? I'm a guy who can turn into water, and there's a chick floating around over there who has to concentrate in order to *not* be vapor. Did you know that?"

"What? You mean she isn't just showing off?"

"No way. Sandman told me about her."

Chemistro made a face. "Sucks for her."

"Yeah. So, anyway, there's them and then there's the guy who can light himself on fire and the woman who can turn invisible . . . I mean, what difference does it make if he's really a demon? Hell might just be a different, y'know, dimension or something. What about the place I hear they're putting all the metas they've been catching who don't sign up for the Initiative or the Thunderbolts or whatever?"

"The Negative Zone."

"Right. Doesn't that sound like *somebody's* idea of Hell?"

Chemistro shrugged. "Maybe. I guess." He watched the zombies lurching around the Baxter Building. "I keep thinking about my mama and the church she used to make me go to when I was a kid, one of those fire-and-brimstone preachers standing up front telling us all that we were damned sinners and we were going to Hell if we didn't accept salvation."

"We were Episcopalians, man," Hydro-Man said. "Don't know anything about it."

"Well, I didn't buy into any of it. Stopped going when I was old enough to outrun my mama. It was a thing with us for the rest of her life. She died a couple years back, and I didn't even know about it until a couple months after. I was on the run; you know how it is."

"I know," Hydro-Man said. "Haven't seen my parents in three years."

"And now I'm thinking, *Well, what if she was right?* What if she's sitting up there at the right hand of the Lord and she knows that this guy we're working with is some kind of demon and we're gonna be condemned for it?"

"It's possible, I suppose. I mean, c'mon—zombies! And I saw some other crazy stuff out there tonight."

"Right. Hell on Earth, man."

"Well, Hell in Manhattan, anyway."

"And we're going to help him bust out of here and spread that craziness all over the country? All over the world, maybe?"

Hydro-Man shook his head. "Bud, you're over-thinking this. I mean, if you want to scamper, you go ahead; I won't rat you out. But, consider this: It won't get that far. I figure when the force fields come down, every frickin' Avenger or Initiative do-gooder in the country is going to come in here and stomp this guy."

Chemistro rubbed his chin thoughtfully. "So, you're saying, take it for what it's worth until then . . ."

"And make sure you're keeping your eye out for a back door. Sure." Hydro-Man slapped Chemistro on the shoulder, leaving a damp patch. "Face it, man: We're B-list guys. Maybe C-list. When the real fight comes, you just fade away and let you-know-who take it on the chin."

The idea settled in, and Chemistro felt some of the old swagger return. "And if things get really bad," he concluded, "we'll just throw Electro at them."

"True enough," Hydro-Man said, and they bumped knuckles. "That cat's crazy."

"Word."

Electro was uncomfortable standing too close to Hellspawn. The red giant's height—he was at least a foot taller than Electro, and the curved horns added another six or eight inches on top of that—was disconcerting, but he also radiated a field of what Electro could only call *dread*. A couple extra feet of personal space cut down the effect, but only enough to make it tolerable.

The pair were looking out the windows of some law firm's third-floor waiting room, staring down at Hydro-Man and Chemistro, who had been eating chestnuts while deeply engrossed in a conversation.

"You don't think they can see us up here?" Electro asked.

"No," Hellspawn said, his voice so deep that it made Electro's stomach reverberate in his gut. "Richards tinted the windows with a photovoltaic coating of his own design. It generates enough electricity to run the whole building."

Electro gave the giant a sidelong glance. "You know, you don't always sound like a demon from a dark dimension."

"I am vast, Max. I contain multitudes."

Electro searched his memory of the recent past and tried to remember when he had mentioned his real name, but was pretty certain he hadn't. *Well,* he decided, *what of it? Not like my name's never been in the paper.* He saw Hydro-Man and Chemistro slap palms like they had just agreed on something. "What do you think they're talking about?"

"They are discussing how they will betray me later," Hellspawn said. "How they'll scuttle away like rats fleeing a burning building."

"You can read minds?"

"I can read *souls,* Max." He turned and looked down into Electro's eyes, and for a second Max Dillon felt like his flesh was being stripped away and his soul being laid bare. His skin crawled and involuntary snaps of electricity popped from the tips of his fingers. "But I'm not worried about them. They'll serve their purpose and then they'll be discarded."

Electro tried to resist asking his next question, but couldn't stop himself. "What about me?"

"What about you?"

"Am I just going to be discarded when your zombie horde gets big enough?"

"Not just zombies, Max. Vampires, werewolves, shadow creatures, razor-clawed fiends—whatever people fear the most or fear they may become. Monsters of every flavor."

"Yeah?" Electro asked. "Then tell me this: Why hasn't anything happened to me and the rest of these guys?"

"Maybe," Hellspawn said, "because I chose to not have anything happen to you. Maybe it is your unique physiology. Or maybe it's because you all already *are* monsters. Have you considered that, Max?"

Electro decided to ignore the question. "And what about the girl?"

"I worry about her the least of all, Max. Vapor does not commit these crimes because she needs or desires anything. She does not eat or sleep or have any physical desires as you would understand them. But she does wish to belong, to associate with others and feel a connection to them. As long as I give her things to do, she is mine."

"Okay," Electro said. "I can see that. So, just one more question: Why are you telling me all this?"

"Because I trust you, Max. I trust your avarice and

your cruelty and I wish you to trust me. We could accomplish a great deal together before the end."

"The end? The end of what? The end of the caper, the job?" Electro didn't understand where the note of panic in his voice was coming from, but he couldn't suppress it. Hellspawn did not reply, only grinned knowingly.

Electro's cell phone buzzed. He checked the display—there were a lot of people he didn't feel like talking to right this second—and was pleased to see that Vapor was reporting in. Hellspawn had sent her into the ventilation system a little while ago to check on the upper floors. They figured Richards would have made the vents in the Fantastic Four's quarters secure, but wanted to see what else was happening in the building.

He answered the phone. "What's up?"

"Hostages," Vapor said, her voice indistinct and wavery. "Two. A man and a woman. He was trying to get her out from under her desk and to an elevator."

"What floor are you on?"

"Twentieth. Number 2010. Watch out for two old ladies with scissor-hands."

*Scissor-hands?* Electro thought. *Whose nightmare did they belong to?* "All right. Give me a minute or two to round up the troops and we'll be there. Sit tight."

"I don't sit," Vapor replied and then hung up.

"Hostages," Electro repeated. "Twentieth floor."

"Go get the other two," Hellspawn ordered. "I'm going to start up the stairs."

"Not the elevator?"

"Would you trust the elevator?" Hellspawn asked.

Electro conceded that he probably would not: Richards would have some kind of defense system in place.

"And Max?" Hellspawn said, ducking his head so he could get through the doorway.

"Yeah?"

"Bring me some of those chestnuts, would you? I like chestnuts."

Max Dillon considered snapping back something about how Hellspawn could get his own damned chestnuts, but then he thought about the word "damned" and decided that it might be better to simply nod and say, "Sure. No problem. Chestnuts all around."

**11**

CASTLE DOOMSTADT AND THE DICTATOR WHO ruled it shared two significant characteristics: their foreboding exteriors and their twisted, labyrinthine interiors. Reed Richards did not know if Victor Von Doom routinely altered the castle to thwart would-be invaders or because he was easily bored and had a mad passion for interior design. Whichever was the case, as always, while hiking from the landing pad to the throne room Reed didn't spot a single familiar piece of furniture or bit of artwork or even a corridor layout he recognized from any of his previous visits.

As they passed the third gigantic portrait of Doom (this one in a bucolic setting and featuring the Em-

peror holding a laughing little shepherd girl on his
knee), guards suddenly snapped into recessed hol-
lows on either side of a closed door. Reed halted, and
a moment later, with a theatrically loud *ka-thunk,* a
hidden dead bolt slid open and the portal eased open
on noiseless hinges. Reed suppressed the desire to
roll his eyes—Doom could be so needlessly, eccen-
trically arch sometimes—and slipped inside, ready to
snap his body into any shape necessary to avoid energy beams or missile attacks. He didn't really believe
Von Doom would assault him, but in Castle Doomstadt one never knew if one was facing the Genuine Article or one of the many robot copies that had
taken up residence over the years.

Having expected to find himself in a throne room,
Reed was taken aback to find Von Doom seated in
an oversized leather armchair. Facing him was a second, slightly smaller chair and between them was a
granite-topped table with a chessboard carved into it.
A single oil lamp hung from a chain and Reed felt a
comforting warmth coming from a low, well-banked
fire burning behind the hearth screen.

Doom sat with his legs crossed at the ankles, his
elbows on the armrests, and his hands clasped before
his face. "Richards," he said, his voice almost a purr.
Reed knew that Doom could modulate his voice
in any number of devious ways with the amplifica-
tion devices in his face mask, but had never before
been on the receiving end of this pleasant, welcom-

ing tone. Despite the heat from the hearth, he felt a shiver run down his spine.

"Victor," Reed replied, making his voice as neutral as possible, carefully keeping his hands in plain sight.

"Won't you come in? Some coffee, perhaps?" He indicated a thermos carafe on the side table. "You are a coffee drinker, aren't you? And you must need a little eye-opener after your long trip."

"Caffeine doesn't really affect me, Victor," Reed said, still not moving from the doorway. "As I'm sure you know."

"So, it's really just about the taste?" Doom shook his head, bemused. "I really don't understand that, but if you like it, perhaps I should relent and let Starbucks open a franchise in the village. What do you think? Could they count on your patronage whenever you were in town?"

*Good Lord,* Reed thought. *He's bantering.* This wouldn't do at all. If he was ever going to reach Susan and the children, they had to get past this. He pointed at the chessboard. "Are we playing a game, Victor?"

"Always," Doom said slyly and indicated the chair. "Sit. Please. Be assured that handcuffs will not pop out of the arms. Sleeping gas will not be dispensed. Not that either would work."

Reed did not reply, but accepted the invitation to sit. Better than anyone else in the world, he understood that Victor was clinically a sociopath, but one who managed his illness by binding his psyche with a strict code of behavior he thought of as his honor. If Victor promised him that the chair was not booby-trapped, Reed believed it. Of course, Reed reminded himself, this was also the monster that had condemned Franklin to Hell on the basis of what amounted to little more than childish double-talk. He would have to remain on his guard and listen carefully to every word. In many ways, the seemingly reasonable Victor Von Doom was more dangerous than the rampaging maniac.

"What are we playing?" Reed asked.

"Can't you see?" Doom asked. "Chess, of course. What other game would be worth our time?"

Reed stared at the empty board. "You seem to have misplaced your pieces, Victor."

"For men of our intellect? How . . . materialistic of you, Richards." Doom held up his hands, both closed into loose fists. "Choose for white," he said.

Reed had seen that Doom's hands were empty, so he had to wonder about the point of the gesture, but he decided that he must permit Victor to play out his charade for at least a short while. Reed tapped Doom's right hand. It struck him at that moment that he had never before touched the armor except when striking it, and was surprised that the surface was warm. Doom opened his empty hand and said, "You chose white." Reed was tempted to reach out and pretend to take the piece from Doom's hand, but resisted. Instead, he folded his hands in his lap and said, "Queen's pawn to e-4."

"King's pawn to e-5," Doom replied immediately.

"King's knight to f-3."

"Queen's knight to c-6," Doom replied after only a moment. Then, he picked up the china teacup on the side table and carefully sipped. "I hear," he said casually while Reed considered his next move, "that you're having a spot of bother back home."

"You could say that," Reed said. "Queen's pawn to d-4."

"Some form of mass hysteria?" Doom asked. "King's pawn takes queen's pawn."

"I don't think so," Reed replied. Something about this game, this series of moves, seemed oddly familiar, but he couldn't let himself be distracted. "I believe it's some kind of dimensional incursion." He closed his eyes and visualized the next move. "King's bishop to c-4."

"I had considered that," Doom said, "but didn't think that such a thing could happen with Stephen Strange in close proximity. King's bishop to b-2. Getting rather crowded there, isn't it?"

"In Manhattan, you mean?" And then Reed realized Victor meant the center of the chessboard. "Oh, I see what you mean. No—queen's bishop's pawn to c-3—I mean, yes, it's getting crowded. S.H.I.E.L.D. has thrown a force field around the affected area."

"That must be getting unpleasant rather quickly. I

take your pawn at c-3. I do hope Grimm remembers to use his deodorant."

"What makes you think Ben is inside the force field? Castle."

"If he weren't, he would be here with you," Doom replied. "I take your pawn at b-2. That's three pawns down, Richards."

"You certainly seem to be up on the situation," Reed replied, mentally reviewing the board. He wasn't certain he wished to win, but he also knew he didn't want to either lose too quickly or let Victor's interest in the game waver. "Queen's bishop takes your pawn at b-2."

"Bishop returns to f-8," Doom said. "Yes, I try to keep current."

Reed held his tongue for a moment, considering his next moves, both on the board and in their sparring match. Finally, he settled on, "King's pawn to b-5." And then, as casually as he dared, "So you don't know—"

"Don't toy with me, Richards. I know a great deal more than you could ever suspect. Queen's pawn to d-6."

"Rook to e-1. No insult was intended. I just wasn't sure if you had taken a look at where the disturbance was centered. Well, began, actually. I believe you'll see that the field has assumed an elliptical shape, with one axis over Empire State and the other moving south and east toward the Baxter."

Doom did not reply for several long moments. Obviously, Reed's supposition had been correct: Victor had not bothered to check where the disturbance had started, but he would never admit that. Finally, he said, "Queen's pawn to d-5."

Reed kept his eyes on the board. "And not just over Empire State. If I'm reading everything correctly through the interference—which was difficult because I wasn't working with my own equipment, but some of Tony Stark's—then the first axis is practically right on top of your old lab." Waving his hand over the center of the board, he continued, "Knight takes pawn."

"Queen takes queen," Doom snapped.

"Oh," Reed said. "Hmph." He held his tongue and for several seconds all he could hear was the slow, dry rasp of Victor's breath whistling through his respirator. Finally he said, "Mate in three moves."

Doom jerked his head back slightly, then raised his hand to his chin and rubbed it slowly in quiet contemplation. A few moments later, he lowered his hand again and retrieved his teacup, but before he took a sip he set it back down and said only, "Gone cold."

"Nothing worse than cold tea," Reed said.

"Unless it's the thought of your wife and children cornered like rodents in a bolt-hole."

"Unless it's the thought of some bright but conscienceless science student successfully performing an experiment that you failed—"

"I DID NOT FAIL!" Doom shouted, smashing his fist down onto the chessboard, sending chips of granite flying in every direction. Reed turned his head away and closed his eyes to avoid any possible shrapnel. When he opened them again, Victor was leaning over the table, his fingers dug into the edges of the board. "I found the dimension where my mother was imprisoned. I spoke with the demon that held her captive and when I commanded it to release her again, it reached out and disfigured me."

"And made the lab explode?" Reed knew the question was dangerous, but the only way he would dare attempt to manipulate Victor was to ascertain precisely what he believed had happened that day.

He was surprised when Doom did not immediately correct him, but instead stared into the middle distance as if Reed were not there. Finally, he muttered, "Forester."

"I barely knew him," Reed said. "He died, didn't he?"

But Reed had misunderstood the roads Victor's mind was traveling. "He must have left notes. Someone found them."

Reed saw where Doom had gone, and while on one level he admired the speed of the man's insights, he also had to wonder at his ability to leap past the consequences of his actions. "I concur," he said. "It fits the facts. But now we have to ask ourselves the question: Who controls the events now unfolding?

Could it be the demon you confronted all those years ago?" This was, Reed knew, a long shot, but anything he could do to bring Victor Von Doom to the forefront would be invaluable.

"He was destroyed when I freed my mother," Doom said and settled back into his chair, but Reed heard the way the teacup clattered in the saucer when Victor lifted it from the armrest.

"And, of course, no one ever makes mistakes where demons are concerned."

Doom's eyes became black slits. "Do not play games with me, Richards."

"I thought that's what we were doing today," Reed replied. "I thought this was game night."

"Why are you here? What do you want from me?"

"Your lab," Reed said.

Doom shook his head, not in refusal, but in disbelief. "You said you were with Stark. What could you possibly want that the great tinker does not possess?"

Reed knew that it was time for some flattery. He hesitated dramatically and then said, as if the words were being dragged from his lips, "Tony isn't . . . Something changed when he . . . He isn't the same man he was." This was undeniably true, Reed knew, but he also knew Doom's ego would put a slightly different spin on the meaning.

"The demands of his directorship?" Doom asked slyly. "Or is he just drowning in the bottle again?"

"I don't know. All I know is that you likely possess tools and equipment that he does not . . ."

" 'Likely'?"

"I can only assume," Reed said. "Not having actually seen your lab."

Doom sat up straight and then rubbed his upper lip with his forefinger. It was an oddly human gesture, especially when Reed considered the accompanying slight rasping sound of metal on metal. "You are attempting to manipulate me, Richards. I can see it as plainly as . . ." He dropped his hand and regarded it carefully. "As plainly as the hand before my face, but I will ignore this insult. For now." Reed almost gave in to the urge to sigh, but held his breath. "A truce, then. For now. But as soon as I find the one responsible for this insult . . ."

"I understand," Reed said. "We deal with him first. One vendetta at a time."


"Dang," Ben Grimm said, staring at the charred tatters of cloth hanging from his arms and around his ankles. "I really liked that suit." This was the first opportunity that had presented itself for Ben to inspect the damage to his accoutrements, and he was finding the entire affair more and more depressing with every passing moment.

Oddly, as he considered his losses, Ben also was pleased to note that he was feeling generally lighter in spirit than he had at any time since the accident with the kid. Maybe there was something to his theory, after all. Maybe they had gotten far enough away from whatever-it-was that he could release Johnny when he came to, though he wasn't sure exactly how he would make that determination.

Ben had known that he didn't have long to work out a plan after he'd walloped the Torch into nighty-night land. The blow he had delivered had been little more than a slap on the cheek and the Torch had proven on many occasions to be made of pretty resilient stuff. Immobilizing the kid and keeping him wet—really wet—was his best bet. Also, trying to get him out of range of the whatever-it-was that had made Johnny act the way he had been acting would be a good idea too. Ben knew he couldn't go very far horizontally, but after you spend a few minutes in the sewers you start to think vertically, and there was never any question about which way was down: He just followed the flowing water.

Poking the rusty iron bars into the concrete and then bending them around the kid hadn't been too hard either. The tough part had been figuring out where to stick him underneath the outflow from the storm sewer. Put Johnny in the wrong spot and he wouldn't stay wet enough; too far the other way and the kid would likely drown. The constant disorientation of being half-drowned probably would help keep Johnny under control, but Ben had trouble with the idea. If worst came to worst, Ben knew he could always (gently) clock the Torch again before he got up to a full burn. At least, that's what he hoped.

The main goal now was to get back to the Baxter Building to see if Stretch or one of the other big brains had figured out what was going on. Ben also had a vague notion that he should check in with Doc Strange—this mess had more than a little stink of the otherworldly to it—but that would have to wait. Most likely, the magician was already engaged on some level and if he wasn't directly interceding, it was because he was tied up with other matters.

With only the low light cast by the emergency lights, but Ben could barely see, but he thought he detected an eye flutter. A moment later, the kid started to cough and sputter, so Ben held his hand over Johnny's face to deflect the stream. The kid's eyes went in and out of focus—Ben could hardly imagine how weird this must all look from Johnny's point of view—and then he wrinkled up his nose and shouted, "Holy mother, you've finally discovered a smell worse than your underwear hamper."

Ben almost laughed out loud. His first impulse was to start bending back the iron bars, but then he decided that Johnny had been acting, y'know, evil, but not stupid. There was no reason to assume he wouldn't know to act chummy if he woke up in a disadvantageous situation. "Whataya remember?" Ben rumbled.

"I remember that you're ugly," Johnny said, sputtering. "I mean, *really* ugly. Like, Thanos-ugly, except he has the decency to wear a full bodysuit, while you tend to walk around without a shirt a lot of the time. And when you *do* wear clothes, your taste in ties *sucks*." He grimaced and spit runoff water out of the corner of his mouth. "Anything else you want to know?"

"You remember getting ready to set those two kids on fire?"

The Torch's face froze, and Ben knew he was replaying the images in his head. Since he could not turn away, Johnny lowered his head until shadows masked his features. Ben was grateful, both for the darkness and for the way the rushing waters swallowed all sound. He gave Johnny another minute or two and then set to pulling the iron bars out of the wall.

Once freed, Johnny sloshed back and forth in the shallow water, slapping feeling back into his arms and legs.

"Why not flame on?" Ben asked. "We could use a little more light." Johnny did not answer immediately, but continued to walk in small circles, his shoulders hunched up high. Ben thought he even saw the kid's teeth chattering. "You hearing okay?"

"I heard you," Johnny said, his tone defensive. "There might be gas down here."

Ben eyed his teammate quizzically. "Well, yeah, of course there's gas down here. So what?"

"I'm not ready."

"Not *ready*?"

"No!"

"Well, when the heck are you going to *be* ready?" Now they were standing practically nose to nose, a typical Thing-Torch confrontational pose. Ben could see not only that Johnny's teeth definitely were chattering and that his lips were blue, but he could see something else, too: The kid was afraid. Ben backed off a step. "What's got into you?" he asked, attempting to soften his tone. "What happened tonight?"

Johnny surprised him by turning away and shouting, "I don't want to talk about it!"

"I don't care if you want to talk about it," Ben growled, grabbing the kid's shoulder and turning him back around. "All signs are pointing to us brawling with a baddie in the not-too-distant future and I gotta know if I can depend on you." Their eyes locked and for the second time in as many minutes, Ben saw something in the Torch's expression he had never seen before; this time he saw uncertainty.

Johnny moved his mouth as if he were searching for the right words but couldn't find them, until finally he said, "I . . . I don't know, Ben. I'm sorry." He shook his head, and then he surprised his friend by leaning forward and laying his forehead on the center of Ben's chest. The Thing had to strain to hear Johnny's low voice through the din of the rushing water, but he made out the words ". . . not sure if I can trust myself. Something happened tonight, something that's never—"

Ben pushed Johnny back so he could both hear and see him, but kept both his hands on the kid's shoulders. "So then you went a little bit nuts tonight."

Johnny continued to stare down at Ben's feet, but nodded his head ever so slightly.

"And it wasn't like some of the other times this kind of thing has happened, like with the Puppet Master. You didn't feel like you were under someone else's control."

Johnny shook his head no.

"And the worst part of it," Ben continued, "is that it actually felt kind of good. There was a part of you that enjoyed it."

Nod.

"And you're afraid of . . . what? That it could happen again if you light up? Like that might be the key?"

"Not necessarily," Johnny said. "I understand it could happen at any time, but . . . I can only do so much damage if I don't flame on. If I start to get crazy again, you might be able to stop me before . . . before I hurt someone."

"So, I gotta be fighting the bad guy, whoever *that* is, and I gotta keep an eye on you?" Ben groused. "Doesn't seem fair to me."

Johnny shrugged, and then a thought seemed to strike him. "Why doesn't it affect you?" He gave a half smile. "Not enough brain to be brainwashed? Extra coating of rock around the brain?"

"Ha, ha," Ben said and gave the kid a gentle shove. "I been thinking about that, and only one idea has come to mind." He started walking in the direction that he thought was north. If Johnny didn't follow, then he didn't follow. If he did, well, they'd figure out later whether he was headed in the right direction or not. "Seems to me that whoever's responsible for this can reach down inside people's heads and somehow uncork whatever kind of monster they got living in there. Everybody's got one to some degree, one way or another . . ."

"But not you?" Johnny asked from not too far behind. Okay, so he was following.

Ben gave a bark of a laugh. "Ha! That's rich. You must be feeling better, kid. You're getting back your sense o' humor. Nah, the way I figure it most people ain't too used to dealing with the monster inside 'em. Me?" He tapped himself on the chest with a giant, square-tipped thumb. "I got a lotta practice with that. Heck, I'm the king."

Johnny gave a little snort and took a couple extra steps so he could walk next to his friend. "Personally," he said, "I think it's the extra coating of rock around your brain."

Ben shrugged. "Could be that, too. Figure I ain't smart enough to figure it out. We'll ask Reed when we find him."

"Hey! That was almost a whole sentence! Good job!"

"Shaddup, punk."

"Lummox."

"Brat."

"Brickhead . . ."

Only seconds after the shields dropped, Sue felt the difference. Returning to the living room, Valeria on her hip, the little girl's face buried in Sue's hair and Franklin trailing behind, she found terrified, expectant faces arrayed around her, eyes fixed and staring.

"What's happening?" the Versace scarf woman demanded. "Are we being attacked? We saw those . . . those horrible things on the TV and . . ." Franklin's patch job must have affected the whole television system, or maybe their attackers could control the building's systems. Sue shook her head. *No, no. That isn't possible. Is it?*

Without knowing why, Sue was suddenly absolutely certain that the monsters in the lobby were going to climb to the thirtieth floor and murder them all, even the children, rending them all limb from limb and scattering the pieces around so that whoever found them first would be forever scarred by the horror . . . *Oh, God,* Susan thought. *The force field fell. Whatever this feeling is, the force field had kept it out.*

The tenants were scattered throughout the living quarters, each of them propelled by his or her need to escape or simply hide. Sue knew she had to stop them before they got too far away. The desire to simply scoop up the children and flee was almost overwhelming, but instead she clenched her hands into fists and dug her nails into her palms, the pain fueling her sense of urgency. She called out, "Everyone, listen to me: You have to come back. I need you as near to me as possible or this won't work. I'm going to project a force field around us all, and the smaller the area, the easier."

Naturally, no one moved. The two or three most panicky-looking ones took a step or two away, but Sue simply held up her hands and wiggled her fingers at them, like she was trying to attract some small, shy animals. "Whatever you're feeling right now," she said, "you have to try to fight it. It's not real. It's not from inside *you*. I know, because I'm feeling it too."

"Then why aren't you *acting* like us?" shrieked the Versace scarf woman. "If you're feeling like I am, how can you sound so *calm*?"

Sue scowled, and the words escaped her lips before she had a chance to think about what she was saying. "Because," she hissed, *"I'm a super hero!"* And with that, she cast the field across the room and rapidly contracted it, roughly dragging the tenants toward her while letting the pieces of furniture slip through. The Versace scarf woman's panic took her over and she began to thrash wildly, so Sue folded the field down over her like a sodden blanket until the struggling stopped.

A moment later, the woman looked around the room wearing an expression of mild surprise, the panic gone from her eyes. "What just happened?" she asked.

"My force field is keeping us safe," Sue said simply. "Everyone feeling better?"

No one said anything, but several people nodded sheepishly.

"Any more questions for now?"

Everyone shook their heads except Franklin, who raised his hand but kept silent until he was called on. "I think I have to go to the bathroom, Mommy," he said. One or two of the adults nodded in agreement.

"We'll worry about that in a minute, dear," Sue said in her best reasonable mother voice. She was just beginning to think she was getting a lid on the situation when H.E.R.B.I.E. fluttered back into the room.

"Mrs. Richards," the little robot said so softly that only Sue and the children could hear him.

"Yes?"

"Intruders have entered the building."

"Yes, H.E.R.B.I.E.," Sue said. "We know. Can you tell me anything about their location?"

"Most of them are merely wandering around the lobby. Several have attempted to gnaw on the receptionist . . ."

"Blondie!" Franklin said, alarmed.

"But she is fine," H.E.R.B.I.E. finished. "She says it tickles."

Franklin made a face that indicated he wasn't sure he was willing to buy into this, but held his peace.

"'Most of them,' H.E.R.B.I.E.? What about the rest?"

"A small number are heading up the stairs at a slow, but steady, pace."

"Anyone we know?" Sue asked.

"Two have been tagged as known metahumans. I would not worry about them, Mrs. Richards."

"But the third?"

"Unknown, Mrs. Richards," the little robot said and then lowered his voice so that Sue had to lean in to hear him. "But perhaps we should see when Mr. Grimm or Dr. Richards or Mr. Storm will be home for dinner." This was a code phrase that Sue had developed for discussing situations such as this one in front of the children. "All three, preferably."

"All three," Sue repeated. *Great.* Whoever the unknown meta was, he was giving off a power rating high enough to warrant Ben, Johnny, and Reed's combined presence. "All right. Thank you, H.E.R.B.I.E. At their current rate . . . ?"

"They seem to be taking their time, ma'am. Fifteen minutes at their current rate. Longer if they haven't been using the StairMaster at their local gymnasium."

"Please give them something to think about when they hit our reception area," Sue said. "I'm going to herd everyone up to Reed's lab."

"An excellent idea, ma'am. The extra shielding—"

Sue waved the robot off. "Go," she said. "Greet our guests."

H.E.R.B.I.E. gave a little midair bob, his version of a bow. "To my last breath, ma'am." And then he floated off toward the elevator.

"Where's H.E.R.B.I.E. going?" Franklin asked.

"To see if anyone else is coming up," Sue said. *And most likely get himself crunched,* she thought. *I hope Reed backed up his memory recently.*

She looked out at the huddled masses and said, "We're going to head up by the back stairs in a couple minutes. Before we go, who needs to use the restrooms?" Half a dozen men and women raised their hands, then Franklin and then Val. After a moment, five more wiggled their fingers or waved. Sue sighed. "Okay," she said. "This way. We can only do this a few at a time. Two bathrooms to the left and one to the right. Do yourselves a favor and don't touch anything in my brother's bathroom."

## 12

"HOW CAN YOU WORK WITH SUCH TINY COMPO-
nents while wearing metal gauntlets?"

Victor did not respond, and Reed wondered if he
had turned off his helmet's aural receptors. For all
Reed knew, the good doctor was listening to tunes
on his iPod, as Professor Richards himself did sometimes (Bach for math; Miles Davis for engineering;
Bowie for astrophysics) when he was immersed in
work.

Taking a break from welding, Reed was drying off
his face and neck with one of the cotton towels that
Victor's butler had left on a tray along with a bottle
of water and a tuna fish salad sandwich he had eaten

a half-hour earlier. Reed chose not to wonder how whoever had prepared the sandwich knew that he liked his tuna salad with fresh dill and water chestnuts instead of celery.

Victor's nonresponsiveness bothered Reed. He had never thought of himself as someone who ever *needed* to talk. Quite the contrary: Reed knew that his days-long streaks of solitude drove his wife insane, but these past four hours and fifty-three minutes of intense, shoulder-to-shoulder work completely bereft of any kind of communication was gnawing at Reed's already frayed nerves.

Sipping from his bottled water, Reed studied the lab, just as astonished now as he had been when he'd first entered. This couldn't be Victor's primary facility—there were no half-finished experiments or incomplete projects scattered about—but the installation was as amazingly well-equipped as any work space he had ever seen, and that included his own. Reed preferred to bring in or build new tools or devices for a particular job as they were needed, but Victor apparently had never heard Alton Brown's admonishment about multitaskers: He seemed to own one of *everything,* and he apparently liked to keep them all out where they could be seen.

Upon embarking on the project, Reed had used exactly ten words to describe the end product when Von Doom immediately began to pull tools and materials from various slots, drawers, and cubbyholes.

Panels slid open at a touch and precision instruments calibrated to within a microcentimeter had seemed to fall into Victor's open palm. He had asked precisely one question—"Are you hungry or thirsty?"—and when Reed said "Yes" (more out of courtesy than actual need), the butler had shown up five minutes later with the items on the tray. Since then, not a word. Reed had tolerated it well at first, but the question about the gauntlets had tickled the edge of his curiosity. As the hours slipped past, the minor inquiry had become a nagging preoccupation.

"Victor?"

"I heard you."

"Then why didn't you answer?"

"The secrets of my armor are none of your concern."

"I don't want to know the secrets," Reed replied. "I just want to know if they really are metal gauntlets and you've somehow learned to work with them or—"

Von Doom stood up straight (he had been bending over a workbench at an unvarying forty-nine-degree angle for the past half hour) and placed his microsealer on its stand. He half-turned away and then, a moment later, Reed heard the soft hiss of air pressure being released. When he turned back, Victor was holding his right gauntlet in his left hand and was holding up the other hand for Reed's inspection. Reed saw that there were smooth silver pads on the tips of his fingers. Reed studied them for several seconds and then said simply, "Contact surfaces."

Victor nodded.

"And the gauntlet is a sensory device. I'm guessing the tips of the fingers contain nanomachines that give you very precise control."

Another nod.

"So you literally only need to *think* about what you want the gauntlets to do and the nanomachines in the gauntlets manipulate the tools."

"A crude description, but essentially correct."

Reed watched as Von Doom reinserted his hand into his gauntlet. "That's brilliant," he said with genuine admiration.

"Yes."

"Do you have any questions for me about the work we're doing?" Reed could not see Victor's expression, but something about the small change in the man's posture made it clear that he was cocking an eyebrow in utter disbelief. Reed sighed. "I just want to make sure we're clear on one thing: This device will only work once. The components I'm building will self-destruct after they've been used."

"Naturally."

"And I've placed scramblers around my work area. No recording devices can—"

"Richards," Von Doom drawled. "There is nothing you could build that I could not imitate—and improve—if I desired. I have no interest in this technology. Of course I knew it existed, but what would it avail me? My goals—"

"I know what your goals are, Victor."

"Do you?"

"Control of the Earth. Recognition of your superior intellect."

"You left out your own complete and utter destruction."

"I was getting to that."

Von Doom retrieved his microsealer. "Excellent," he said. "Then we are of one mind. But I cannot take control of the Earth if the forces unleashed in Manhattan damage it. I cannot have the misuse of one of my earliest inventions sully my reputation. And what use would it be to destroy you—as I could at any moment—if no one would ever know that Doom had triumphed?"

"Imagine the intense sensation of security I'm experiencing right now," Reed said, retrieving the microwelder. A moment later both were back at work and the only sound heard was the scritch and whir of exotic machines.

Vapor wafted down from an air vent and coalesced into a suitably human form before addressing the large red figure the others had named Hellspawn. She focused, said "Hello," and waited for a response. The edges of her lower limb wavered and blurred in the slight breeze from the vent.

Hellspawn was leaning against the wall, munching contentedly on chestnuts (he didn't remove the shells), while a very winded-looking Electro sat in a corner near the stairway, panting out enormous clouds of carbon dioxide.

"What do you have to report?" Hellspawn asked. When he spoke, he released tiny puffs of complex sulfuric gases that Vapor found mildly intoxicating.

"The ventilation system is secure. I could not pass without being ionized."

"Would this kill you?"

Vapor pondered the question. "Perhaps. I would definitely be rendered unconscious."

"Can we destroy the junctures where the ionizing chambers are?"

"Yes, but the vents are arranged in such a way that they would close farther down the line. It would take a long time to open them all."

"And our prey would hear us coming."

"Don't they already know we're here?" Electro asked. He had risen and was now walking slowly back and forth while massaging his calves.

"Of course," Hellspawn said. "But they probably don't know the full extent of our powers. Besides, I was only considering our options. I do not think we will need to use air vents or break holes in walls."

A second later, the light above the elevator door dinged and the doors parted. Hydro-Man and Chemistro prodded out a disheveled middle-aged man and a plump, but wilted, middle-aged woman who was wearing only one high-heeled shoe. As soon as the woman laid eyes on Hellspawn, she fell to her knees and began to blubber prayers. Brannigan—Vapor remembered asking him his name and getting a courteous response—knelt down beside her, not to pray with her, but to lay his hand on her shoulder in a supportive way. Both were breathing too quickly, taking in huge gulps of oxygen. Vapor thought about telling them to calm down or risk passing out, but then was distracted by a passing whiff of methane. A moment later, there came a thunderous crack and a gale of brimstone, and Hellspawn was suddenly holding a giant hammer in his hands. He hefted it up onto his shoulder, then brought it up and slowly around so that it was a bare centimeter from the bald top of the pudgy man's head. "You want to guess who I am?"

Hunching up so that his ears were level with his shoulders, Brannigan did not look away while he shook his head.

"I'm the guy who's going to toss your lady friend back to the zombies if you don't do exactly what I tell you to do. Understand?"

The man nodded, but then followed that with a simple, "Yes. I understand."

"You've been a tenant here for a long time?"

"Longer than most."

"Are there security devices in the reception area upstairs?"

Another pause. "Probably," the man said. "I've only been there once or twice. They don't invite many people up."

"But you've been there. Are you friends with any of them?"

After appearing to consider his answer extra-carefully this time, Brannigan finally said, "No, not friends. We say hello, but that's all."

Hellspawn reached down, grabbed the man's tie, and hauled him up from his squatting position beside the keening woman. "So," he rumbled (and the sound made Vapor's loosely packed atoms vibrate), "you think it's time to go say hello?"

"No," Brannigan said. "I don't think the Fantastic Four would care one way or another." Vapor was surprised by the little round man's courage. She noted that both Hydro-Man and Chemistro took an uneasy step away from Hellspawn, as if they didn't want to take a chance of being sprayed with anything unexpected or nasty.

Hellspawn laid the flat of his free hand on the top of the sobbing woman's head and loosely draped his long, massive fingers around the sides of her head. "Then you would prefer that I just butted this one's head against the front door until something broke open."

The man shook his head slowly. "I don't want you to do that, either."

"Well, it's one or the other," Hellspawn said. "Your choice."

"A few minutes ago," Brannigan replied, "you were going to throw the lady to zombies. Now you're going to just out-and-out murder her. You've probably already decided to kill me. I'm not seeing how I have a choice about anything except maybe how I'll be judged in the afterlife: as a man who betrayed his friends and a coward or as a man who showed some dignity at the end."

It had been many years since Vapor had interacted with a "normal" human being, and she had become accustomed to think of them as mindless sheep that scampered away at the first sign of trouble. Seeing one show something like backbone was a novelty. Even the sound of the woman's blubbering had changed, like she was listening to the man and taking some courage from what she heard.

"So you think there's such a thing as an afterlife?" Hellspawn asked.

"Some would say you were absolute proof of that."

"Let me tell you everything you need to know about the afterlife, my friend," Hellspawn said, his voice low and reasonable. "It's a pit. And I don't mean like 'a pit of damnation' filled with tormented souls. Oh, no. If only that were so. I mean, it's drab. Dull. A lot of people—well, people and other things—are all packed together in a very small space and none of them much interested in anything except themselves, their misery, their fate. And I'm not talking just about the wicked. I wish. If it were just the wicked, the evil, or even just the rude, there might be a reason to hang out there, something worth listening to, but no one can hear those stories because they're drowned out, overwhelmed by the miserable drone of tales like yours: unbelievable, dishwater gray wastes of life. Do you hear what I'm telling you?" He leaned over, his face so close to Brannigan's that he could have bitten off the little man's nose. "The afterlife—your afterlife, in any case—is something you want to avoid for as long as possible." Releasing Brannigan's tie, he stood up straight, but kept his hand on the plump woman's head like he was holding the top of a cane.

Brannigan looked up at the oversized red man, and Vapor could tell from the peculiar mix of gases he exhaled that Hellspawn's words had affected him. Finally, he said simply, "You're lying." Vapor was expecting more, but that appeared to be all the little man had in him.

Hellspawn rolled his eyes. "Fine. I'm lying. Whatever." He clamped his hand tightly around the plump woman's head and lifted her off her knees. She tried to touch her toes to the floor to support her weight, but Hellspawn had pulled her up too high. Vapor heard a strangled gasp and then calmly noted the interesting, agitated swirls of carbon dioxide gushing from between the demon's fingers. *This will be pretty,* Vapor thought and then she heard a sharp *shooop!* of compressed air explode somewhere behind her. She turned just in time to see a hidden door pop open.

A squat little robot about the same general size and shape as a canister vacuum cleaner hovered on a column of compressed air. Vapor was vaguely amused to see that it had a digital display screen for a face and two gigantic, fierce eyes with slanted brows meant to convey anger. None of the others—villains or prisoners—seemed to know what to do, and they all jumped when the robot zoomed toward them screeching, "Defend!"

Walter Brannigan had heard stories about the Fantastic Four's robot, had even seen photos of it in the newspaper, but had always assumed it was a story cooked up by promoters or marketing teams to sell a stuffed animal or toy construction set. But now here it was zooming toward him, much more frightening than he could have expected from something that looked like it had been constructed from a cast-off Mac computer monitor and a bread machine.

Hellspawn lifted up poor Miss Floyd by the head and held her out like a shield between him and the attacking robot. Judging by what happened next, the robot had anticipated this cowardly response: A slim servo-arm flipped out of its body, and Brannigan saw that at its tip was a metal disc the size of a soup can lid. The robot touched the disc to Miss Floyd's back. As the air shimmered, Brannigan felt his ears pop and saw a flickering luminescence that forced him to turn away. When he turned back again, Miss Floyd was gone.

"Holy crap!" said the heavyset man in the silver and red costume. "He disintegrated her!"

Electro shouted, "No! She teleported! Don't let him touch you!" He pointed a finger at the robot and a bright blue flash arched across the hallway. The robot tumbled away end over end and crashed into the far wall. It weaved drunkenly in midair for a moment, then regained its orientation and zipped forward once more.

The heavyset man stepped around Electro and shot a column of water out of the end of his arm. The robot tried to dodge, but the edge of the geyser caught it and sent it into a spin. Before it could stabilize again, the man with the gun fired some kind of ray. Brannigan flinched, expecting an explosion, but was surprised when all he heard was a dull *thunk!* When he opened his eyes, he saw the robot lying on the ground, its thrusters firing madly, but ineffectively.

"I turned its case into lead," the man with the gun said. "Figured it wouldn't be able to fly then, but would still be functional."

"Good thinking, Chemistro," Hellspawn said, hefting his hammer. He stepped forward and prodded the robot with his toe. "What happened to the woman?"

"She's safe now," the robot said, its voice calm but slightly throaty-sounding through the lead speaker grill.

"Safe where?"

"Safe where you'll never find her." Its electronic eyes flickered toward Brannigan. "Sorry I couldn't get to you, sir, but, you know, ladies first."

"Sure," Brannigan said. "I understand."

"Do you think any of them will try to come out and get him?" Electro asked Hellspawn.

"I can answer that," the robot said. "The answer is no. I've already transmitted my memory to central storage. Dr. Richards will replicate me a new body as soon as he's finished sorting all you out." He sighed. "I do so hope he'll let me have pinstripes this time. I keep telling him how good I'd look in pinstripes."

"Anyone buying any of this?" Electro asked the group.

"As if it matters," Hellspawn said, raising his hammer over his head. "Any last words?"

"Yes," the robot said, its voice light and airy. "But I'm too much of a gentleman to use such language"

Hellspawn brought his hammer down.

Lead is a very soft metal, but Brannigan heard the components inside crunch and splatter.

"So," Electro asked as the red giant scraped the robot off his hammer. "Now what?"

"We follow through with the plan. We head into the reception area and call them out. If no one comes, we continue on until we find whatever is controlling the force fields. If we can't find that, we grab whoever might be around and make them tell us."

"So you still think the big force field is being controlled by something here?"

"You don't?" Hellspawn rumbled.

Electro shrugged. "The field around the building came down, but the one around the city didn't. Or maybe it did. Is there any way we can know for sure?"

"I'd know."

"Fine. So, one's down, the other isn't. Doesn't that suggest something?"

Hellspawn seemed to consider the point for several seconds, which surprised Brannigan. Upon first meeting the red giant, he had been convinced the villain was only a muscle-bound colossus, but here he was displaying something like caution. "You may have a point," he conceded. "But we should at least check before moving on. I don't have any particular desire to fight the Fantastic Four, but I'm not afraid of them, either."

The others all nodded, even the gaseous woman who had become semitransparent. The brief fight seemed to have bound them more solidly together and, looking back at it, Brannigan was impressed by how well they had coordinated their attacks. If Mrs. Richards or the rest of the F.F. were really home, they would need to be careful.

Hellspawn lifted Brannigan off the ground by the scruff of his neck. "Let's go, you. And just remember this: If I see any other robots flying at me, I'm not going to hold you up as a shield like last time. I'm going to toss you at a window and see how thick the glass is. Got me?" Brannigan nodded, and his reward was to be dropped down onto his feet. "Good," Hellspawn said and pointed at the wide door that led into the Fantastic Four's residence level. "Get moving."

" 'Ooh, ooh, ooh, I feel my temperature rising,' " Johnny sang in a trembling tenor, his teeth chattering around the lyrics. " 'Help me, I'm flaming, I must be a hundred and nine. Burning, burning, burning, and nothing can cool me. I just might turn into smoke, but I feel fine.' "

Slogging along behind his friend, Ben Grimm did his best to suppress the urge to pick the kid up and carry him. This was taking way too long and he was afraid the cool, wet air was making his friend sick. Johnny probably hadn't been chilly a second of his life since becoming the Human Torch and didn't take well to having the sniffles. Ben considered asking the kid about flaming on one more time, but changed his mind. Instead, he said, "Didn't know you liked the King."

Johnny shrugged as best he could with his arms wrapped around his shoulders. "I like the early stuff, the Sun Studio ones. Don't much care for the later ballady numbers."

"'Burning Love' was from pretty late in his career," Ben observed.

"Yeah," Johnny agreed. "But I've got other reasons for liking that one."

"Do you know the words to every song that has 'flame' or 'burn' in it?"

The Torch shook his head. "Nah, just the ones girls would like."

They lapsed into silence for a stretch. Finally, Johnny said, "How far you think we've gone?"

Now it was Ben's turn to shrug. "Don't know exactly. Couple miles."

"Think we should take a chance and head up to the surface?"

"You think you're ready?"

Johnny stopped and turned. Ben saw that his skin was so pale his lips looked black in the dull light. "If I don't get out of here soon," he said, "I'm going to pass out. And then who will serenade you?"

"I was just going to say that," Ben replied. "All right. Next ladder we come to, we go up."

They slogged along for several more minutes until Ben asked, "Hey, you ever hear of this show called *Futurama*?"

"Sure," Johnny said. "It's on all the time on cable. Why you ask?"

"The kid you were going to roast mentioned it. I just wondered."

"S'funny show. Franklin likes it. There's a guy in

it who reminds me of Reed. Well, a very old version of Reed. If we were in an episode of *Futurama* right now, we'd be running into sewer mutants any second now."

"Sewer mutants?" Ben asked. "Didn't there used to *be* sewer mutants under Manhattan?"

"Morlocks," Johnny said.

"Right."

"I think they left."

"Good thing."

"I heard they weren't so bad," Johnny said. "Like the sewer mutants in *Futurama*. Ugly, but not violent."

"Sounds like my kind of people," Ben said. He pointed ahead. "I think I see a ladder."

Johnny surprised him by turning around. "Hey," he said. "Before we head up, I just wanted you to know that all that stuff I said before . . ."

"It wasn't you," Ben said. "Don't worry about it."

"I know," Johnny replied. "But, y'know, it was, too. It had to come from somewhere." He tipped his head down to look at the water rippling around his feet. "There's a monster in all of us somewhere, I guess."

"Oh, please," Ben grumbled. "The profundity is too much for me."

"You know what I mean, you big gorilla. And I know you know what it's like to deal with it." He squared his shoulders and looked Ben in the eye.

"But you know what? I didn't. I didn't and I let it take me over and . . . well . . ."

"Yeah," Ben said. "I know." He clapped a hand down on the kid's shoulder. "It's cool." Johnny laid his hand on his friend's arm and tried to squeeze, but he was trembling too hard. Ben finished, "If you try to hug me, I'll have to slug you."

"Understood," Johnny said and dropped his hand. "Let's go find some bad guys. You can hit them really hard for me."

"Beautiful," Ben replied. "And you can give a couple the ol' hotfoot. When you're feeling up to it."

# 13

"EVERYONE," SUE SAID, SWITCHING FROM CALM, managerial mode to her "I'm the mommy" voice, "I've said this now three times and I *do not* want to have to say it again: DON'T TOUCH ANY-THING."

Reed's lab was not meant to hold quite so many people, certainly not so many panicky people, and definitely not so many panicky people who didn't seem to be able to follow simple orders. Upon enter-ing the lab, Sue had dropped her force field, hoping that its thick walls would filter out the worst effects of the whatever-it-was that was happening outside and give her a moment to catch her breath. Unfortunately, less than five minutes after she had shut the vaultlike door behind the last straggling tenant, the feeling of dread had began to creep up the back of Sue's head. She felt a tug on her left leg and found little Val clinging there, her eyes wide and starting to tear. Franklin joined them a moment later, though Sue wasn't certain whether it was to comfort Val or to be comforted himself.

"Where's H.E.R.B.I.E.?" he asked.

"I sent him outside to see if he could gather some more intelligence."

"How will he get in here with us?"

"He can't, honey," Sue said. "But he can hide in one of his tunnels until this is over." Franklin nodded once, but his mouth was a thin, unsatisfied line of worry.

Most of the tenants appeared to be doing their best to stand in the exact middle of the aisles, as far away from various lab stations and exotic-looking experiments as it was possible to get. A handful settled down in a corner near the door to the hangar and were conversing in hushed tones. Sue had considered taking one of the aircraft—Ben's hoverbike, perhaps—outside to check on the exterior of the Baxter Building, but decided that her guests could not be trusted unsupervised. Besides, leaving Val and Franklin behind wasn't an option.

The feeling of dread leveled off and stayed constant, neither getting worse nor easing. Looking around at the faces staring back at her, Sue feared that many of the tenants would crack before long, but she decided, *I need to rest for as long as I can.* If something wicked was on its way, whether metahumans or zombies, she couldn't fight if she was exhausted. Better to let everyone suffer a little now.

There wasn't much comfort to be had in Reed's lab, but she had already done as much as she could for her exhausted tenants. There was a sink with water and she had erected a screened-off area for those who needed to relieve themselves. Reed being Reed, he had never bothered to install a lavatory. Lack of food would be a problem sooner or later, though if they were stuck here that long, other issues would probably force her hand first.

Question number one: Were there any weapons in the lab if they needed to defend themselves? Knowing her husband, the answer was probably yes, but also knowing her husband, anything that might be used for attack or defense wouldn't be recognizable as such. More than once, Sue had been tempted to come into the lab with a label maker and just start clicking away with it, but Reed had always managed to talk her out of it. "Some things," he said, "shouldn't be labeled." Undoubtedly this was true, but, Sue felt, some things *should*. Like guns. Or bombs. Or anything that could be used as an escape hatch . . .

*Escape hatch.*

Tiny tumblers clicked into place inside Sue Richards' mind. Should she consider *that* option if the situation got bad enough? She had confidence that the door to Reed's lab could stand up to almost any kind of normal attack, but she knew that metas were probably on their way. Right off the top of her head, Sue could think of half a dozen villains who would be able to yank the door out of the wall, and while she normally wouldn't have worried about protecting herself and the children if any of them got through, she wasn't sure she could protect the rest. Maybe if she could get them out of harm's way for even a short time . . .

But, no. The idea was crazy. She wasn't even sure she could get through all the security protocols and . . .

*THOOM!*

Sue felt Val's fingers dig into her thigh. Every man and woman in the lab—including herself—either shrieked or groaned.

*THOOM! THOOM!*

Someone or something was pounding on the lab door. The vibrations from the blows simultaneously rippled down through the top of Sue's skull and the bottoms of her feet. One of the women in the corner near the hangar began to sob hysterically, crying so loudly that Sue could hear her over the sound of the next blow.

*THOOM!*

She picked up Val, took Franklin by the hand, threw up a force field around the three of them, and approached the lab door. The security monitor was disabled, but Sue Richards didn't need security monitors to see what was happening on the other side of the door. A moment's concentration and a narrow slit of wall at eye level became transparent.

A red giant who obviously shopped at the same big-n-large stores as the Hulk was standing there holding a huge hammer and was aiming it at the lab door's handle. The curved horns on his head scraped the ceiling as the weight of the hammer pulled him around.

*THOOM!*

*Amateur mistake,* Sue thought. The area around the door latch is always the most reinforced part of a door frame. Still, whatever he lacked in brains, he clearly made up for with brawn.

The giant lifted his hammer for the next blow, but then stopped mid-swing. He had just noticed the narrow window in the door. To his credit, he did not reach forward to inspect the hole as most people would have. A moment passed, and then the creature lifted his free hand, two fingers extended heavenward, waved, and grinned broadly. Then he pointed, drawing Sue's attention to the edge of the room. Sue expanded the invisible field and saw a stocky man in an unimpressive silver and red costume holding out a short, round, middle-aged man so Sue could see him.

Sue's heart sank: They had Mr. Brannigan. He stared miserably at Sue, disheveled and dirty, but apparently unharmed. The red giant lifted his hammer and waved it over Mr. Brannigan's head, his grin so wide that Sue could see his molars. Val tightened her grip on her mother's leg and whimpered softly.

A millisecond before she dropped the invisibility field, Sue saw a blue-white flash and felt a sharp jab of pain between her eyes. Feedback. Someone had attacked the door with an energy weapon while she had been in contact with it. The pain cleared in a moment, but Sue knew that whoever it was who had attacked was also fairly powerful. Something told her, though, that whoever the attacker was, he had jumped the gun She sensed that the red giant was the leader of the group, but there was at least one member of his team who didn't know how to restrain himself. *Every team has a Johnny,* she decided and began to work on ways that this information could be useful.

One of the tenants tried to approach, saying, "Mrs. Richards?" but bumped into the force bubble. Sue dropped the field and immediately felt dread sink into her bones again. Val clutched harder, and Sue instinctively cast a protective field around her daughter. She looked out of the corner of her eye at Franklin and saw that the boy seemed to be bearing up all right for the moment.

"Yes?" Sue said to the tenant, the tall African-American man who was wearing the sweat suit. "Mr. Jenkins, isn't it?"

"Yes," he said. "Do you know who those men were?"

"Never saw them in my life," Sue said.

"I think the man in the costume is called Chemistro," Mr. Jenkins said. "I forget his real name, but he has a brother named Curtis Carr who made the weapon he uses. Curtis works for Stark Industries now. We visited him—Curtis, I mean—at his office a couple months ago and he had a picture of himself on the wall in that getup. I asked him about it and he said he likes to keep it around as a reminder of how stupid he used to be."

"So Curtis was a villain?"

"I think so. Briefly. Got beat up by Luke Cage and shot off his own foot," he said. "Did some time, reformed. Unfortunately, his brother—the guy out there—he's not as smart."

"Thank you, Mr. Jenkins. That might be very useful."

*THOOM!*

The red giant was at work on the door again.

"Any idea how long that door will hold?" Mr. Jenkins asked.

"A long time," Sue said, lying convincingly. "And

I'm going to start supplementing it with my force field." This wasn't a lie, though Sue knew it would mean focusing her undivided attention on the attackers, not giving her much time to consider other defensive measures.

"You think there's anything in here we can use for weapons in case they break through?"

"I was considering the same question, but my husband isn't a weapons maker; he's a researcher." Mr. Jenkins' shoulders sagged slightly, and Sue realized she had made a mistake. These people needed hope, not harsh reality. "That said, who knows what might be useful under the circumstances? You strike me as a very careful man, Mr. Jenkins."

"I try to be, Mrs. Richards. I work in one of the start-ups downstairs and we handle some fairly . . . unpredictable substances."

*THOOM! THOOM! THOOM!*

Through her force field, Sue felt the concrete around the door frame begin to fragment. "I have to go see to this, Mr. Jenkins," she said. "If you promise to be *very* careful, I would like you to start opening cabinets and . . . well, you get the idea. See what you can find. If anything starts to beep or a siren goes off . . ."

"I'll back away quickly," Mr. Jenkins said, and Sue thought she saw something that almost looked like a smile.

*THOOM! THOOM! THOOM! THOOM!*

"You'd better get to work," Sue said.

"Good luck, Mrs. Richards."

"Good luck, Mr. Jenkins."

"I'm going to be finished in five minutes," the wearisome Richards said. "Can you run diagnostics on your work in that time?"

Doom was exchanging his work gauntlets for his battle gauntlets. Though he considered irritation an emotion for lesser men, he had grown weary of Richards' constant nagging. Only the knowledge that he had to bear the man's presence for only a few more minutes made finding the patience possible. "My work is perfect," Von Doom said. "Diagnostics are not required."

Richards rubbed his stubbly chin. "Victor," he said, sighing, "I know you don't care about what may be happening to my family right now, or even to the people of New York, but I feel the need to remind you *yet again* that completing this work accurately is the only way we're going to find out who or what may have stolen your research. It might even mean rescuing your mother from—"

*"I rescued my mother,"* Von Doom rumbled. "As I have told you."

"Yes, you told me," Richards said. "But what had her, Victor? Did you consider that? It was a demon, wasn't it? And what do demons do? What's their specialty?" Von Doom did not respond instantly, which

Richards took as an invitation to continue talking. "They *deceive,* Victor."

"Your friend and ally, Stephen Strange, assured me—"

"Stephen has been wrong before," Richards said, "and he'll be wrong again. If you asked him, I'm sure he would confirm this. In fact, I spoke to him about this very question just a few weeks ago. The chances that a demon as powerful as the one who held your mother could create a simulation—"

*"No demon could deceive Doom!"* Von Doom shouted and struck the lab table with his fists. The table cracked and splintered, sending tools flying in every direction.

Richards fell silent. Finally. Of all the many things that had bothered Von Doom about the man, the most unbearable was his ability to chatter on, seemingly at random, without regard for another person's interest or patience. The sound of his own voice appeared to be the only thing he truly, truly loved. His professed affection for his wife and children was as nothing compared with the pleasure he seemed to take in hearing his own incessant yammering.

Von Doom picked up the component he had completed only minutes earlier. "Thanks to your disruption, Richards," he said, "I will need to recalibrate the unit and run a complete diagnostic on it."

"Of course," Richards said. "My apologies. Will five minutes be enough?"

"Certainly," Von Doom hissed. "Now be silent. I must concentrate."

"Okay," Johnny said, emerging from the Fifth Avenue station up onto Madison Avenue, "I admit it. This is pretty good." He could see the New York Library behind them and the Baxter Building only a block away. Best of all, there seemed to be relatively few ghoulies wandering around, and none of those seemed interested in attacking. Sadly, Ben had been forced to educate the trio who had jumped them when they emerged from the sewers into the subway station, though he had tried to be gentle. Relatively.

"What's pretty good?" Ben grumbled, still rubbing the spot on his neck where the pseudo-vamp had been gnawing on him.

"Your sense of direction. I mean, the whole time we were down there, I had *no* idea where we were and you kept saying, 'I know where we are, I know where we are,' and I figured you were just—"

"I was," Ben admitted. "I had no idea where we were."

"Really?"

"Really. Just wanted to keep you underground as long as possible. We got lucky. About damned time, too. Just so we're all clear about this, I haven't been having the best day ever and . . . aw, crap." Ben stopped rubbing the side of his neck. "It's got me again."

"What?"

"The feeling. The, you know, the black mood. Just like before in the rec center. How are you doin'?"

Johnny considered the question and realized that the answer was simple: He felt good. The warm, stagnant air blowing up from the subway was drying him out quickly and for the first time in a couple hours he was tempted to flame on. He felt confident, pretty damned sure of his superiority compared with the rest of the human race right here, right now, standing at the top of some subway station stairs. He tried to imagine how much better he would feel if he just flamed on, flew up into the night sky toward the Baxter Building, and fried any creep or ghoul that . . .

"Aw, nuts," Johnny admitted. "It's back."

"Can you keep it together?" Ben asked.

"Can *you*?"

Ben gave a deprecating guffaw, but didn't really answer.

"I don't think I should flame on," Johnny said. "Will that be okay?"

"Depends," Ben said.

"On what?"

"On whether or not those are real zombies shuffling this way."

Johnny looked in the direction Ben was pointing and saw the mob of slow-moving, disjointed figures headed their way. "Ah, nuts. Well, at least they're not the kind of zombies in *28 Days Later*. Remember them?"

The zombies suddenly stopped shuffling and started running toward them at breakneck speed.

"Kid," Ben said, balling his hands up into fists. "Ya gotta stop thinking of that kind of stuff."

"Just remember," Johnny yelled after him, "we don't know that they're really zombies. They might be transformed people . . ."

"I won't muss a single hair on their disgusting, revolting heads," Ben called back. And he was good to his word. Rather than engaging the horde in direct combat, Ben bent low when they had closed to within twenty-five meters, dug his fingers into the pavement, and ripped out large chunks of concrete. Familiar as he was with the Four Freedoms Plaza, Ben knew there was an underground parking garage below. Most of the zombies were moving too fast to change direction and tumbled headlong into the chasm like lemmings into the sea. The drop was no more than ten or fifteen feet, which meant the chances of anyone's being critically injured were relatively minor. Also, it looked to Johnny like there were benefits to believing you were a zombie; most of the horde bounced back to their feet as soon as they hit the ground.

When the rest of the mob swarmed over Ben, he casually tossed them down into the hole with their buddies. Only three got close enough to Johnny that he had to bother with them and he knew enough hand-to-hand fighting to take care of them without a problem. Popping the middle-aged lady in the designer dress felt odd, but it got *much* easier after she tried to take a chunk out of Johnny's forearm.

"You okay?" Ben called as he dropped the last yellow-eyed maniac down into the hole.

"Yeah. No problem."

"Feeling any better?"

Johnny paused for a moment to survey his inner landscape, an activity he would freely admit was not one of his specialties. To his surprise, he found that the urge to fricassee the zombies was not very compelling. "Okay," he said. "So far, so good."

"So, you gonna light it up?"

Johnny shook his head. "Not if I don't have to."

Ben shrugged. "Your call, kid; trust your instincts. C'mon. We gotta get moving."

They entered the main lobby expecting to encounter more resistance, but found only a single stray zombie standing in a corner, arms limp at her sides. When she spotted them, she began to shuffle toward them, but Ben held up his hand and said, "Lady, don't push it. I ain't in the mood." Surprisingly, she turned, moaned once in a supplicating manner, and shuffled back into the corner.

"What do you suppose that means?"

"Means they ain't really zombies. There's something still human inside some of them, so you were right when you said not to hurt anyone too bad." He pointed toward their private elevator. "You gonna call that thing?"

"You think it's a good idea to take the elevator if there's someone upstairs waiting for us?" Johnny asked.

Ben rolled his eyes. "Hey, I've walked up all thirty flights before. You usually just fly. You up to it?"

Johnny pushed open the door to the stairwell, careful to check the corners before stepping through. "If I get tired halfway up, you can carry me."

"I told you that you should have let me transform the door into glass," Chemistro said. "Could have been through here half an hour ago, but now we have to wait until—"

*THOOM! THOOM! THOOM!*

Walter Brannigan pressed the palms of his hands over his ears in a futile attempt to cushion his eardrums while Hellspawn pounded away at the heavy door. The three other men did the same—the sound was deafening in such close quarters—though the woman called Vapor didn't seem to mind. In fact, she smiled a sly little grin as each blow vibrated through her.

"Until he cracks through the Invisible Woman's force field."

"We were going to have to do that anyway," Hydro-Man said. "Thing I can't figure out is how she's casting the field through the door."

"She isn't," Electro said. "She's using one of the cracks the boss made in the wall."

"She can push out a force field through a little crack like that?"

"That's what I heard."

"Wow. I didn't know that."

*THOOM! THOOM! THOOM!*

"Well, then," Hydro-Man continued. "Here's the thing I don't get. What's to stop her from pushing a force field in through our noses and giving us all, y'know, swelled heads? Like, *'Pop!'*"

Chemistro made a sour face. "That's a disgusting thought."

"But she could do it, couldn't she?"

Electro nodded halfheartedly. "Suppose so."

*THOOM! THOOM! TA-THOOM!*

Hellspawn paused in his labors. Mr. Brannigan found the demon's expression of unmitigated happiness unsettling. "She won't do that as long as we're out here," Hellspawn said. "If we get in, maybe— especially if we threaten the kids. So this is the plan: Vapor goes first. Richards will either try to contain her in a field—if she has anything left when I'm done here—or she'll be protecting her kids. Hydro-Man, you flood the room and then withdraw. While everyone is wet, Electro . . ."

"I get it," Electro said.

"What about me?" Chemistro asked.

"You watch for anyone trying to get through the door. If anyone gets out, turn them into something creative—phosphorus, maybe. Then we can toss

them back into the room and watch the fireworks."
Electro and Hydro-Man grinned at the joke. Vapor
became briefly more transparent, then resolidified
sporting a distracted smile. Only Chemistro appeared
to find the idea mildly distasteful, but wisely kept his
opinion to himself.

"Can you feel the field weakening?" Electro asked.

"Definitely," Hellspawn said. "That last shot,
something gave way. I think we may be looking at
just a door soon, and that thing's not going to hold
up to too much more." He set the head of the hammer on the floor, raised his hands to his face, spit in
them, rubbed the palms together, and then gripped
the handle firmly. The giant grinned smugly, lifted
the hammer onto his shoulder, took his stance . . .

. . . And disappeared.

Electro, who had been slouching against the wall,
jumped to attention, his hands sparking. "What the
hell?" he shouted.

Chemistro unholstered his alchemy gun and
began to wave it menacingly back and forth, shouting, "What's going on? Is she in here?" while covering his nose with his free hand. Only Hydro-Man
kept his composure, carefully backing into a corner
and studying the room for movement. Something
flickered in the center and both he and Electro attacked immediately.

Someone screamed and they attacked again.
Chemistro set his sights on the area they were as-

saulting and was just about to fire when Vapor surprised them all by flowing into the middle of the room, turning into a whitish cloud, and encircling a flailing figure. The mist stung their eyes, but revealed what Vapor was attempting to show them: The figure that had briefly flickered into sight was Hellspawn. As soon as they paused in their attack, all of them could hear their leader screaming imprecations: "You idiots! She turned me invisible! And then she let you see me for a second!"

Mr. Brannigan couldn't contain his pleasure when the demon became visible again: He looked like a wet cat, the thin ruff of hair at the back of his head hanging down in soaked and singed tatters. His oversized coat was burned black in several spots. Hellspawn closed on Electro with three giant steps and clenched a giant hand around his neck. "You want to find out what it's like to fly?" he shouted, pointing at one of the wide windows. "I'm pretty sure I can get you through that glass with the first throw, but if I can't, I'm willing to try again."

The electric caster was not easily intimidated and clearly felt he had as high a status as the demon. Holding one hand high, he let a ball of blue-white light dance on his fingertips. "Just try it, jumbo!" he said. "And then we'll see how fireproof you are!"

"*Stop, you fools!*" Vapor hissed, her voice airy and diffused. "*Can't you see that this is what she meant to happen? She's trying to turn us against each other!*"

"Ya know," a gruff voice said from the far end of the room. "We could just let them settle this and then come back up when you're done. Whataya think, kid?"

Hellspawn let Electro slip from his grasp as the rest of the gang turned and looked at the figures standing in the doorway. The Thing was standing there, gently tapping his clenched fist into the palm of his open hand. Johnny Storm stood beside him, his arms crossed over his chest, calmly studying the scene. He did not reply for several moments, but then raised his hand and pointed at the red giant. "You," he said. "I remember you."

Hellspawn grinned wickedly. "I remember you, too. Didn't look too great the last time I saw you."

"I got better," Johnny said. He slowly tightened his hand into a fist, a single tongue of orange flame curled around it.

"Ya gonna say it, kid?" the Thing asked.

"Are *you* going to say it?"

"Yeah, I'm going to say it," Ben said. "The time has come for some clobberin'."

"Clobberin' time, you mean."

"Yeah," the Thing said and grinned impishly. "That."

"I concur," Johnny said as his fist ignited and the fire rushed down the length of his body. *"Flame on!"*

# 14

BEN GRIMM KNEW THAT NOT MANY PEOPLE thought of him as a meticulously organized person, but none of them understood that you didn't get to be an Air Force test jock if you weren't. Many years ago, when Ben switched professions from pilot to meta-human adventurer, he brought those same administrative skills from the old job to his new one. Though he usually looked like he was rushing headlong into a fight, Ben had learned to study a battlefield and decide where his particular skill set would be required. Scanning the room, he quickly assessed the range of foes arrayed against him and made a plan.

None of these guys, Ben saw immediately, was

here because they were heavily invested in a mission or felt any kind of team unity. Part of the reason groups of bad guys usually took it on the chin from teams like the F.F. or the Avengers was because they had no reason to fight much more important than the desire to make a quick buck or to prove how tough they were. On the other end of the scale you had mobs like H.Y.D.R.A., who were a little *too* invested in the group, and individuals like Namor, who fought primarily in service of some ideal or a sense of personal honor. By their subtle body language and quick glances, the villains revealed that the red guy was the Big Boss, and that made him target numero uno. When he went down, the rest would peel off faster than nuclear-powered bananas.

Hydro-Man was a known quantity, dangerous but predictable. Johnny would likely go after him and Ben knew that if things got too heavy, ol' Hydro was the sort to cut and run. On the other end of the scale, there was Electro, a deadly psychotic, one of those guys who let whatever goals he might once have had get swallowed up by the whole costumed villain deal. He would have to be dealt with right away.

He had never before seen the gun-toting guy in silver and red, but Ben noted the way he stepped back from the rest of his team. This guy wasn't invested in the fight and if not attacked directly, Ben knew he might just stay out of the melee until he saw how things were going to go. Chances were good that if he got a clear shot at the door, he would be gone.

Then, there was the misty girl. Ben could see from her stance that she was perilously into the whole idea of a knock-down, drag-out fight. When her color shifted from misty gray to an ominous green, Ben saw there was some kind of attack coming, and worse, that she didn't care how much collateral damage there would be to her team. That made her potentially the most dangerous of them all. "Torch," he grunted, pointing at the girl.

"On it," Johnny said and released a wide swath of flame that cut through the center of the mist girl. Most of the gas boiled away under Johnny's assault, the edges of the cloud turning a shimmering blue. Mist girl shrieked and swirled away toward the ceiling.

A jolt of electricity sizzled down the tip of Ben's finger, through his body, and into the floor, leaving behind a trail of curling steam. Ben said "Ow" in a very sincere manner, then bounded across the floor in three quick steps and smacked Electro in the face with the back of his hand. The Thing knew that most of those who had never fought him one-on-one thought he was chunky and slow, and used that fact against them. He might tip the scales at five hundred pounds, but most of that weight was composed of a substance that acted a lot like muscle (or so Reed told him), but was much faster and more flexible.

Electro slumped to the ground. Ben looked up at the red giant and said, "Glass jaw, I guess."

"Really?" the giant said. "Imagine that." Ben had hoped he had a talker on his hands, the kind of putz who could be goaded into yammering for a second or two until Ben could get himself set. Alas, no such luck: The hammer came up and around much faster than Ben would have expected, crunching down on his right shoulder. Ben's arm went numb and his knees wobbled.

A second after taking out the mist girl, Johnny turned his sights on his ol' pal Hydro-Man and peppered him with a fusillade of fireballs. Hydro-Man, bless his soggy heart, did the predictable and went completely liquid. The Torch was tempted to just cook his juices until there was nothing left but a wisp of water vapor, but that kind of heat would have baked everyone else in the room, too, so Johnny left water boy to his own devices.

Mist girl was still coalescing. He had ten, maybe fifteen seconds before he would need to think about her. Out of the corner of his eye, Johnny saw Ben take out Electro. Good. He was the only bad guy in the room besides Hydro-Man that Johnny had ever taken on, and he knew how utterly ruthless the guy was. He flicked his gaze to the dude with the gun and sent a quick set of mini-fireballs in his direction. Turned out this was a mistake.

Up until then, the guy had been holding the gun low, but now he brought it up and started waving it around. Johnny sent up a wall of flame more to block his opponent's view than anything else, and he was sure he heard the guy shriek. "Amateur," Johnny muttered and turned back around to mist girl and Hydro-Man.

Just as he spun around, he saw Ben drop down to one knee, the red giant's hammer bouncing off his back. Rage flooded through the Torch, a firestorm of anger that exploded from his fingertips and was aimed at the giant's face. Johnny was surprised when his opponent reeled backward—some part of him had been expecting the creature to be fireproof—and shrieked in pain. Ben cocked his head toward his teammate, raised a hand to signal he was okay, and then rolled those rocky digits up into a haymaker. The fist connected and the giant flew across the room to crash against the lab door. Ben stood up, brushed an imaginary speck of dust off his shoulder, and grumbled, "I *told* you what time it was."

The shadow that had hollowed out Stanislaw Klemp wanted to find a dark place, pull it up around itself, and never emerge again. Never in its long existence had it known anything like the intensely unpleasant sensation it had felt when the rock-hided creature had struck him. One of the reasons it had decided on this damnable undertaking was that the idea of corporeal being had sounded so sensuously attractive—and, up until that moment, the experience had been everything it had expected. Some of the smells had been a little off-putting, but, overall, three dimensionality had been quite agreeable, especially the parts where it was able to use its powers to terrify and intimidate the solids. But this, this *contact,* was unbearable. For a moment, the shadow thought it would lose control of its physicality; indeed, it had felt a sound come out of its throat, a kind of bleat or shriek. It decided that it would do anything, *anything* to prevent that sensation from occurring again. Looking around, it saw the rock creature—"the *Thing,*" Klemp's mind called it—moving closer, filling its vision. The monster was grinning, as if in anticipation, and grinding his fist into the palm of his hand. "I understand," the Thing said, "that you've been giving my pal Torchy a bit of trouble." He bent down, grabbed the lapels of the creature's singed coat in two large bunches, and pulled it close enough that the creature could smell the monster's breath. "And, judging by the look of the lab door, you probably owe Susie and the kids some kind of apology too. Not to mention most of the folks who live here in the building, folks who mostly have been pretty decent to me. Not *everyone,* mind you, but most."

The Thing let go of the coat's left lapel and rubbed his chin as if in thought. "Come to think of it," he continued, "I guess you're the one who's been causing a lot of the grief that's been going on here in ol' En-Why-Cee. That kinda cheeses me off." The creature looked from side to side to see what its erstwhile allies were doing. Unfortunately, the only one who might have been motivated to act—Electro—was unconscious; the rest were remaining as motionless as they could (even Vapor, which must have been quite a trick). "I mean, c'mon, I love this freakin' town. Can you imagine any other city in the world embracing a mug like this and becoming, as I'm sure you've heard, the idol of millions?"

The creature didn't know exactly how it was supposed to respond to this question, but, to its great surprise, the Torch came to its rescue. "Ben, stop messing with his head. We need to finish this."

"Aw, cripes, listen to you bein' all responsible. Weren't you the guy who was afraid you were going to come over all evil if you lit up your flame?"

"Yes," the Torch said. "And I can feel the temptation to give in to . . . that feeling snapping at my heels, and I figure he's the cause of it. So I'd really appreciate it if you'd just—"

"Well, welcome to *my* world, then!" the Thing shouted, and the creature felt a black surge of hope well up in its chest. "Imagine what it'd be like to feel that way—like you want to clock every guy who looks at you sideways—every *frickin'* day of your life!" The Thing's grip on the creature's lapels loosened as he turned around to face the Torch. "You have a bad afternoon, a couple of lousy hours, and you're all 'Boo-hoo, check out my angst.'"

"Ben . . ."

"'What a crappy slice of life I got dealt . . .'"

"Ben!"

"'I actually didn't *like* myself for a couple of minutes today!'"

*"BEN!"*

The red giant kicked upward and made contact with Ben's midsection with his bony knees and quickly scrambled out of range of the Thing's long reach. Sue hadn't been able to hear what Ben was saying, but she had been able to read the alarm on Johnny's face as the tirade had continued. Now the creature was on its hands and knees, crawling with remarkable speed across the floor toward the corner where Mr. Brannigan had been curled up trying to be small and inconspicuous for as long as possible.

The Invisible Woman was exhausted. The long ordeal of shielding both her children and the lab door and then, with the last ounce of her reserve, tricking the villains by turning their leader invisible had taxed her to the limit. Simply making the lab door invisible so that she could see what was occurring outside was almost more than she could bear at the moment, but Sue knew that neither Johnny nor Ben seemed to comprehend what was about to happen to their tenant. Inhaling deeply, she let the shields around the children drop and refocused the energy, then shoved it through the tiny cracks that the red giant had made in the wall.

Sue couldn't take her eyes off what she was doing, but she couldn't stop listening to the crowd around her. The tenants groaned in horror as the red giant closed in on Mr. Brannigan. She knew that there would be a gasp of surprise in a moment, which made her smile. Then, sooner than she had expected, there came a gasp, but Sue knew from its tone and intensity that it hadn't come from the front row of her audience, or even from the braver souls closer to the wall. This gasp had come from far back in the row, from those nearest . . .

First there came a scream of alarm, and then the heavy clang of a large door creaking open. Sue knew what that sound was, but she didn't dare turn around. *One calamity at a time.*

Mr. Brannigan had been watching the events of the last couple minutes unfold around him through the spaces between his fingers. Any other way would have been too much for his heart. Hellspawn crawled toward him, his intentions obvious, but Mr. Brannigan found he was unable to look away and unable to move. Only when the giant reached toward did Mr. Brannigan finally find he could move, but the only direction to go was backward. The vertebrae in his spine were pressed flat against the wall, his chin touching his chest.

\*      \*      \*

Ben tried to find his footing, tried to set himself for a final, desperate leap, but his knees were unaccountably wobbly and the floor seemed to dip and turn under his feet. What had he been saying a moment ago? Why had he been acting that way? The monster . . . the monster was getting away, eluding him. The monster . . . the monster . . . he found himself staring at the backs of his own hands. The monster . . . was right here.

The shadow that huddled inside Stanislaw Klemp reached out to seize the pudgy man by his throat. What it would do next was not precisely clear, but it knew that clasping the pudgy little man's throat meant the day might still be won. A gentle squeeze was required and then the man's pink face would go purple. Then, events would grind to a halt and the woman behind the door would have to see she had lost, that she had to come out and let the shadow have its way. Electro had been right, it saw: Using the hostage had been the right way to go after all. It felt warmth on the balls of its fingertips and joyfully anticipated the moment when its talons would pierce the man's flesh. Maybe it would just kill him after all. The temptation might be irresistible . . .

Mr. Brannigan felt an odd, not unpleasant warmth spread across his throat as the creature's hand closed around it. There was a slight sensation of restriction, but it was firm and gentle, a caress rather than a stranglehold. He felt, for want of a better word, safe, and the experience was so lovely and rare that he lowered his hands from his face. Looking down the length of the giant's arm, Mr. Brannigan stared into its red-rimmed eyes and saw confusion and something very much like fear.

The shadow tried to clamp its hand around the man's throat, but it couldn't constrict his airway, couldn't even pinch the fold of flesh that waggled under his chin. It squeezed harder, willing the mighty hands it had sculpted out of Klemp's feeble form to crush the life out of the revolting little bug. Anger surged up from the center of its chest, and it finally understood the frustrations that had motivated Klemp to make the choices he had made. Maybe that was the answer— maybe a human's rage could do what a demon's could not. It gripped harder and suffered the tortures of the damned when the pudgy man began to grin. The man wasn't even looking into the creature's eyes anymore, but was staring over its huge shoulders. *Why?* The shadow had to turn around to see, and then the small part of Klemp that was forever drowning in black depths curled up and turned into a sniveling ball.

*"BEN!"* Johnny shouted again and pointed at the lab door, which was now glowing ominously. "Look out!"

The light grew unbearably bright, but Johnny sensed no heat radiating from it. Even with his eyes screwed tightly shut, small white beads of luminosity danced at the corners of his vision. The light suddenly disappeared and the Torch cautiously opened his eyes to find a neatly carved hole where the lab door had once been. Framed in the exact center of the hole was Doctor Doom, his arms raised over his head, the twin coronas around his gauntlets quickly fading.

Before Johnny could react, Reed Richards stepped around their archenemy and said, "You're showing off, Victor. I'm sending you a bill for that door."

Doom only lowered his arms and said, "Bah."

Electro had come to about halfway through the Thing's tirade and had decided that the most prudent form of action would be inactivity. Studying the scene through half-shut eyes, he weighed his options. Doom's appearance was unexpected, but, then again, Doom's appearances usually were. The Torch and the Thing certainly didn't look like they'd expected the good doctor to be behind the door. Even more strangely, Mr. Fantastic simply slipped past Doom without a glance. Shouldn't they be trading blows or, at the very least, exchanging multisyllabic insults? Nothing felt right.

Sadly, Hydro-Man didn't seem to be picking up on the same cues. His response to seeing Doom was to cheer moronically and act like he and the Latverian monarch were BFFs. "All right!" he roared and went liquid from the waist down, then churned up his lower half like he was going to sweep all the heroes out to sea. The Torch, naturally, decided this was a cue to stoke his fire and levitated six inches off the floor. Hydro-Man grinned like an idiot and cocked a semiliquid fist. Electro tried to figure out the best way to get out of their path.

Doom took care of the problem with, literally, the wave of a hand. He must have had some kind of spray or microbomb in his hand and when it hit Hydro-Man . . . well, one minute he was roiling and the next he was a first-place entry at an ice sculpture contest. The worst part about it was the sound, a *sha-woosh!* with an underlying crackling note as the crystals locked into place. From where Electro lay, he could make out some of the minute details, like the folds in Hydro-Man's shirt and the hairs on his arms.

Richards said, "That wasn't necessary, Victor. We had the situation under control." *Victor,* for God's sake. When did these two get to be on a first-name basis?

"The churning sound annoyed me," Doom said without looking at either Richards or Hydro-Man. Instead, he stepped over Electro without shortening his stride and headed toward Hellspawn in a way that made Electro think the big guy was the only one in the room who mattered to Doom, which, honestly, was fine.

Hellspawn couldn't take its eyes off Von Doom. The part of it that had been Klemp knew as much as there was to know about the man. All that accumulated information made the monster wish it could simply disengage, let the flesh melt away and slip into deeper shadows. When Doom paused for a moment to deal with Hydro-Man, the shadow heard a soft buzzing tone in its ear. For a moment, it thought the old man was mocking him, but then it realized that the whispery voice belonged to Vapor. She must have been at her lowest density level, because Hellspawn's eyes could not detect her presence.

She said, "I think this party has come to an end. I've been enjoying myself, so I'm going to try to help you as I take my leave. Consider it a parting gift so you'll remember me if our paths ever cross again."

The shadow wasn't sure whether it should say "I will" or "They will," but it didn't have time to say either, so it simply nodded once. Then, it felt a light tickle as Vapor wafted away across the room toward the Thing and the Torch. It suddenly had a clear idea of what was about to happen, and screwed its eyes tightly shut.

First, Johnny Storm heard a voice. It said simply, "You hurt me." A moment later, a ball of rippling, swirling green gas hung in the air before him. Johnny didn't have time to do anything except push himself back about three inches from the ball before it expanded outward into a whitish sheet that filled the space in front of him from ceiling to floor. The center of the sheet had eyes and a mouth that turned upward at the corners into a Cheshire cat grin. "So guess what I'm going to do now?" the mouth asked in a whispery sigh. The sheet disappeared—or, rather, Johnny had the distinct impression that it had simply turned into another gas, something odorless and colorless. Something like . . .

He tried to shut down his flame, but later he had time to reflect that it wouldn't have mattered much one way or another. Hydrogen doesn't need much more than a spark.

Doom assessed the tableau laid out before him. There had been a flash and a bang, but very little in the way of actual damage unless you were right at its center, as the Torch had been. He lay unconscious on the floor, arms and legs akimbo in a ridiculous fashion, while the bestial Thing stood mere inches away muttering "Wha' happened?" and waving his hands in front of his face like the imbecile he was.

Richards had reacted with the preternatural speed that came along with his flexible form and, naturally, had interposed his body between the explosion and his family, despite the fact that Susan Richards should have been more than up to the task.

Electro also lay on the floor, though no longer feigning unconsciousness. Doom supposed the blast must have hit him rather hard, as the idiotic mask he habitually wore had been flash-fried and torn into tatters. Perhaps he would reconsider something more sartorially pleasing when he next emerged from prison. The watery fool, who had been so annoying a moment ago, was pitted in places, and a large section of his head was now dripping despite the use of Doom's best freezing reagent.

Farthest from the explosion had been the silver and red garbed man, who now sat in the corner rubbing his tearing eyes, his rather interesting-looking weapon by his side on the floor. If circumstances had been different, Doom might have considered picking up the weapon for study, but currently there was no time for such idle luxuries.

The red giant, the one who was so clearly the catalyst for the day's events, had disappeared. *He must be very fast for one so large,* Doom decided.

Inside his armor mask, Doom smiled, and the scarred corners of his mouth ached painfully from the unaccustomed strain. He stepped around the Thing and passed through the chamber door, his armor's sensors scanning for spore. *Very well, then,* the Emperor decided. *A hunt it shall be.*

# 15

REED RECOVERED BEFORE ANY OF HIS FAMILY, cursing himself for being taken in by such an obvious ploy. The problem had been that he didn't know enough about the players. Of course, he had read Vapor's file and knew what she could do, but Reed was surprised that she had so willingly sacrificed herself for another. Everything he recalled about her indicated she suffered from a dissociative condition related to her tenuous physical state. Later, he would have to scan the room for remnants of her genetic structure, though he expected that most of Vapor's vapor would be drawn into the air scrubbers and dumped outside. He considered:

If she could reintegrate, that might have been her plan.

After quickly checking on Sue and the children, Reed stretched across the room to grab Ben by the shoulders and steady him. "Ben, stay still. You might tread on someone."

Ben nodded, but did not otherwise respond. Reed knew that his friend had a mild phobia about damage to his eyes and would be having a difficult time with this situation. Reed checked Johnny's vitals and determined that the lad might be a little shocky, but otherwise fine. He reached across the room and opened the first aid cabinet, retrieved one of the insulated blankets, and tucked it around his brother-in-law's unconscious form.

Who else? The clock was ticking and Reed knew he had only a few more seconds before he had to be on his way. The villain in the red and silver costume didn't appear to be even thinking about moving, so Reed ignored him. The older, somewhat familiar-looking gentleman whom the red giant had threatened earlier seemed to be in better condition than Ben. This made sense, since he was the farthest from the explosion and the giant and Ben would have absorbed much of the concussive force.

So, Reed returned to Susan to confirm his initial assessment. "Are you all right, darling? I felt your field go up just before I threw myself in front of you."

"Fine," Sue said. "But very tired. All of us . . ."

She pointed toward the tenants, who were all now huddled in the corner farthest away from the heavily shielded doors that Reed and Doom had emerged from. Reed knew that sidestepping S.H.I.E.L.D.'s force field by traveling through the Negative Zone wasn't the most sagacious plan he had ever conceived, but it was the only route he could have used that would bring him directly to the heart of the Baxter Building, and, more importantly, it was a route he could control completely.

"Let me get the shield generators up again," Reed said. "That should give you some relief." Sue nodded and Reed stretched back into the main lab area to inspect his apparatus. As he had suspected, the generators themselves were fine, but the coupling to the power grid had overloaded. Reed made a mental note to improve the failover system when the opportunity presented itself. Since H.E.R.B.I.E. had not already addressed the problem, he concluded the little robot had either been overwhelmed with other tasks or incapacitated. As he passed the robot's main control panel, he checked the indicator and determined that the problem was the latter option. He slapped the big red button labeled REBUILD and moved on.

Stretching across the room to the tenants, Reed performed a quick visual scan, then asked, "Any injuries here? You're safe now—"

"That was Doctor Doom!" said a woman, her

voice shrill with anxiety. "You brought Doctor Doom into the same room where—"

"No," Reed said, calmly prevaricating. "That was not Doctor Doom. That was an android I constructed to look like the good doctor for precisely these sorts of situations. Nothing terrorizes the lower-echelon metahumans quite like having an angry Doom stride into a room." One of the tenants actually chuckled at Reed's unintentional rhyme. Another pair looked at each other quizzically, then exchanged brief nods. *If you can't dazzle them with logic,* Reed thought, *then baffle them with . . ."* Reaching around the crowd to a locker to retrieve a small backpack, Reed explained that S.H.I.E.L.D. agents would be arriving soon (unfortunately, possibly another lie). After making some minor adjustments to a power cell and transmitter array already stowed in the backpack, he cinched it shut and strapped it on.

"Stretch," Ben called from the outer room. "C'mon, we gotta haul butt."

"Excuse me," Reed said, then reached back, laid a hand on his friend's shoulder to steady himself, and retracted into the outer room. "Haul what where?" he asked Ben.

"After Doomsie and my new best friend," Ben said, pointing toward the elevators. "We have to make sure they stay out of trouble."

Reed shook his head. "I agree with the general statement, but we can't both go. I need you to stay here and make sure Johnny, Sue, and the children all stay safe." Nodding toward the main lab, he continued, "Not to mention the tenants. We don't know whether the red giant is coming back, but if he does, you're the only one here who can handle him."

"Wow, Stretch," Ben said, dropping his voice to a low whisper. "Please tell me you ain't playin' the 'I'm the only one who can set this right' card, 'cause if you do, I might have to biff you into next week."

Reed smiled wanly. "I'm afraid I might be, old friend."

Ben rolled his eyes. "Aw, cripes, and then you bring out 'old friend.' I hate it when you say that. It always means you need me to do something stupid."

"Only what I just asked: Stay here and keep an eye on things while I see how this plays out. Don't worry about me, though. I'm not the one who's going to finish this."

"Then who?" Ben asked. "Doom?"

"Doom."

"And you're following after because . . . ?"

"Because I'm partly responsible. None of this would have happened if I hadn't given Victor—"

"Aw, jeez, Reed," Ben said, giving up any semblance of a whisper. "Have you ever tried *not* feeling so damned responsible for everything that happens in the world?!"

"What did Reed do now?" Sue called from the main lab.

"Nothing!" Ben and Reed called back in unison, and then Ben started to giggle.

Wiping the corner of his eye with the flat of his palm, he said, "Okay. If you're going to go, then you better be off. Settle this and then get back here fast. I've had a *really* crappy day and I need someone to rag off to."

Reed nodded; no further words necessary. Not wishing to have the same discussion again with Sue, he stretched back into the main living quarters, but paused midway when the middle-aged gentleman who had been huddled in the corner waved frantically. "I'm sorry," Reed began, "but I have to—"

"Ms. Floyd," the gentleman said quickly. "The flying robot touched her with some kind of disc and she disappeared."

"Ah," Reed said and called to Ben. "We have a guest in the holding center. She's probably a little frantic. You and Mr. . . ."

"Brannigan," Mr. Brannigan said.

"You and Mr. Brannigan should probably release her."

"Ya think?" Ben grumbled and beckoned to their guest to follow him. "Those cells are a little cramped even for regular-sized folk."

"Cells?" Mr. Brannigan asked, but Reed didn't stay to answer. Passing through into the living room, he punched the access control for one of H.E.R.B.I.E.'s chutes and shot inside, then curled up into a compact ball. Careful to be sure his hand was on the remote control, Reed rolled into a ball and quickly moved to the rooftop exit. Grabbing the edges of the hatch, he catapulted himself skyward and swiftly re-formed into a trim airfoil which was immediately carried aloft by a warm updraft. He felt for the control stud that would power up the force field generator in his backpack, but then curiosity overwhelmed him and Reed decided to taste the effect of the intruding dimension.

The sensation was . . . unsettling. He was aware that his mental state was changing, that he was becoming more self-absorbed, losing interest in the welfare of Susan, the children, and, generally speaking, everyone else. Far below, Reed watched tiny specks scurry up and down the streets of Manhattan and couldn't help but think how much better he was, how much smarter, how much more rarefied a sensibility he possessed . . .

The alarm on the sensor rig in his harness beeped and Reed pressed the control stud without thinking. The generator powered up and sheathed his soaring form in a low energy field that filtered out the frequencies of radiation responsible for the mayhem. The sheath slightly warped the shape of his airfoil, so he needed a moment to adjust his form, but then took new bearings and headed northeast over Central Park.

Carefully tapping a second control stud on the control unit, he listened for the directional beep that would guide him toward Doom's armor. Reed was certain the pseudo-demon would head toward Empire State, but he couldn't ignore the possibility that Victor would overtake his quarry before he reached his goal. Another factor that needed to be considered was how fast they were moving and what would happen if a metahuman encountered Doctor Doom en route. If other egos grew as large as Reed's had during his brief exposure to the alternate dimension's effects, he wouldn't want to consider the outcomes. Fortunately, judging by the tone and frequency of the beeps, Victor was moving steadily northwest, as predicted.

Reed estimated that with a decent tailwind, he would reach Empire State minutes before either Victor or his quarry, so he set his mind to the next problem: what he would do when all the alma mater were gathered together.

Stanislaw Klemp was awake again, and nothing the shadow could do would make him return to the void. Inside its head, all the shadow could hear was Klemp frantically chanting over and over, *It's Doom! It's Doom! It's Doom!* Of course, the shadow knew who Doom was and that he was somehow responsible for the gateway it had used to travel to this world. Unfortunately, it could not break through Klemp's mania long enough to ask his host the very basic question of why they should flee this Doom rather than attempt to ensnare him. The shadow was certain it could stop Klemp if it exerted all its will, but the results would be unpredictable. The effort might render the body unable to move at all and easy prey for Doom or any other aggressor in the vicinity.

Sooner or later, the shadow knew, Klemp's frenzy would run its course, and then it would be able to take back control, soothe the frazzled idiot, and consider their shared or divergent futures. Retreat back to its own dimension was a valid option, especially if it could take back with it the knowledge of how to open these gates again in the future. Klemp, it knew, did not have the information stored in his mind, and the notebooks had likely been destroyed in the fires of the shadow's emergence. This Doom, however, seemed to know the secret. The shadow judged that Doom would be more difficult to dominate than Klemp, but such a prize might be worth the effort.

It lapsed into thought as it leaped over a barricade some enterprising students had erected. *Much to decide,* it thought as its feet pounded down the broken streets. *And not much time.*

Much time had passed since Doom's last visit to Manhattan, and he found that he was enjoying this one much more than any of the previous. Notably, there were fewer tourists. Indeed, fewer people, period. The population of exotic, even monstrous creatures had definitely increased, but Doom noted that these tended to take pains to give him a wide berth, which he appreciated. Also, since the architecture had altered toward the grotesque, the creatures looked at home, a perfect melding of dwelling and dweller.

Doom flew at a relatively low speed, buoyed along above the streets by his antigravity harness, taking in the sights while monitoring the position of his quarry. He could, if he chose, overtake the beast, but Doom had decided shortly after leaving Richards' wretched domicile that he would rather face it in its lair. What if destroying it made the dimensional gateway collapse? Doom could not take the chance; he had to be certain his mother was truly free before crushing the usurper.

Floating north up Central Park West through the smoke-choked sky, Doom spied what appeared to be a young man clinging to some sort of flexible line and repeatedly swinging down toward the street, catching up a wandering soul, and depositing him or her on the opposite side of the street. The utter futility of the act made Doom chuckle. The young man's general demeanor reminded him of the costumed fool Spider-Man, but it was difficult to be certain if it was truly him, as there were so revoltingly many meta-humans clogging the streets and skyways of Manhattan these days. This was, of course, another reason to avoid the place under most circumstances, but Doom decided he would keep an eye peeled for others of their ilk. Not many would be this amusing, naturally, but one could always hope.

The red indicator on the HUD overlay inside his mask blinked twice, then remained fixed. His prey had stopped moving and, as Doom had anticipated, his coordinates were the site of young Victor Von Doom's most devastating defeat. Doom accelerated through the swirling miasma, a thrilling sense of anticipation rising within him.

A geyser of hot ash had opened up beneath the Sheep Meadow and sent Reed into a steep upward spiral that required several minutes to recover from, so instead of being the first to arrive at Empire State he was the last. He recognized the contours of the campus under the changes wrought by the dimensional rift, but the details were lost, like the features of a beloved face lost beneath calloused burn tissue. The walls of the graduate laboratories, once as familiar to Reed as his children's faces were today, had lost structural coherence and slumped to the ground like so many lumps of cottage cheese left in the sun.

After landing and retracting into his bipedal shape, Reed ran around the building to find an entrance, the directional beeper on his harness changing pitch as he paced the perimeter. The only entry he could find was a narrow gap half-hidden by a jagged lump that must once have been the main doors. Reed sighed; if no way could be found to reverse the effects of the dimensional intrusion, Empire State's fund-raising department would be giving him a call.

Flattening his body and slipping through the gap, Reed wondered how the red giant and Doom had gained entrance, but as soon as he was inside and concealed in a dark corner, he saw the answer: The ceiling had collapsed when the walls had altered shape. After taking one more reading, Reed muted the beeper and headed toward the center of the building, more or less in the direction of Victor Von Doom's old lab.

Reed expanded his feet to the size of beanbag chairs and with long, long strides silently prowled the debris, guided only by the gnarled fingers of light flickering through the melted roof. Two voices echoed in the distance, both low, both domineering. *Wonderful,* Reed thought. *An egofest.* He decided that the most rational course of action would be to remain hidden for as long as possible and see how events were unfolding. Moving slowly to minimize the distinctive sound of his flexible body stretching, Reed extended his neck to first peer through and then slipped through a slight crack near the ceiling on the inner wall. Once inside, he pressed into a dark corner, his body taking on the irregular contours that made it difficult for observers to see a human form.

Doom and the red giant were speaking in low, clipped tones, each man wreathed in protective energy. Doom was enclosed inside the shimmering green field Reed had seen so many times before. He was fairly certain that Doom employed some kind of cycling resonance modulation device that made energy weapons useless, but Reed's repeated attempts at reproducing the effect in his lab had proven unsatisfactory. The only foolproof method for breaking through that Reed had discovered was the kind of unrelenting pounding only an enraged Ben Grimm could deliver.

The horned giant sat cross-legged, hovering a few centimeters off the ground in a glowing circle of turquoise energy. What appeared to be mystical symbols swirled around the circle's perimeter, fading and then growing stronger as they slid over and under one another. Previous encounters with mystical forces had led Reed Richards to conclude that though he would never completely understand "magick," he had to admit it existed and that the forces it represented could be manipulated by logical processes. Obviously, the being who had brought chaos to Manhattan understood these forces: The undeniable result of his labors—a hole in space—gaped open behind him.

"What assurances do I have that you can do what you claim?" Doom asked, even as the sensors in his armor analyzed both the creature and the rift behind it. He had no intention of believing anything the creature said; the only thing one could definitely trust about demons—or creatures that claimed to be demons—was that they could never be trusted. The scans revealed two significant facts: the creature was basically a human hybrid, and the rift it sat before was charged with exotic energies that might be extra-dimensional in nature. In brief, the creature's claim that it was a demon occupying a human host might be accurate, though whether it could move freely through the dimensions remained to be seen.

"Oh, I offer no assurances," the demon replied smugly. "The only way you'll reach your goal is by partnering with me. If this thing you desire is truly important, then you'll make the commitment without any thought of assurances."

"Do you take Doom for a fool? You sound more like a human lawyer than a creature of the pit."

"Ah, the advantages of being an absolute ruler!" the demon shouted with glee. "Obviously you haven't dealt with lawyers often enough if you think they sound any different than we pit-dwellers!" It shook its horned head and rubbed its chin with satisfaction. "Oh, Victor. Truly, this is the most fun I've had in . . . well, ever. It's such a pleasure to finally meet you. Heard so much about you . . . over the years, you know. Between her screams and pleas for mercy and her begging for relief."

Doom moved with the speed of an adder, thrusting his hands into the energy field and bearing down on it with all the considerable force at his command. Finally, he had to concede his efforts were in vain. Whatever the nature of the creature, whether demonic or scientific, it had considerable energies at its disposal.

The creature chuckled. "All done, Victor? Tantrum over? Good. Sorry about that last remark. It was quite unnecessary, but then sometimes unnecessary remarks are the most enjoyable."

*Enjoy yourself, monster,* Doom thought as he studied the sensor readouts. *Enjoy yourself now while you still may.* Interesting. During the period when Doom had been attacking the field, the configuration and type of particles emanating from the portal had changed significantly. Doom's assumption was that the creature was drawing power from the portal, but the question was what kind and how often the system needed to be replenished. The answer to the second question, clearly, was *frequently.* No sooner had Doom put pressure on the system than it needed to be revitalized. *Excellent,* Doom thought. *Most excellent.*

Von Doom's next words were music to the shadow's noncorporeal ears. "Very well, then," he said. "I agree to your terms. I will assist you in your quest for a new host. I shall either create one for you using my peerless abilities in robotics or, failing there, find you a suitable candidate. I have a few ideas in that area. The repugnant Thing might suit you well; he is more massive than your current host and would likely be easy to dominate. There are other options, of course; this world simply teems with muscle-bound clods." Inside his head, Klemp screeched and clawed at the interior walls of the shadow's mind. Now that the fool was awake, there didn't seem to be any way to shut him up again. The shadow couldn't wait to be rid of the gibbering idiot.

"Excellent," the shadow said. "And in return I will confirm whether or not your mother truly escaped the malodorous dimension to which she was condemned all those years ago." It extended its massive hand. "Then the only remaining thing is to shake on the deal." Von Doom tilted his head curiously, as if the creature were speaking a foreign tongue. "Oh, come now, Victor. The traditional ways are the best. Didn't your father used to say that?"

Von Doom shrugged and extended his hand. "My father said a great many things, creature."

The shadow shook its head (and felt like Klemp was rattling inside like the clapper of a bell). "Not with the gauntlet on, Victor. Skin to skin or it doesn't take." The way Von Doom glared into the creature's eyes, it briefly wondered if the good doctor could see Klemp staring back out. Then, predictably, Victor sighed, touched a control stud on his wrist, and slipped the gauntlet off his right hand. Von Doom's skin was surprisingly pink, smooth and youthful, not nearly as shriveled and scarred as the creature had expected. It wondered what the good doctor's secret was, but then resolved to be patient. Soon enough, all of Von Doom's secrets would be his.

From his secluded spot near the ceiling, Reed could barely believe what he was witnessing. Was Victor truly this desperate, this *foolish*? He very much doubted he would be able to prevent what was about to happen, but he knew he had to try. Realizing that surprise might be his only hope, Reed sprang out of the corner, launching himself at the pair with all the considerable kinetic energy at his disposal and shouting, "Stop!"

As soon as Victor heard Reed's voice, he withdrew his hand and tried to slip his hand back inside his gauntlet, but the red giant bounded forward and gripped Victor's bare wrist in an iron grip before he could move away. The blue-green field flowed out around Von Doom and he collapsed to his knees, releasing a soul-shattered groan that made the lab's warped walls reverberate.

Reed stretched his arms back behind him and gripped two large pieces of loosened masonry, then contracted his muscles, tearing the chunks away and catapulting them at the demon. Both chunks burst into concrete hailstones against the blue-green field.

Victor dangled at the end of the creature's outstretched arm, legs spasming, hands hanging limp at his side. His groan turned into a low, breathless scream of agony. Without instrumentation, Reed couldn't be sure what was happening, but the sound of Victor's misery made him think the giant was displacing Von Doom's soul and filling the void with its own black heart. As Reed watched helplessly, the red giant shrank, lost mass and definition, deflated like a pierced Mylar balloon. Within seconds, the giant was almost human-sized and no longer red. Moments later, it crumbled to the ground, a demon no more, but only a slight young man with a sunken chest and a weak chin.

Victor had ceased screaming, but was on the floor on his hands and knees, his back heaving spasmodically, his heavy green cloak quivering. Reed checked his comm system and saw that the interference from the portal prohibited any calls for help. Whatever process the giant had begun was almost complete, and Reed would have to attempt to deal with the outcome or flee.

Von Doom gasped and Reed thought he was going into a new paroxysm, but the spasm eased and turned into a sigh. Surprisingly, the next thing Reed heard was not a sound of pain, but a guffaw, a laugh of genuine triumph. "Good Lord," he said. "What have you done now, Victor?"

The laugh rolled on for several seconds while Von Doom—or whatever now lived inside him—gathered his strength and pushed himself up onto his haunches. Reed realized that the giant's force field had dissipated and he might now be able to deal some damage. Also, he noted that the dimensional portal still swirled before them. If he could find a way to shut it down, the creature might be cut off from its power source. If all else failed, he might be able to force Victor through and block the entrance until a mystical expert could be found. While Von Doom's laughter grew louder and stronger, Reed gathered himself and considered which option would be most beneficial. Then, having made his decision, he rearranged his leg muscles into tight coils, enlarged and hardened his hands, and selected his target.

A moment before Reed launched himself, Von Doom abruptly stopped laughing and imperiously raised his hand in a gesture of dismissal. "Stop, Richards. Did you truly think Doom would be so easily overcome?"

Reed released some, but not all, the tension in his legs. Cocking his head to the side, he replied, "That's one of those questions that one can never answer politely, so I'll just say this: If you weren't overcome, then resisting it certainly wasn't pleasant."

Doom stooped slowly—and, Reed thought, with some evidence of discomfort—to retrieve his dropped gauntlet. "Pain is for lesser beings," he replied.

"Perhaps. But you know I need to be clear about what just happened. Where is the giant or demon or whatever it was? It touched your arm and it looked as if it was trying to take you over, dominate you." Reed pointed at the recumbent, apparently sleeping, form. "Like it must have *that* poor devil."

"It attempted a lame trick," Doom said haughtily. "But it did not take into account Doom's genius." He pointed at his forearm. "Though this may look like skin, it is really a superconducting sheath that interfaces with my wondrous armor. Through it, I have complete control over every system, every device, with nothing more than a thought."

"Very nice," Reed said. "Tony Stark recently created something very similar."

"Bah! Mine is infinitely more sophisticated."

"So, rather than being taken over . . . ?"

"Correct. Doom is in control. Even as we speak, my analytical software is extracting the information I seek."

"And that information would be?"

Before Doom could speak, Reed felt a familiar tingle at the nape of his neck. A moment later, a translucent head as high as Doom was tall appeared before the dimensional rift. *Ah,* came the familiar voice, though Reed did not hear the words with his ears, but rather inside his mind. *So this is what has been causing all the problems.*

# 16

"HELLO, STEPHEN," REED SAID ALOUD. JUDGING by the way Victor suddenly froze, he could also see the Sorcerer Supreme hovering before them. Or his head, anyway. "I assume you knew something about this?"

"Didn't Ben tell you that he and I spoke a few minutes ago?"

"We've all been busy."

"As have I," Strange said. He cast a glance at Doom and then the prostrate form on the ground before him. "Victor, I can only assume you had something to do with this."

"I brought the threat to an end," Victor said.

"Truly?" Strange turned to look at Reed, who

nodded minutely. "Well, then, thank you. I am weary from dealing with all the other extra-dimensional menaces that looked to take advantage of this situation. Since most of them were largely ethereal, I trusted to our city's more corporeal defenders to look after things until I could get back."

"Your timing," Doom said, "as ever is exquisite."

Strange smiled thinly and turned back to Reed. "And now this portal must be closed before it attracts any more invaders. It opens onto a rather peripheral dimension, one I have never visited. There isn't much there, actually."

"No," Doom said. "There isn't, is there?"

Reed asked, "So, you've finished processing its memories?"

"Yes," Von Doom said. "It is not what it claimed to be. Or, at least, it is not from where it claimed to be from. It never held my mother's spirit captive and could not even say where it is."

"What are you talking about?" Strange asked. "We freed your mother's spirit together, Victor."

"Or so we thought," Victor said. "The creature suggested we may have been misled. I sought definitive knowledge."

"By doing *what*?" Strange asked impatiently.

"Victor absorbed the demon—or whatever it was—into his armor," Reed explained. "He's been reading its memories."

"*What?!*" Strange exclaimed. "That's extraordinarily dangerous, Victor. You may think you have control of it now, but these creatures are much hardier than you would expect. Even if you completely dissected it, reduced it to atomic dust, its essence—"

"I do not care," Doom said, stepping through Strange's head. "I must begin my journey now."

"Journey?" Reed and Strange asked simultaneously.

"I must be sure that my mother is at rest," Doom said. "From this creature, I have gained the knowledge I need to manipulate these gates, to move from dimension to dimension. I will go forth and find—"

"You must stop him!" Strange shouted inside Reed's head (an uncomfortable sensation, to say the least). "If Doom carries that thing into another dimension and it gains control of his armor, it could do irreparable damage to the multiverse!"

"Be silent," Doom said, standing before the portal, readying himself like a diver on a high board. "Nothing of the sort will happen. I am Doom!"

"Can't you stop him?" Reed asked. "Can't you close the portal?"

"I need time!" Strange cried. "Why does everyone think that sorcery is something that can simply be tossed off like . . . like . . ."

"Like magic?" Reed finished for him.

"Be clever later, Reed," Strange said coolly. "Or, rather, be clever *now*. Stop him however you can. Use *science*."

Reed thought, *Why does everyone assume that super-scientists carry around exactly the device they need to stop any threat that comes down the pike?* He removed his palmtop from his belt clip and said aloud, "Probably because we do."

"Because we do what?" Strange asked.

"Never mind, Stephen." He sighed deeply and called out, "Victor, Stephen says I can't let you take your armor through the portal. I'm inclined to think he's right about this one."

Doom looked over his shoulder, then shrugged contemptuously. "And what do you propose to do about it?"

"Just this," Reed said and tapped a control surface on the palmtop.

Several seconds later, something deep inside Victor's armor began to buzz. Reed heard a rapid succession of pops and clicks, like the sound of two score attaché cases snapping open at once. "I'm sorry, Victor," Reed said, and then, without any other preamble, most of Doom's armor fell away and clattered to the ground. Beneath his voluminous green cloak, Reed could see that his entire body was coated in the silver superconducting nanolayer.

The mask started to fall away, but Victor caught it with both hands just as the magnetic locks released. Turning to Reed, he hissed, *"Richards! What have you done?!"*

"You spent almost ten minutes inside my lab, Victor, which was more than enough time for my scanners to analyze the bond between your armor and the superconducting layer. It might have taken me some time to get through all the data, but you showed me how it worked back in Latveria . . ." He shrugged. "Scrambling the programming was pretty easy." As if it had been waiting for a cue, silver ooze began to run off Victor's body and pooled on the floor around his feet.

"Very well," Stephen said, looking slightly embarrassed. "I can see I am no longer needed here. Not in my ethereal form, in any case. I shall be there soon to deal with the portal." And with that, he disappeared in an overly theatrical blink of light.

"Curse you, Richards," Doom hissed. "I thought we had struck a bargain!"

"I am going to feel just awful about this, Victor," Reed said. "Eventually."

Doom leaped over the pile of armor, one hand holding his mask, the other stretched toward Reed, his fingers curved like claws, ready to rend or tear any part of his enemy he could reach. Reed simply stepped away, unwilling to engage his old foe, but not so foolish as to think Doom could not still deal damage. "Stand and fight, coward!" Victor sneered. "The great Reed Richards! Afraid to engage a defenseless normal human!"

"Don't insult me, Victor. We both know there's nothing either defenseless or normal about you."

"Stop calling me that! You will address me as Doom! *DOOM!*" Lurching toward Reed, Victor stumbled and fell forward onto his hands and knees. He lost his grip on his mask, which skittered away and came to rest only inches from Reed's foot.

The shock of the fall knocked the wind out of Doom's lungs, and Reed listened to the sound of his foe's labored breathing for several long seconds. Then, slowly, he leaned down and retrieved the mask. "As far as I know," he said, "you've committed no crime, so you're free to head to the Latverian embassy. However, I will be keeping tabs on you until you leave American soil. S.H.I.E.L.D. should be entering the city, so I would advise you not to dawdle. They may not be as gracious as I am if they catch you out and about . . . or even recognize you. Do we have an understanding?"

Doom continued to gasp for breath, and Reed found himself wondering how long it had been since the man had breathed unfiltered atmosphere. But then, he seemed to collect himself and the heavy gulping slowed. "I do not now nor have I ever considered you a man of honor, Richards," he said with an asthmatic wheeze, "but I ask you to look within yourself and try to decide what a man of honor might do. I must go through that portal. I must know what happened to the soul of my mother. Would you bar my way? I ask you: If the circumstances were the same for Susan or Franklin or little Valeria, would you not battle through any obstacle to reach them? Would you not even go so far as to beg Doom, your mortal enemy . . . ?"

"As I recall," Reed interrupted, speaking through clenched teeth, "you *did* condemn my family to Hell and I believe I *did* do everything I needed to do to save them. Including defeat you." He threw Doom's mask into the dirt within his foe's easy reach. "If you want to go to Hell, *Doom,* I won't try to stop you."

Doom reached forward and gripped his mask, pressed it to his face, and rose slowly, but (Reed had to concede) with a majesty that few men he had known would have been capable of. "I do not need my armor," he said imperiously and stepped carefully through the debris toward the portal.

Before he could step through, Reed said, "Victor, wait." He slipped off the harness that held the force field generator and threw it at Doom's feet. As soon as he dropped the generator, Reed felt the effects of the energies emitted from the gate, but was confident he could withstand the effect until Strange arrived. "Take this. I'm not sure that the field will be strong enough to protect you from whatever you'll find through there, but it might give you a slight edge."

Doom bent and picked up the harness, then stood for a moment regarding it with what Reed thought was a mixture of mild amusement and not very mild contempt. Then, with a quick flip of his forearm, he tossed it against the far wall. One of the more delicate circuits must have been damaged, because Reed heard a faint pop and the mild scent of fried plastic. Doom chuckled lightly, shook his head in wonder, and murmured, "As if Victor Von Doom could fear anything Hell has to offer." With that, he stepped through the portal with a curious lightness in his step and was gone in a swirl of fire and a snap of brimstone.

Five minutes later, Stephen Strange hovered into the room, suspended by his cloak of levitation. He found Reed Richards sitting on what might have once been a lab stool, staring across the room into the angry red eye of the dimensional rift. Strange looked from side to side of the dimly lit room, noted with mild interest the softly whimpering man lying near the portal, and asked, "Where is Doom?"

Richards shook his head and focused on Strange as if he were a man waking from a dream. "What?" he asked. "Oh. Doom. He left."

"Really?" Strange responded. "Pity. I would have liked to have heard his opinion of this rift." He crossed his legs and began to prepare himself for the brief but complex spell he would need to seal the opening. "A bit of a doctor's consult, I suppose you would call it." He chuckled lightly at his own remark.

"Ah," Reed said. "Yes. Well, you just missed him. Perhaps another time . . ."

As is often the case with magical events, as soon as the source of the problem was removed and things began to revert back to their pre-event status, people began to forget what had happened or invented new, slightly more plausible explanations for the destruction and mayhem. S.H.I.E.L.D. happily enabled this behavior, reasoning that if half the people in Manhattan were more comfortable attributing their recent lapses in good conduct to a H.Y.D.R.A. nerve gas attack rather than to a dimensional incursion, so be it.

Time passed. Buildings that had undergone significant transformations either fell down or were pulled down. The victims—and there are always victims— were taken to morgues and paperwork was filled out listing vague causes of death. The heart at the center of the city continued to beat.

Johnny Storm and Ben Grimm strolled down Yancy Street, both in what passed for civilian clothing, both of them carefully studying the streetscape, alert for clues from the locals about how much they remembered of the events that had transpired a couple weeks earlier. No one appeared to recall much. An elderly gentleman sitting on a bench outside a deli stared at the Thing accusingly as he passed, but he looked to Ben like the sort who would stare at anything he hadn't seen walk past his front stoop every day for the past twenty-five years.

Ms. Sullivan was waiting in front of the rec center in the middle of the charred spot that marked where the Yancy Streeters had tried to set fire to Ben. Judging from the way Johnny was warily regarding the black smear, Ben guessed that the kid was recalling his threat to firebomb Julio and Marcus and not feeling too good about it. It didn't matter how many different ways Reed explained how the radiation from the other dimension affected serotonin and hormonal production—the kid remained sure he should have been able to control his baser instincts. Ben decided early on that maybe that wasn't the worst lesson his teammate could have drawn from the experience, and allowed Johnny to have his little guilt trip. The way Ben saw it, sometimes a little guilt can be a good thing.

"So, Mr. Grimm," Ms. Sullivan said, standing up even straighter than usual as he and Johnny approached. "Are you ready to inspect the damage?"

"Are you sure this is really necessary?" Ben asked. "Like I said on the phone, I figure I *caused* most of the damage, so it's not like I don't know what happened."

"It would probably be in everyone's best interest if we didn't mention that in the official statement to the insurance company, Mr. Grimm," Ms. Sullivan said sternly. "And since they *will* be expecting you to file a report, yes, this is really necessary."

"I don't need to file an insurance report. I got more money than I know what to do with, so if we want to rebuild the place, I could pretty much just give you a blank—"

"'If'?" Ms. Sullivan asked archly. "'Could'? The conditional nature of these statements does not bode well, Mr. Grimm. Are you *actually* reconsidering the pledge you made to the people of this neighborhood?"

"Naw, naw, not that," Ben said, shaking his head. "I want 'em to have the rec center, but, y'know, I got to thinkin' maybe it would be better if I just did it a little more, y'know, anonymously. Events might not have unfolded the way they did if I hadn't been making such a big deal about, well, *me*." He shrugged and stuffed his big hands into his trench coat's oversized pockets.

Ms. Sullivan did not respond for several seconds, but only stared at Ben with her mouth hanging slightly open. Obviously, she had something to say, but wasn't quite certain how to express herself. Ben wanted to reach out and gently push her jaw shut with the stubby tip of his finger.

"Cripes, Ben," Johnny said. "That's about the dumbest thing I've ever heard you say. And that's based on what I would characterize as a broad experience of listening to you say dumb things."

"Back off, flame brain," Ben groused. "This ain't any of your business."

"Of course it is," Johnny retorted. "Ben, we need

you to do *more* of this stuff. It's not like Reed or Sue
are going to do it. Reed's too busy taking care of . . .
*whatever* he does. And Sue is too busy taking care of
Reed. And the kids. And then there's me . . ."

"Yeah?" Ben turned on his friend, his hands invol-
untarily curling into fists inside his pockets. Sometimes the kid was so ridiculously selfish, didn't think
of anyone but himself . . . "What *about* you?"

To his surprise, Johnny also had his hands
jammed in his pockets, and he was staring fixedly at
the charred spot on the pavement. "I'm like the rest
of these people, Ben. Sometimes, I need someone to
remind me . . ." He shrugged, struggling, but then
continued: "It's not always easy to be a good guy, but
it's something worth trying to do." He looked up at
his friend and said, "You're my hero, Ben Grimm."

For exactly one half a millisecond, Ben almost, *almost* bought into the performance, but then the kid
let slip one of his ridiculous cocky grins. The Thing
growled and lurched forward, with both his hands
reaching for Johnny's scrawny neck, but the Torch
was too fast for him.

"Flame on!" he shouted out, laughing, streaming
a tail of red and gold flame as he soared up into the
morning sky.

Ben and Ms. Sullivan watched the fire trail disappear toward the north. When it was finally out of
sight, he turned toward her and said, "Yeah, okay.
Let's do this thing."

"Very good," Ms. Sullivan said and looked at the first item on the list she had attached to her clipboard. "First, we'll need to replace the statue in the foyer."

"Okay," Ben said.

"And the floor in the gymnasium."

"Sounds good. Say, listen, do you know that little kid, Julio . . . ?"

"The one they call Bender?"

"Yeah. You ever meet his brother?"

"The Iraq War vet? Not in person, but I've heard about him."

"Could we name the gym after him?"

"It's your building, Mr. Grimm. You can name it anything you want."

"Yeah," Ben said and felt a grin creep up onto his face. "That's true, ain't it?"

Working in her office, Sue tried not to eavesdrop on Reed's conversation in his outer lab, but Tony Stark made that difficult. The director of S.H.I.E.L.D. didn't have an "inside" voice, especially when he was on the visi-phone. She suspected that Stark was slightly hard of hearing, no doubt because of all the heavy metal he pumped into his armor's headset when he made cross-country flights at cruising speed. "The work crews should be finished with the refits within the next twenty-four hours," Stark said, finishing up the review on the force field generators. "Our only concern is that we might need to keep some of the units permanently shielded. Now that the locals know where they are, some of the kids have taken it as a challenge to figure out how to strip them."

"Disguise them as police call boxes," Reed replied. "I've done research that pretty conclusively proves that humans are genetically predisposed to ignore them."

There was a long pause before Stark finally said, "This is a pop culture reference, isn't it? I'm always confused when you do those."

"You need to get an eight-year-old son," Reed said. "Then you would understand."

"I'll take that under advisement. How is Franklin, after everything that happened?" Stark scored ten million points with Sue for asking about her son and another ten million for remembering his name. She found herself thinking back to the days when she hadn't actively disliked Tony, but only found his playboy inventor act to be slightly annoying.

"As well as can be expected," Reed reported. "He's strong, like his mother." Sue couldn't see Reed's face, but she easily pictured the undefended, wistful smile he would be wearing.

"And, no doubt, resilient, like his father," Stark replied, which got him an additional five million points, but only five because it was as much a bit of sucking up as it was a compliment to Reed. Stark knew he had made a mistake to install the force field generators without consulting with the leader of the Fantastic Four, and had done the right thing by asking her husband to help with the recalibration and repair work. She had come to decide that in concept, the idea was sound, though the idea of his installing the generators without telling anyone rankled her. "So, is that everything?"

"I believe so," Reed said. "Oh, except for the boy, the one from Empire State. I've been meaning to ask you what became of him."

"Klemp? We scanned him six ways to Sunday, but couldn't find any traces of metahuman tissue. He claims he doesn't remember much of what happened, and psionics couldn't get anything else out of him, so we cut him loose."

"He's back at Empire State?" Reed asked, slightly alarmed.

"No," Stark said. "I understand he flunked out. Went back home to live with his grandmother or something like that."

"Ah," Reed said. "Well, then I suppose he'll be all right."

"I suppose," Stark said distractedly. "If we're done, then thanks for your time, Reed."

"Not a problem. Give my best to Rachel the next time you see her."

"I would," Stark said, "but she just recently resigned. Said something about getting a job offer."

"Really?"

"You wouldn't happen to know anything about that, would you?"

"Are you accusing me of poaching your employees, Tony?"

"Maybe a little," Stark said. "Anything you care to say about it?"

"I leave all the hiring and firing decisions to Sue," Reed said, but Sue could hear the smile in her husband's voice. "Do you want me to have her give you a call?"

"Oh no," Stark replied hastily. "That's okay. Your wife scares me."

"As well she should, Tony. Good night."

"Night, Reed."

Sue listened to her husband rustle around in his room for another ten minutes or so, but she could tell from the sounds of items being put in equipment lockers and computers powering down that he was finished for the day. Or, to be more accurate, that he wasn't planning to start anything new at this particular moment, which made her glad. She felt the need to spend some time with him, maybe snuggle on the couch with a movie and a bowl of popcorn and gear back down to what passed for normal in their world. Then, as if on cue, Reed rapped lightly on her half-opened office door. "Sue?" he called. "Are the kids asleep?"

Sue smiled. Both Franklin and Val had come into his lab to say good night not an hour ago. As she had the night before, she'd been obliged to stay with her little daughter until the girl dozed off, but, unlike last night, there hadn't been any calls from H.E.R.B.I.E. to come back and comfort her. No doubt the ordeal of the bunny-eating vampires had left a mark, but it didn't appear as if it would be permanent or severe. "They went down pretty early tonight."

"I can imagine," Reed said, settling down into one of her guest chairs. "Why don't you call it a night. Don't we still have episodes of *Lost* on the DVR to watch?"

"Only all of season three."

"Excellent. I just hope we can get some explanation of what's happening this year."

"You say that every time we watch it, dear."

"Do I? Sorry."

"I'll be finished in just a couple minutes," Sue said, scanning another lease contract and then signing in the blank spaces next to the bits of sticky tape.

"Did everyone re-up?"

"Most everyone. The firm Ms. Floyd was working for decided they couldn't stay, but I'm pretty sure that had more to do with the parent company's fourth-quarter financials than anything that happened here. I hear she decided to quit and is now working for Mr. Brannigan."

"Ah, that's fine then. He seems like a nice man. A little lonely, perhaps."

"Not so much anymore," Sue said, signing the last contract in the pile. She enjoyed seeing Mr. Brannigan and Ms. Floyd together in the lobby. They were so kind to each other, so solicitous. It was reassuring that something so lovely could come out of such a stressful experience. Sue realized that the entire world had not been at risk (as was so often the case with their adventures), but the ones that came so close to home, that affected the children even a little, these she hated . . .

Before she could finish her thought, the intercom on her desk bleeped the two special tones that indicated H.E.R.B.I.E. was calling. "What is it?" she called.

"Mrs. Richards?" the robot said softly. "Franklin is awake and says he would like to talk to his father. Is Dr. Richards—"

"Tell him I'll be right there, H.E.R.B.I.E.," Reed said.

"Will do, sir. Thank you."

Reed stood and brushed invisible dirt off his lab coat. "Remember when you used to find H.E.R.B.I.E. annoying?"

"I never found him annoying. You're thinking of Ben."

"Really?"

"No. It was me. You've done wonders with him, dear. Best. Invention. Ever."

Reed chuckled. "Meet you on the couch?"

"I'll bring the popcorn. Extra butter and light salt."

"Excellent."

*　　*　　*

Reed found his son sitting up in bed with the desk lamp on his side table lit. He was wearing his disconcertingly direct expression, the one that sometimes made Reed forget that Franklin was really only eight. "Hey, pal. What's going on? Your mother said you conked out so fast that she almost left you on the floor beside your bed. You're too big for her to carry now."

"Mom wouldn't do that," Franklin said very seriously. "She'd just lift me up with her force field."

"Of course she would," Reed said, realizing that joking wasn't going to get any traction until whatever it was that was bothering Franklin had been aired. He sat down on the bed next to the boy and said, "So, talk to me. What's on your mind?"

Without preamble, Franklin asked, "Have you heard from Doctor Doom yet?" Franklin rarely asked about the team's various villains and nemeses, but he had always seemed especially loath to discuss or even listen to tales that included Doom as a topic, so the question was surprising.

"No. As far as I've been able to determine, he's off in another dimension, probably lost, probably for a long time." Reed thought, but did not add, *Though knowing Victor, he'll find his way back.* "Why do you ask?"

"I was just wondering," Franklin said. "I heard you talking to Iron Man about how Doctor Doom might be in one of the Hell dimensions."

"Yes," Reed said. "I did say that, though you shouldn't listen in on Daddy's conversations that way."

"Mr. Stark talks very loud."

"All right, that's true. Still . . . But that's not your only question."

"No," Franklin said and his voice trailed off. Reed was almost struck dumb when he saw that tears had started to leak from the corners of his son's eyes. "It's just . . . it's just . . ." He wiped his eyes, and Reed reached out and gripped the boy's shoulder. "You remember when he sent me to that place, the bad place . . . ?"

"The Hell dimension he had found," Reed said softly. "Of course I remember. I could never forget that."

"And then you came and got me," Franklin said, his voice cracking slightly. "And you brought me home. You remember?"

"Of course. I came and got you."

"If he . . . if Doctor Doom ever did something like that again . . ."

"He won't," Reed said. "I've made sure of that . . ."

"But if he *did*," Franklin said earnestly.

"Then I would come and get you."

"No matter what."

"No matter what," Reed repeated. "And this time I'd bring Mommy along and she would kick Doctor

Doom in the butt so hard that she'd leave a dent." Reed did not like resorting to the use of the word "butt"; however, he too had been a boy once (despite many comments to the contrary) and knew that few things could guarantee a laugh from an eight-year-old like an adult saying naughty words.

As anticipated, Franklin smirked and chortled and was suddenly very self-conscious about the fact that he might be crying. Wiping the corners of his eyes with his pajama sleeve, he said, "And bring Uncle Ben, because he would leave a *really* big dent in Doctor Doom's butt. And Uncle Johnny, because he would give Doctor Doom a hotfoot on his butt, and H.E.R.B.I.E., because he would just keep telling Doctor Doom that he was a big butthead . . ."

"Yes, Son," Reed said and began to tickle the boy because there was no way to get kids to stop saying "butt" once they started except to tickle it out of them. "That's exactly what I'd do."

He needed a few minutes to get Franklin to calm down again after the tickle session was over, and there were extra-special requests for the reading of the transmogrifier strips from *The Essential Calvin and Hobbes* and a drink of water, but eventually the boy conked out again and Reed was able to tuck him in and turn off the desk lamp.

Standing in the open doorway, his shadow streaming before him and cast over the foot of his son's bed, Reed Richards reflected on the boy's question and considered the future. What if Doom returned, as he always had in the past? What if he should somehow gain control of the Hell dimensions that he traveled through and was able to muster their various denizens to his call? What if he never found out what really happened to his mother's spirit and decided that the lack of knowledge was really his archenemy's fault? What if Doom decided to take out the frustration and rage generated by his twisted psyche on Reed's friends, Reed's wife and son and daughter, as he had so many times before?

Reed Richards closed the door to his son's room and walked toward the living room, where his wife waited for him with a bowl of extra-buttery, lightly salted popcorn.

*What if?*

And because he was Mr. Fantastic, he started to formulate a plan . . .

# About the Author

Jeffrey Lang started reading comic books when he was eight years old (*Daredevil* #45, 1968) and, with the exception of a brief spell in 1972 when he decided he was "too old for comics," has never stopped. So, yeah, writing a novel about Marvel Comics' "first family" is the fulfillment of a lifelong dream (thanks, Marco!). Lang's other work includes comic book scripts for DC Comics, Wildstorm, and Dark Horse Comics, as well as several novels and short stories for Pocket Books' *Star Trek* line. Lang lives in Bala Cynwyd, PA with his partner, Helen, his son, Andrew, and an ever-growing menagerie of pets, including three cats and an anxious dog.